# I THOUGHT I WAS PREPARED FOR HIM. I WAS WRONG.

Standing in front of me, he simply occupies more space than I expected. It takes everything I have to keep my expression calm and neutral when everything inside me is strung tight enough to snap. I want to leap across the distance between us and claw my nails down his cheeks and demand answers. How did he survive? Why did he lie? Did he know it was going to happen?

What is he hiding and why?

A warm flush pools along my lower back, spreading out in all directions. I want to run. Hide. Take a moment to regroup, refocus. But I can't do any of these things and so I stand, feet rooted in place, and wait while his gaze sweeps over me.

"Libby." The name escapes his lips on a breath of air, and behind me comes the collective movement of each guest straining forward to hear.

A memory from the cruise rises unbidden: the two of us together on deck, the night sky infinite as he kisses me for the first time. His forehead had been pressed against my own for what felt like an eternity. The distance between our lips minuscule, yet infinite. His fingers found their way to my temple, slowly sweeping my hair back behind my ear. Goose bumps trailed in the wake of his touch.

# OTHER BOOKS YOU MAY ENJOY

# DAUGHTER

## OF

## DEEP

## SILENCE

## CARRIE RYAN

**speak**

SPEAK
An imprint of Penguin Random House LLC
375 Hudson Street
New York, New York 10014

First published in the United States of America by Dutton Books,
an imprint of Penguin Group (USA) LLC, 2015
Published by Speak, an imprint of Penguin Random House LLC, 2016

THE LIBRARY OF CONGRESS HAS CATALOGED THE DUTTON CHILDREN'S BOOKS EDITION AS FOLLOWS:
Ryan, Carrie.
Daughter of deep silence / Carrie Ryan.
pages cm
Summary: At fourteen, Frances survived a slaughter that claimed the lives of her parents and best
friend, Libby, but she took on Libby's identity and wealth while plotting revenge against the powerful
Wells family and now, at age eighteen, is ready to destroy them, including her first love, Grey.
ISBN 978-0-525-42650-9 (hardcover)
[1. Revenge—Fiction. 2. Identity—Fiction. 3. Survival—Fiction.
4. Orphans—Fiction. 5. Love—Fiction. 6. Death—Fiction.]
I. Title.
PZ7.R9478Dau 2015
[Fic]—dc23   2014048067

Speak ISBN 978-0-14-751160-7

Printed in the United States of America

3 5 7 9 10 8 6 4 2

Designed by Theresa Evangelista
Edited by Julie Strauss-Gabel

For two amazing friends without whom this book wouldn't exist:

Diana Peterfreund for being my inspiration,
guru, constant confidant, and unerring supporter

&

Ally Carter for listening to my wild idea, saying,
"Yes, write that!" and never letting me waver.

*Deep vengeance is the daughter of deep silence.*

—VITTORIO ALFIERI

# ONE

When they pull me onto the yacht, I can't even stand I've been adrift in the ocean so long. A young crewman sits me on a teak bench while he calls out for someone to bring him blankets and water. He asks me my name but my tongue is too thick and my throat too raw from screaming and salt water to answer.

*I'm alive*, I think to myself. The words run on an endless loop through my head as if with repetition I'll somehow believe it. *I'm alive, I'm alive, I'm alive.*

*And Libby isn't.*

I should be feeling something more. But it's all too much too fast. Inside I'm awash with numbness that cocoons a brightly burning knot of rage and despair. Protecting me. For now.

A pair of crewmen pull Libby's body from the life raft, rolling her onto her back on the yacht's gleaming deck. I think about how birds have hollow bones and how easy it must be to break them.

That's how she looks right now: hollow. Her cheeks sunken, her wrists twigs wrapped in tight skin that's turned to leather from relentless heat and exposure.

A crewman presses his fingers against her neck, a palm in the center of her chest. His expression slides from desperate hope into a mask of efficient resignation. He looks up to where an older man with a ring of white hair around his otherwise bald head hovers, waiting. The crewman shakes his head.

The older man lets out a cry, his face crumpling as he falls to his knees by Libby's side. He only says one word over and over again as he pushes a tangle of wet hair out of her face: *no*. His voice cracks and his shoulders slump, shaking, as he sobs.

If I had any tears left in me I'd be crying too, but I'm so dehydrated that all I can do is shake, my lungs spasming with hiccups. I try to talk, my mouth forming a *wh-* sound over and over again.

"Shh." The crewman who rescued me drapes a blanket around my shoulders. "It's okay, you're safe now."

I want to believe him. But all I can do is stare at Libby's body. An hour earlier, and they'd have found her alive. She might have survived. Seven days adrift in the middle of the ocean, and she'd lost it in the last hour.

It doesn't seem fair. We were supposed to make it together. We'd promised.

Her body is so light and brittle it takes only one person to carry her inside the ship. The older man does it, clutching her against his chest, his eyes red and lips pressed tight together.

"*My baby*," he whispers against her temple. Understanding hits with a physical force: This is Libby's father. He glances at me as he passes, his expression bewildered, and I know he's wondering the same thing I've already been thinking: Why am I the one who survived? Why couldn't it have been her pulled alive from the raft?

I want to apologize, but seeing him with Libby—a father cradling his broken daughter—I can't. The unfairness of it is monstrous. I would give anything to have my father here now, to feel him holding me and protecting me the way Libby's father does.

And he would give anything for his daughter to still be alive.

I close my eyes, unable to stand it. Because in this moment I truly understand just how alone I am. How no one will ever again hold me and care about me the way Libby's father does her. My parents are dead. Libby is dead. I have no relatives—no other family waiting for me.

I am alone. Utterly and irrevocably alone.

Memories storm through me, fast and sharp, in an unrelenting strobe of sensations—sounds, smells, fragments of sentences. I feel my mother's hand against my forehead checking for a fever some night, years ago. I hear the way she sneezes, big and loud, and my father laughing in response the way he always, always does.

There's the smell of the car on the winter morning we go to pick out a Christmas tree, my father singing along to the carols on the radio with his voice always just slightly out of tune. I taste french fries—my fingers slick with fast-food grease—my mom's treat to me as she drives me home from summer camp.

I lick my lips and gag at the taste of salt. The memories come faster, running over one another, drowning me. Panic claws its way up my throat. My nails are soft and cracked from so long in the water and they split past the quick as I try to dig them into the skin along my thighs, wishing I could gouge it all out of me. The memories. The loss. The pain. The refrain that's been unspooling in my head for days: *gone, gone, they're all gone, your life is gone.*

And inevitably, images from the attack come next: the gun pressed to my father's head. The blood drenching my mother's shirt. She'd begged, but it hadn't mattered. It didn't matter for anyone on that cruise ship. They'd all been massacred.

*Three hundred twenty-seven.* That was the total number of passengers and crew on the *Persephone*. It was one of the things we'd learned during the safety drill before leaving port. In the end, it never mattered how many people a life raft could hold. It never mattered where each cabin's muster station was.

Nothing we learned during the safety drill mattered.

The attack had come swift and hard in the middle of the night. One minute life on the *Persephone* was normal, the next the ship was rocked with explosions. The attackers blocked the exits while armed men went room to room, systematic in their assault. Faces passive, expressions detached from their actions, they'd pulled triggers and reloaded magazines with sickening efficiency.

Killing them all.

*The bodies. Oh God, the bodies. And the blood and the screams and the smell of it all, like overripe peaches stuffed with pennies.*

I gasp and shudder. It was only luck that allowed Libby and me to escape. We talked about it relentlessly during those next seven days adrift, the impossibility that we'd somehow survived.

All of that and she'd ended up dead anyway. It's so brutally unfair.

The young crewman pushes a plastic bottle of water into my hand, forcing me back into the present. My throat clenches. The bottle's cold—freezing against my palm—and there's condensation dripping along the outside. I fumble to open it, my fingers useless, my muscles too weak to even lift it. Finally he takes mercy and twists the cap free.

"Drink slow," he says, but in my world there's no such thing and I press that bottle hard to my lips. If I'd died the instant that water rushed across my tongue I wouldn't have cared. I'm sharply aware of each drop as it cascades down my throat and into my hollow belly. Nothing exists then but that taste—that sensation.

"Easy now," the man says, gently prying the bottle from my lips. "You don't want to make yourself sick." He's too late; already my stomach revolts in painful cramps. I turn and vomit.

The man rubs my back as I heave, telling me again that I'll be okay. That I'm safe. "What's your name?" he asks when I've recovered enough to sit up again.

I press the back of my hand to my mouth. My skin tastes like salt, making me retch. "Frances," I try to tell him, the sound nothing more than a tattered thread.

The storm that had been threatening at the edge of the sky all day finally breaks, sending fat drops of water crashing to the deck. "Let's get you inside," the crewman says as he slides his arms gently under my shoulders, lifting me as easily as Libby's father lifted her. As he carries me, I tilt my head back, letting the rain wash across my sun-cured skin.

If it had come a few hours sooner, this rain would have saved her.

I barely pay attention as the man maneuvers me through a large salon, down a flight of stairs, and along a hallway to a stateroom. He sets me carefully on the bed.

"I'm a medic," he explains. He pulls over a large red bag emblazoned with a white cross and slides on gloves. "Is it okay if I examine you?"

I nod and he's ginger as he probes at the sores covering my legs and back, unable to hide his horror at what's become of my body. "You'll be okay," he tells me again, but I get the impression it's more to convince himself than me. He unzips his bag and begins pulling out various medical supplies.

"You're severely dehydrated," he explains as he runs an alcohol-soaked swab across my inner arm and presses a needle against the flesh. "So the first priority is to start getting fluids in you." It takes him several tries, his forehead creased in frustrated concentration as he searches for a vein. I feel none of it.

Eventually he's satisfied and drapes an IV bag from a hook on the wall. "For now, just rest." He starts for the door but I force the sound up my throat.

"How many survived the attack?"

He looks at me, not understanding the question. "Attack?"

"The attack on the *Persephone*," I croak in a salt-crusted voice. "How many others survived?"

Frowning, he opens his mouth, reconsiders, and closes it. Finally he says, "Two others: Senator Wells and his son."

I don't even dare to breathe. "*Grey?*" I whisper.

He nods and I slump back into the nest of pillows, pressing the heels of my hands against my eyes. Grey's alive. *Grey's alive!* It seems so impossible, that after losing everything else, this one small part survived. Like suddenly there's a bright spark of hope in the cavernous blackness my life has become.

*"Hey, I'm Grey," he says, standing next to my deck chair, casting me in shadow. I have to squint when I look up at him and though I've been ogling him all afternoon I still can't stop my eyes from dropping to his chest, skimming down to the strip of bare skin just above the waistband of his swim trunks.*

*They skim low on his hips, almost like a promise.*

*I'm fairly certain he notices and my cheeks heat. But I know the reason he's here—what he's really after. He's made that abundantly clear.*

*"Her name's Libby," I tell him, gesturing to where Libby's hanging out over by the towel stand. She has her elbows propped on the counter and is leaning forward slightly, hoping to catch the hot attendant's attention. "I'd move quick if I were you," I add.*

*"Oh, um." He shifts from one foot to the other, and I assume he's nervous because he can't figure out how to politely ditch me to go after my friend. But I'm already expecting it—I've noticed him looking our way for a while now.*

*"Do you mind if I join you?" He points at Libby's empty chaise next to mine. It's so unexpected, I stare at him perhaps a beat too long. Finally I realize he's waiting for my response and I shrug.*

He's barely settled before I ask, "So, what do you want to know about her?"

He smiles and ducks his head. "Actually," he says, "I was hoping to learn more about you."

While on the raft, I'd daydreamed of Grey rescuing me, even though I knew it was impossible—that he must have been killed with everyone else on board. Over and over as we drifted toward death on the empty ocean, I'd imagined him coming for me.

It didn't matter than I'd known him barely a week, it had been long enough to fall for him with an intensity I'd never experienced before.

He was my first love. And he'd told me I was his.

*He's alive.*

In the black horror of what my life has become, that single point of light now shines. I've lost my parents. I've lost Libby. Nothing will ever be the same again. I have no other family, no long-lost relatives to take me in. There is nothing left.

But Grey. I still have Grey.

I cling to the thought as though it is a life raft, knowing that if I hold on tight enough and don't give up, I'll somehow be able to survive.

I drift asleep imagining our reunion. Already feeling his arms around my shoulders, his hands pressing against my back, holding me tight against him. He'll brush his lips against my temple and whisper over and over that it's okay, he'll keep me safe, and I'll believe him.

Because he also saw the horror. He also survived it. He also *understands*. In the protection of his arms finally, *finally*, my tears will come again.

The same four words cycle endlessly through me, giving me comfort for the first time since that opening shot was fired on the *Persephone*: *I am not alone. I am not alone. I am not alone.*

# TWO

I wake in darkness, raw and confused. There's this moment of lightness as I roll over, the soft bed beneath me and the sheets sliding along my skin. For a fraction of a heartbeat it feels right.

And then I remember. It comes as a physical sensation first, a crushing on my chest as my mind struggles to bend and stretch to take it all in.

*The gun pressed so hard against Dad's head that it caused the skin around the barrel to wrinkle and pucker. All down the hallway, shots firing, one after another after another. Systematic. My dad's top teeth scraping against his bottom lip, starting to say my name.*

Gasping, I bolt upright, pressing my palms over my ears as though that could somehow stop me from hearing. But of course it doesn't.

*The gunshot, shattering bone.*

It never will.

Beneath me, the yacht rocks softly, the thrum of its engine a low vibration through my bones. The stateroom is empty, the windows dark. It's too quiet. I'm too alone. Memories of the attack circle around like hungry sharks and I reach for the television remote, hoping that sound and distraction will keep them at bay.

When it flickers on, the TV hanging on the far wall is glaringly bright and colorful, stinging my eyes. But it's something other than silence and that's what I crave. I flip through channels absently until a familiar name stops me. *Persephone.*

My hand falls limp to the bed. Heart pounding, I watch as a news anchor shuffles papers while an image of the cruise ship floats behind her. "Breaking news on last week's *Persephone* disaster," she announces. "Sources are confirming that another survivor from the ship may have been located. As of now, authorities haven't released any information about the potential survivor or survivors. While we wait for more information to trickle in, let's take a look at the dramatic footage of Senator Wells and his son taken shortly after their own rescue."

The scene on the TV shifts to a sprawling marina bustling with activity. The camera zooms in on the gangplank of a large US Coast Guard ship, focusing on a small group making its way toward the pier.

Senator Wells leads the pack. Even with a sunburned face he manages to appear debonair in an almost-dangerous way, the salt-and-pepper scruff of his unshaven face emphasizing the sharpness of his cheekbones. The camera pans past him and my breath catches.

It's Grey. Alive.

It's one thing to be told he survived, yet another to see it as truth. That same surge of relief washes through me, the sudden realization that I'm not alone. Someone else out there understands.

I devour his appearance. Grey looks much worse than his father. He clutches a thick blanket around his shoulders, his steps slow as he trails after the group. His hair sticks up from his head at odd angles and his eyes look bruised above the shadowy scraps of stubble strewn across his cheeks and chin.

Reporters rush the two en masse, shouting questions and Grey rears back, alarmed by the sudden onslaught. I press my fingers against my lips, feel them trembling. One of the coast guard men tries to push the camera away, but the Senator stops him. "We'll answer," he says. Grey winces and his eyes squeeze shut.

"The world deserves to know the truth of what happened to the *Persephone*," the Senator explains, pulling Grey toward the reporter's microphone. "It happened fast," the Senator begins. I find myself nodding even though at the time it had seemed like hours. Days of gunfire. Years of blood.

"It was late and I was out on deck with my son, helping him look for his phone he'd forgotten by the pool that afternoon. There was a terrible storm and we were just about to give up and go inside." He pauses, shakes his head. "The wave came out of nowhere. I've never seen anything like it. It just . . . took the whole ship out."

*Wave?* I find that I can't breathe, his words grinding my thoughts to a halt. *That's not what happened. There was no wave.*

Senator Wells steps aside, leaving his son facing the microphone. Every heartbeat echoes through my water-slogged veins, causing my entire body to throb and rock as I wait to hear what he has to say. Grey blanches, but doesn't retreat. The familiarity of his gestures is jarring. The way he holds himself with his weight slightly on his right leg, the furrow between his eyebrows as he sorts through his thoughts before speaking.

The way he unconsciously rubs his skull, just behind his ear, whenever he's about to lie.

It's amazing the little things you can pick up about someone in such a short amount of time when you're falling in love. Every nuance, every sound and movement a code to understanding them.

"Like Dad said, it happened fast," he starts, and then he clears his throat, choked up. In my head I see it all. I *hear* it all and taste it all. Again.

*Grey pulls me against him and threads a strand of hair behind my ear. When he brings his mouth closer, I stop caring about the rain. All I care about is devouring this moment as though to imprint it into my memory forever.*

*Rivulets of water wash down his face, dripping from his chin and coursing along his neck. The way his shirt plasters to his chest allows me to see the outline of every muscle. I press my fingers against them, tracing the edges.*

*I laugh, a bubble of euphoria too large to keep contained. He kisses me right then, like he could take my laughter into himself and make it a part of him. And still, all around us the rain crashes but we don't care.*

The reporters huddling around Grey barely breathe as they wait for him to continue. "The rain was awful, and as Dad mentioned, we were . . . uh . . . out on deck by the pool." He glances toward his father before continuing. "It was unlike . . . anything. It came out of nowhere—this massive wave. And it just was there—a wall of water. It rose higher than even the top of the ship—much higher." He pauses as if reliving the moment, eyes haunted.

I'm trembling now. I don't understand. Why isn't he talking about the attack? Why isn't he mentioning the guns?

Grey inhales slowly, his shirt lifting just enough to lay bare the strip of pale skin along the edge of his shorts. He begins to rub that spot behind his ear again. "And then . . ." His voice breaks.

*And then the guns. Men slamming through the corridors, cutting off the emergency exits, and locking the ship down. Panicked passengers in robes and nightgowns run, screaming. Making it no more than a few steps before bullets tear them apart.*

*Water drips down my back, my hair still wet from kissing Grey in the rain. I press myself against the cold metal wall of the dumbwaiter, watching through the mirrored window as a tall, narrow man makes his way efficiently down the hallway. He kicks a broken body aside. Forces his way into a room. It takes seconds—a loud spattering of gunfire—and then he's in the hall-way again, moving on to the next.*

*Moving on to my family's room directly across from where I'm hiding.*

*A high-pitched whine climbs its way up the back of my throat, coated in acid. I clamp my hands over my mouth, knowing with-out question that if they hear me, I am dead.*

*I'm dead either way.*


As Grey speaks, the reporters hang on his every nuance and gesture. They're enraptured by him. I wait for him to mention the armed men. The gunshots. The murder.

But he never does. "It's like what Dad said. The wave just swallowed her whole. Like a toy in a tub. And then . . . the *Persephone* was gone." He shakes his head, as though he him-self couldn't believe it. "Just *gone*."

In the silence that follows, the Senator squeezes his son's shoulder. One of the reporters shouts, "How were you able to survive?"

Grey's eyes widen, his expression one of bewilderment. The Senator steps in. "Had to be luck, plain and simple. It was late and because of the rain everyone else was inside, probably asleep in their cabins. I was so angry at Grey for losing his phone, but if he hadn't . . ." He inhales sharply. Grey stares at his feet. "We wouldn't have been up on deck and thrown free when the wave hit."

"No!" I shout, the sound raw in my throat. "That's not how it happened!"

"Once we got to the surface and saw the wreckage . . ." Here the Senator pauses and takes a water bottle one of the rescuers holds out to him. "We tried to find other survivors, but . . ." He shakes his head and a shudder passes through Grey. "The only choice we had was to try to stay alive. We found a life raft that must have broken free and just prayed that someone would find us."

I'm gasping for air. "But . . ." I close my eyes remembering. Libby and me dragging our arms through the water, trying to put distance between us and the burning *Persephone*. Flames choking out her windows, undaunted by the rain. It wasn't until dawn that we saw the extent of it: nothing.

Not a scrap of the ship remained. No hint of other survivors. No other life rafts anywhere in sight. *How had Grey and his father survived without either of us seeing them?*

On TV the tenor of the reporters changes as the camera pans and zooms in on a middle-aged woman running down the pier, her perfectly coiffed blond hair loosening in the breeze. She's wearing a skirt that hits just above her knees and she pauses briefly to kick off her heels so that she can run faster. "Alastair! Grey!" she cries, the sound primal.

The cameraman knows how to do his job and he instantly focuses in on Grey's face, capturing the moment it crumples and he mouths the word, *Mom?* And then they're hugging, sobbing, reunited. His father's arms around them both.

The video pauses on this perfect image. The intimate snapshot of an all-American family newly reunited, their heavy grief finally lifted. A miracle. The Senator with his sunburned face and lightly tousled hair. His wife barefoot, tendrils of hair pulled loose around her tearstained face. And their beloved only son between them.

My chest tightens as though it were collapsing in on itself. Father. Mother. Child. All together. All safe.

It becomes impossible to breathe.

*I'll never hug my parents again. My mother will never come running toward me. My father will never place his hand on my head and tell me he loves me. I'll never feel safe ever again.*

*I've lost everything. And somehow, Grey hasn't.*

The anchorwoman's voice cuts into my thoughts, and I listen with a mounting sense of incredulity as she continues. "News of another survivor certainly comes as a surprise. As you may recall, the coast guard called off the search for survivors last week after interviewing Senator Wells and his son and concluding that a rogue wave capsized the *Persephone*, sinking it before those belowdecks could escape."

The camera switches angles and the anchor swivels, continuing. "Though they're considered a rare occurrence, this isn't the first time a rogue wave has been suspected in the disappearance of a ship. In fact, it's widely believed that it was a rogue wave that took the SS *Edmund Fitzgerald* in 1975, and just as with the *Persephone*, there was no wreckage found in that case either."

It takes a moment for this information to take shape in my mind. For the implications of it to settle in. The coast guard called off the search days ago. When Libby and I were still out there. When we both still had a chance to be rescued alive.

All because of Senator Wells and Grey. Because they lied.

I don't even realize that I'm screaming until firm hands pull me from the TV. My fists flail at it and smears of red mar the screen, blood from where I'd ripped out my IV in my scramble from the bed.

"They're lying," I shout, still flailing. "The ship was attacked. There was no wave. It was men with guns—they killed everyone!"

A crewman holds me steady as the medic slips a needle into my arm. "Shh," he murmurs. "It's okay."

"No," I whimper, shaking my head. But everything feels so much heavier now. My protests, fuzzy and indistinct. "You don't understand." He carries me to the bed, and when he tries to leave, I fumble for his wrist, holding him. "You have to believe me. They're lying. Please." A tear leaks from my eye, the first since I've been rescued.

He gently frees himself. "It's okay," he says softly, pulling another blanket over me. "You're safe now."

But I know that's not true. May never be true again. "*They killed them all and sank the ship,*" I whisper, my voice weakening. "*They killed my parents.*" It comes out slurred. "*Please believe me.*"

# THREE

I t's still dark when I wake again. The yacht rides the swell of the waves, rocking me gently. And I suddenly realize how strange it is to be alone. Not just here in this room, but in life. There is no one who cares about where I am right now. No one to notice whether I come home or not.

There is no one in charge of me, to tell me what to do. Where to go. How to recover. As the breadth of my isolation yawns open ahead of me, I begin to tremble. I will no longer live in my house. Sleep in my bed. Pull clothes out of my dresser. Brush my teeth in my bathroom. Leave shoes lying at the base of the stairs.

Where will I live, I have no idea. A foster home? Do they even have orphanages anymore? The thoughts come faster and faster, tumbling over one another, inciting panic. I find myself wheezing, the room spinning.

*My parents are gone. My life is gone. Everything. Everything—it's all gone.*

I pull free of the IV again and push from the bed, stumbling toward the door. I ache for anything familiar, someone to tell me it will be okay. But there's no one left.

*Greyson Wells*, a voice whispers in the back of my head and an image of him from the TV flashes in my mind. My stomach roils, and if there'd been anything in it, I'd have vomited.

I shuffle down the hallway, fingertips pressed against the wall to keep myself steady. My steps are halting, pained, and I don't even realize what I'm searching for until I'm there. Standing in the doorway.

She's on the bed, an insignificant lump under the crumpled covers. Her back is toward me, the sharp tips of her wing bones barely visible under the stretch of her shirt.

*Libby*. Even dead I feel that pull to her, the connection that drew us tighter and tighter as our lives slipped through our hungry fingers and into the ocean. Her blistered cheeks are masked by a tangle of hair, and I want to tuck it behind her ear. She hated it in her face. But even as I stretch my fingers toward her temple, I know I can't bring myself to actually touch her. Doing so would make it real.

"*It should be you standing here*," I whisper, my fingertips hovering a breath away from the curve of her jaw. She had family and friends waiting for her. I have nothing.

"You remind me of her," a quiet voice says from the doorway. My heart jumps and I stumble, spinning to press my back against the wall. Libby's father stands just across the threshold.

"When they pulled you in," he continues, stepping into the room, "I thought you were my Libby at first." He sighs and gestures toward a chair. I sink into it and he takes the one facing me. "Frances Mace, right?" he asks. The words come out weary, the sound of them as heavy and thick as the bags under his eyes. I nod.

"Your family was on the *Persephone* as well?"

I nod again.

"And they didn't make it?"

It's cold in the room, the air-conditioning running full blast, and I cross my arms tightly over my chest as I shake my head.

"How old are you?"

"Just turned fourteen," I mumble.

"Where are you from?"

I tap my fingers against my thumb, nervous. "Small town south of Columbus, Ohio, sir."

"You have family there?"

My fingers still and I stare at them, motionless, in my lap. "No, sir." I take a sharp breath. "My parents were both only children."

"Any siblings? Grandparents?" He's frowning.

I shake my head. "There's no one." Clearing my throat I test the word out for the first time: "I'm an orphan." It's horrible, making my stomach churn.

His lips purse together as he ponders this.

"It wasn't a wave," I blurt into the silence. I lift my eyes, watching confusion flicker across his face. I lean forward, needing him to understand. "The *Persephone* was attacked. They killed everyone on board." My voice breaks and I swallow, trying to hold the memories at bay.

*The guns. The blood. The screaming. God, the screaming.*

"The coast guard interviewed Senator Wells and his son and there hasn't been any mention of armed men or—"

"They're lying," I interject bitterly.

He shakes his head. "Why would they lie about something like that?"

It's the question I've been asking myself; one I don't have an answer to. So instead I lift a shoulder and tell him the only explanation I could come up with. "Maybe they were somehow involved. The attackers weren't wearing masks. Maybe they're afraid that because they're witnesses those same men will come after them."

It sounds even more far-fetched when I say it aloud and a blush flares up my neck.

But Libby's father doesn't laugh. He considers the idea for a moment. "And you," he adds. I glance up at him sharply. "If you're also a witness," he clarifies, "it stands to reason they'd come after you as well." It's not clear whether he believes it's a possibility or is merely placating me.

A chill tightens the skin between my shoulder blades. But what I feel more than anything else is exhaustion. For the past week all I've done is fight to stay alive. The prospect of having to keep up that fight is overwhelming.

My eyes flick toward Libby and I find that a part of me is jealous of her. That she was able to escape. How nice it would be to slide into oblivion. "It's not like I won't be hard to find," I mumble.

There's silence for a moment, the only sound our breathing.

Confirmation that we're alive and Libby is not. "Do you know if my wife . . . if Barbara . . ." He trails off, unable to ask the question.

My eyes flutter shut, the memory coming against my will.

*The screaming doesn't stop. Neither do the gunshots. I curl into a ball, arms over my head as though that will make it all go away. But it won't.*

*All I see over and over in my mind is my mother kneeling on the floor of our room across the hall, tendrils of blood writhing like venomous snakes across the front of her shirt. Her eyes wide as she glances toward the dumbwaiter—terror not for herself but for the fact that the gunman might discover my hiding place.*

*And now she's broken. She and my dad both. And I'm next if they find me. But moving is unthinkable. What if they hear me? What if they see me? What if they kill me?*

*The smoke billowing down the hallway grows thicker, dark tendrils coming for me in my little metal box. I choke on the terror of being trapped and press the up button, cringing at the sound of grinding gears. When it wrenches to a stop at the top I wait, hand over my mouth, for someone to find me.*

*Nothing happens and I force myself to run. The silence in the hallway is shrouded in cotton, thickening the air so that it feels like moving through water. It's only a few yards to the O'Martin's suite and I blow through the doors.*

*And she's there—Libby—like she's been waiting for me. She's halfway into the next room, already running for the balcony.*

*Someone bangs on the door behind me, screaming to get inside* to safety. *I hesitate, not knowing what to do, but there's panic in the woman's voice and I open it to find Libby's mother. In her eyes there's that heartbeat of relief.*

*Then there's a noise. And then nothing. Not even Libby's mother.*

*I stare at her lifeless body sprawled across the hallway. Her chest ragged and raw, the side of her jaw nothing but shards of bone. Blood and bits of her flesh splatter down my arms and across Libby's lovely clothes she'd let me borrow.*

Fingers yank at my arm and I think it's Libby, come to drag me to safety. But I open my eyes to find her father instead. Kneeling in front of me, physically pulling me from the memory.

"My wife?" he prods. My entire body trembles.

"She was killed like the others." I force the words through chattering teeth. "I watched it happen."

He drops his head, inhaling sharply. After a moment, he slips an arm around my waist, helping me stand. "We'll be in port soon, we should get you cleaned up." He shuffles me down the hallway, back to my room. Gesturing to the narrow bathroom, he says, "Everything you need should be in there. I'll have some food brought up in the meantime."

In the bathroom I turn the faucets greedily, shoving my hands under the spray. Needing to feel that instant gratification. I cup handfuls of water into my mouth, careful to drink only small amounts and using the rest to swish around in an attempt to purge the pervasive taste of salt.

Then I glance up. I'm not sure what I thought I'd look like

after everything that's happened but it's certainly nothing like the creature I find staring back. My hair, dark with sweat and grease, lies in clumps, the ends tangled and knotted around my shoulders. My lips are split, my normally narrow nose swollen from sunburn.

Immediately I understand why everyone's treated me like a wounded animal—my eyes are wild and fierce and unlike anything I've seen in myself before. I don't recognize my own expression and that, more than anything else, unsettles me.

I watch as my reflection lifts trembling fingers to probe against the ridge of my cheekbones, so starved and sharp they cast deep shadows over sunken flesh. It's as though my skin were made translucent and stretched across an oversized skull, every fissure and ridge of bone standing in prominent relief. Something between a gasp and a cry gurgles in my throat, and I turn away, unable to bear it.

Behind me is a small shower and I grasp for the handles, turning the water full blast. I don't even bother removing my clothes. Pressing my back against the wall, I slide until I'm sitting, knees clutched to my chest, and let the water punish me with heat and steam.

Not caring at the sting of all my sores or at the protest of my sunburned flesh. Because this pain means that I'm alive. That I made it.

If only I knew what that means.

# FOUR

When I finally shut off the shower and peel off my clothes, I don't bother drying before pulling on a thick robe I find hanging on the door—I like the feel of water on my desiccated skin.

Stepping back into the bedroom, I'm surprised to find Libby's father waiting for me. The dome of his head gleams faintly with sweat, and the folds on his face hang thickly, as though gravity somehow exerts more force on him than anyone else.

As soon as he sees me, he stands, helping me to a plush chair next to a table where there's a glass of water waiting. I cup my hands around it, but my stomach's not ready for more yet.

He moves to sit but then changes his mind and paces toward the porthole window before turning. "I didn't introduce myself earlier. I'm Cecil." He gestures down the hallway. "Libby's father," he adds, and I nod. "I . . ." He seems to reconsider whatever he was about to say and paces across the room again.

When he reaches the table, he grips the back of the empty chair, leaning on it. "I've been thinking about what you said about the *Persephone* being attacked." He watches my reaction carefully. "Is it true?"

I hold his eyes a moment before answering. "Yes, sir."

He presses his lips together and lets out a long breath. I stare down at the water in front of me, watching tiny ripples radiate against the glass from the sway of the yacht.

"And the men—these attackers—they weren't wearing any masks. You could identify them?"

I nod.

"So you, Senator Wells, and his son are the only witnesses to what happened. And for whatever reason the two of them seem intent on keeping quiet about it being an attack." He pauses. "Which leaves you."

This time I don't respond. What is there to say?

He pulls out the chair, finally, and sits. For a long while, he considers me while I keep my attention focused on the glass of water. "Which means that if I ever want to find out the truth about what happened to my wife and daughter, I'll need your help."

At this, I jerk my eyes up. "Me? What can I do?"

"I don't know," he admits. "That's what I've been trying to figure out."

I shift, suddenly uncomfortable. I don't like the idea that I'm the only thing standing between the world and the truth about the *Persephone*. It's too much of a burden when I'm carrying enough already. I shake my head. "I don't—"

But he holds up a hand and I let the protest die on my lips. "I started to call the coast guard to give them the details of the rescue and let them know we were bringing you in so they could have someone there to pick you up."

He shakes his head slowly. "But then I thought about how you're the last person who saw my baby alive. The last person to talk to her. You're the only one who knows what those final moments were like for her." His voice breaks and he glances away, his eyes glistening with tears. "You're my last connection with her."

I pull my feet up to the edge of the chair, wrapping the robe tighter as I hug my knees to my chest. So that I take up the smallest amount of space possible.

"I lost my family out there." He chokes on a sob. My own throat tightens, my eyes burning as I swallow again and again. If I let the ache in my chest rise too far, it will drown me.

"You know, we're alike that way," he adds, struggling to turn the sob into a laugh and failing. He presses his fingers to his eyes, taking measured breaths. "I don't want to go home and face my daughter's empty bedroom."

I shove the heel of my palm in my mouth, biting what's left of the flesh in an attempt to stave off the tide of grief.

He stands, walking across the room. Composing himself. "Did Libby ever tell you about Shepherd and Luis?" The change in subject is so abrupt that I blink, a few times, wondering whether I've misheard him. I nod slowly, confused about where this is going. Shepherd, his older brother, Luis, and Libby had practically grown up together. During our time adrift, there'd been nothing to do but talk and she'd told me everything about them.

Especially about her and Shepherd falling in love.

"Their parents worked for me," Cecil explained. "Their mom was my personal assistant and their father ran my estates.

But it was more than that—they were practically family. When their parents were killed in a car accident, Shepherd and Luis didn't have any relatives in the US; the state planned to send them back to live with their extended family in Mexico, which didn't seem fair to them."

He lifts a shoulder. "Or to us. Shepherd and Luis were like sons to Barbara and me. We couldn't bear the thought of losing those two boys as well—how empty the house would seem. And so Barbara and I took them in and became their legal guardians. It wasn't even a question for us. Those boys needed us, and we needed them."

I'm not sure whether I'm supposed to say anything in response to his story or not, so I stay silent. "I thought that, maybe, we could help each other out," he continues. "You took care of my baby as she was dying. Please let me take care of you. I can protect you if the attackers come after you as a witness. You wouldn't have to go into foster care or have to worry about the state—everything would be taken care of. I wouldn't have to say good-bye to the last memories of my daughter just yet."

He pauses, hands clenching into fists. "And maybe together we can find the bastards who did this."

"Are you talking about . . ." I struggle for the right words. "Becoming my guardian, like you did with Shepherd and Luis?" Suddenly, the idea of having a place to go, having a house and a room and a dresser and a person who knows the truth of what happened and could protect me—it's too much to hope for.

So when Libby's father shakes his head, it's like the last bright spot inside of me shattering.

"There would be too much paperwork. I learned that with Shepherd and Luis. You'd still end up in the system, a ward of the state. And who knows if they'd even consent to me taking care of you. In the meantime if there are people out there looking for you, they'd find you easily," he points out.

"No, what I'm suggesting . . ." He leans forward and sets something on the table between us. I recognize it instantly: Libby's signet ring. "Is that you switch places with my daughter. That you become Elizabeth Anne O'Martin.

"It's the only way to keep you safe." He pushes the ring toward me. "It's the only way to figure out who did this and make them pay."

## FIVE

*Four Years Later*

Senator Wells's voice drones through the car speakers, causing my stomach to churn. It's another one of his campaign ads and it follows the same theme as all the others: *blah blah blah . . . Persephone . . . blah blah blah . . . rogue wave . . . blah blah blah . . . survivor.* I clench my fists listening, wanting to punch something.

*Four years ago my son and I were on a family cruise when the unthinkable happened: A rogue wave struck our ship, sinking it almost instantly and leaving my son and me stranded in the middle of the ocean. During those three long days lost at sea, I came to truly understand what is important to me in life: the health and security of my family. That's why every day in Washington I fight for the health and security of your family the same way that I fought for my own—because I know how much it matters.*

*They say that the measure of a man isn't in how he faces the expected; it's in how he faces the unexpected. Four years ago I turned the tragedy of the* Persephone *into the opportunity to better serve my family, my constituents, and my country. If re-elected, I won't stop fighting for South Carolina, and I won't stop fighting for you. I'm Alastair Wells, and I approve—*

"Turn it off," I tell the driver. His eyes flick to the rearview mirror before he reaches for the knob and silences the radio. Leaving us enveloped in the sound of tires zooming across concrete as we cross one of the myriad bridges leading to Caldwell Island. Libby's home.

*My home now,* I remind myself.

Below, spartina, crisp green in its newness, shimmers across mud flats as the tide drains from the marshes. It's so different from the mountain meadows I'm used to in Switzerland. Perhaps I'd find it beautiful, even relaxing, if I didn't know that somewhere on the other end of the bridge the ocean is waiting for me.

It's time for her to give up her secrets. She's been a silent participant in everything: the attack; Libby's death; my rescue and transformation. And every summer since, she's been witness to Grey and his father, living out their lies without consequence.

I've come back to put an end to it. Maybe if Senator Wells had left things alone I wouldn't have returned. Maybe if he'd just let the past stay the past, I'd have kept my fantasies of revenge tucked neatly away, never daring to brush them off and consider putting them into action.

I'd moved on. Or at least I'd convinced Cecil I had. When he saw what my obsession with finding the attackers was doing to me—how it was only feeding the rage festering inside, he called off the search for the truth. Or rather, excluded me from it.

He wanted me to have a normal life, the life his *real* daughter never had. And so we pretended, together. I pretended that I was okay. He pretended that the violent loss of his wife and daughter wasn't slowly killing him. Both of us pretended we weren't still searching for the attackers. School breaks became elaborate performances by the both of us, each playing our part for the other.

Until he died seven months ago and I didn't have to pretend anymore. But I'd tried—out of love and respect for Cecil and everything he'd done for me—I had tried to truly move on.

The breaking point for me had been the movie. They'd made a documentary about the Senator's rescue, its release perfectly timed to hit as his reelection campaign began heating up and the media started to speculate about whether the Senator had his eye on the presidency down the road.

The movie had been everywhere: inescapable.

In it, the Senator waxed on with great detail about the final moments of the ship. How fortunate it was that he and Grey had been up on deck at the time. The sound and fury of the wave as it approached. Experts weighed in with elaborate simulations of what must have happened when the rogue wave hit—all the possible ways the ship could have broken apart while it sank.

As part of the dramatization they'd stuck the Senator and

his son in a life raft and reenacted their rescue. It had been a complete farce—not even the tastefully ragged clothes they'd dressed them in could hide the healthy roundness of their cheeks, the paleness of their skin unmarred by sun-spawned blisters.

Watching Grey's face when they "spotted" their "rescuer" for the first time had made me violently ill. And as I knelt on the hard, cold tiles of my dorm's bathroom I realized a new truth: I was done.

I was done pretending to be okay. I was done attempting to move on. I was done trying to forget. I was done searching and finding nothing but dead ends. I was done being afraid of Senator Wells.

I was done staying away from him.

I'd spent four years struggling to find the truth and all I had were bits and pieces. Enough to know that Grey and his father hadn't seemed to lie out of fear of the attackers coming after them. Yet not nearly enough to understand what that meant. To know what role they played.

One thing is obvious: If there's any truth left about the *Persephone*, it lies with Grey and Senator Wells. Perhaps our confrontation was always inevitable and that's what Cecil had tried to keep me from by sending me off to boarding school in Switzerland and urging me to move on with my life.

But how could he really understand that the only way for me to move forward is to go back?

So I'd taken all of my elaborate revenge daydreams and began to boil them down into a single plan. Once I turned eighteen and had unfettered access to the trust funds I'd inherited from Cecil, I began to put that plan in motion, laying the groundwork. And now with graduation behind me, it's time to go home and pull the trigger.

The driver slows, putting on his blinker before turning down a long driveway lined with moss-draped oaks, their limbs gnarled from age and the constant barrage of salt-crusted breezes. I've seen pictures of the house, of course, but I'm still not prepared for the overall scope of it. It feels as though it belongs on a movie set with girls in tight corsets and hooped skirts.

Fluted columns two stories high run along a wide front porch that seems to stretch out forever. Once upon a time it had been the only house on the island, part of a much, much larger plantation. The ancestors of the original owner had broken the land into large lots, selling them off to create beach-front estates. This house had been slated to be torn down until Shepherd persuaded Cecil to buy it. They'd spent the last several years trying to put as much of the original plantation's land as possible under a conservation easement.

It certainly helped when Senator Wells purchased a lot farther down the island and was willing to throw his weight behind the cause. After all, limiting development only served to increase the value of his own property and provide tax breaks for his wealthy neighbors.

And this presented the perfect excuse for me to come "home" after so many years away. It's only natural that I'd throw the Senator a fund-raiser in thanks for his support of a cause my father held dear.

Already there's a bustle of activity around the side of the

house. Caterers, florists, and decorators setting up for this evening's event. I've been told by the party planner that the guest list is full; scores of the South's wealthiest families willing to pay an exorbitant price to the Wells Senatorial Reelection Fund for the chance to witness the survivors of the *Persephone* reunite for the first time.

It's an opportunity I knew the Senator himself would never turn down. The man loves a good photo op as much as he loves money and power.

The car pulls around to the front of the house and as the driver unloads my luggage I take a deep breath and climb the front steps. Before I even reach for the door, it opens to reveal a guy around my age.

His hair is dark and cut short—practically buzzed—and a light coating of stubble washes across his chin and cheeks. It makes his jaw look sharp and emphasizes the shadows under his cheekbones. He's wearing a green T-shirt with a faded recycling symbol printed across the front and as he clutches the edge of the door, the muscles in his arms flex against the thin fabric.

Though I've never come face-to-face with him in person, I recognize him immediately. During the interminable hours lost at sea, Libby had shared everything about him until I felt that I must have known him as well as she did. Even so, a thread of anxiety knots in my stomach: If there's anyone who can end this charade in an instant, it's Shepherd Oveja. He'd been in love with Libby, once. And she'd loved him back.

But that was all before the *Persephone*.

"Hello, Shepherd." I muster a crooked smile.

Emotions tumble across his face: a flare of surprise, followed by a flash of hunger, leading into something wary and guarded. I'm keenly aware of the way his eyes devour me, taking in every tiny detail.

I twist at the gold ring on my finger, the one bearing the O'Martin family crest. When he notices the nervous habit, his jaw clenches and he inhales sharply. He struggles to shield his anger behind an expression on the cold side of neutral.

To be fair, he has every right to be mad. For months after the rescue he'd tried to reach Libby, desperate to know how she was doing. Desperate to hear anything from her.

And not once had I responded.

He nods, sharply. "Libby." That's all he says. No "hello" or "nice to see you after all these years."

No "I missed you."

I frown at the small kernel of disappointment I feel. Not at his cold reception, but that he falls so easily for my deception. It makes me feel sorry for Libby, that she'd once loved this guy with the kind of intensity that only exists when you fall in love for the first time.

And he can't even recognize that I'm not her.

For a moment, neither of us moves. He stands blocking the door and I stand on the wide porch, the hired car idling behind me.

"Welcome home." He practically spits the words as he turns and stalks into the house, leaving the door open.

## SIX

I follow Shepherd into the house and find myself in a marble-draped foyer. To my left, a wide curving staircase leads to the second floor while ahead of me the foyer spills into a massive living room.

The entire back wall is a row of alternating windows and French doors that lead to a large flagstone patio curving around a sparkling blue pool. Beyond that lies a low row of dunes and then it's the ocean, stretching out into forever.

I cross to the windows and press my hand against the cool glass. Even from here I can feel the slight vibration of the waves crashing to shore and a shiver passes through me, the remembered taste of salt sharp against the back of my throat.

*Now it begins*, I think to myself. *Go.*

*"Go!" Libby screams. "Jump!"*

*She already has one leg over the railing and I follow, a horrified sense of impossibility as I teeter over the black emptiness below. Libby must sense my terror of heights and before I can think about what I need to do, she shoves me, hard.*

*My body twists and I flail.*

*The drop is interminable and I wait, wait, wait for the slap of water that I can't see. I'm nothing but dark and rain, screams and blood, and then I'm water. I sink down and down and even farther down, the life preserver not buckled tight enough and ripping free. My lungs already burn as I kick to try to stop my momentum.*

*Sound comes back more as physical force than anything else. A* chug-chug-chug *of the ship engine and I wonder how close I am to being chewed by the massive propeller. It seems impossible that I'm so deep in the water but with everything so dark I have no idea how far it is to the surface or even which way is up. I'm pretty sure I won't make it. Already my lungs are bucking, every cell screaming to inhale* now.

*My fingers touch the air first and I claw at it, bring my chin free long enough to gasp and choke before going under a wave. I kick hard, flailing to stay afloat. The hull of the ship towers over me, the propeller* chug-chugging *close enough that it pulls at me like a current. I scour the surface for Libby but the night is too thick with dark and rain to see anything but the* Persephone.

*Her lights flicker, a burst of smoke and fire roaring near the bow. Even from down here I hear the panic, as thick as the salt in the air.*

*"Libby!" I scream, but the sound is swallowed by a wave and then another, ripping me farther and farther into the black emptiness.*

*At first I try to swim after the ship, thinking that somehow the nightmare will break but it's useless. And the more energy I expend, the harder it is to keep my head above the swells and I know it's only a matter of time before I have nothing left in me to fight.*

*I wait for the life rafts to descend. To see others jump like I did. I wait to not be on my own any longer. But the more time passes, the more distance grows between me and the* Persephone. *The more I realize how alone I am.*

I'm pulled from the memory almost physically, Shepherd's warm hand circling around my shoulders. My palm has turned rigid against the window, fingernails like claws scratching the glass. As though I could rip the past from my head, rip the sea from the world.

*"Libby?"* He says the name on a whisper.

He's so close behind me that I catch a hint of his warm, soapy smell. I can almost feel the way his breath quivers, gently brushing the delicate hairs along the nape of my neck.

I blink, swallowing several times before I'm composed enough to face him. There's a hesitation in his expression, one laced with concern. "You okay?" The edge to his voice that had been there earlier is only slightly blunted.

I pull away and move toward one of the chairs. "Sometimes the ocean—it's too much," I tell him, rubbing my hands over my bare arms. He sits across from me, a gleaming glass coffee table festooned with family photos between us.

None of me, of course. At least not at first. It would have been too easy for someone to later compare them and note the differences. My jaw is wider, eyes are duller, nose sharper. All changes easily attributable to the passage of years or explained away by the excuse that I'd been injured when the *Persephone* sank and had undergone some reconstructive work.

I twist the ring around my finger as I stare at the sea of Libby's faces, trying to control the nerves flooding through me. Trying to convince myself I can pull this off.

"I wasn't expecting you," I finally say, breaking the awkward silence.

He lets out a snort, practically rolling his eyes. "I live here."

"I know. I just . . . thought you . . . might be out." I lift a shoulder. "Managing one of the other estates or something." I'd thought that perhaps he would have wanted to avoid me. I should have known better.

Shaking his head, he pushes to his feet and paces to the window. His shirt is so worn that I can see the shadowy ripple of the muscles between his shoulder blades tensing as he grasps at the back of his neck.

"I've been running the conservation efforts," he says. "Like fighting with the state over a couple hundred acres on the mainland they set as forever wild but are now trying to sell off for a strip mall. Which you'd know if you bothered to get in touch. Or to come home at all in the past year."

I stare at my hands clasped in my lap, chagrined. Cecil passed away seven months ago, not long after I'd returned to boarding school in Switzerland for my senior year. He'd been cremated and buried in the family plot, but I hadn't been there for the funeral. I'd been so devastated by his death that I wasn't strong enough to attend.

He was the last family I'd had. The last one who truly knew my past. Who truly knew me, who I was, where I'd come from.

I couldn't have pulled off being Libby anyway—especially not around those who'd known her before. And I couldn't risk failing. Not with so much at stake.

Shepherd has every reason to hate me for missing the funeral and deciding to stay in Europe during all the breaks. Like me, he was also mourning. He'd been six when Cecil and Barbara took him and his brother in—Cecil was practically the only father Shepherd had ever known.

"I'm sorry." I drop my eyes. "I just couldn't face it then," I add, my voice cracking. I take a deep, wobbling breath. While most everything about me is a carefully composed amalgamation of subterfuge, my heartache over Cecil's death is real. "I should have been here."

Silence descends between us until Shepherd sighs and rubs a hand across his close shaven head. "Libby—" he starts, but then he presses his lips together. "I mean . . . it's been four years."

"I know," I say.

He steps closer, agitated. "*Four years.*"

I know what he wants me to say. He and Libby had grown up together. They'd been best friends. And as they'd grown older they'd fallen in love. He may not have thought that Libby died out there on the ocean, but he'd still lost her all the same.

"I'm sorry," I tell him again.

His eyes widen and he almost laughs. Like this is all too much for him. "So for four years I hear nothing from you. You don't even bother coming home. And suddenly now?" He crosses his arms. "Why are you really here?"

The question startles me and at first I think I've failed at convincing him that I'm Libby. That he's somehow figured out my underlying motives and that my plan is ruined before I've even begun.

But then I see the desperation in his eyes and I understand: He wants me to have come back for *him*. Some part of him still loves Libby. Still wants her.

He's looking at me as though I'm the answer to his everything. The last person to look at me that way was Grey, and just thinking the name causes an angry rod of steel to slide down my spine.

Sometimes the best lies are wrapped in the flavor of truth. "Because I thought it was time to stop running away from the past."

# SEVEN

It's impossible to be in this house and not think of Libby. Pictures of her adorn the living room: as a baby, as a toddler missing her two front teeth, her face scrunched up in concentration as she learns to ride a bike. She stands next to a gleaming brown horse and holds a trophy for dressage, she leans against Shepherd on a ski slope on some impossibly high mountain.

But the picture I keep coming back to is the one of her at the beach. It's hard to be sure, but she looks to be around thirteen, probably just a few months before the cruise. Her back is to the camera, sun-pinked shoulder blades drawn tightly together, as she races into the crashing waves.

There's no hesitation, no fear. Her head is tilted slightly to the side so that I can barely catch her profile. She's beaming, mouth open with laughter, and I wonder who or what, just outside the edge of the photo, has caught her attention.

It's the last picture of her and it sits in a place of honor on the mantel. I'm standing, staring at it, when a woman clears her throat behind me. "Sorry to interrupt, Miss O'Martin."

I turn to find Cynthia the party planner, with her clipboard clasped in her hands. She's one of those middle-aged women who looks unnaturally bony. Her black hair is cropped short on one side, with a perfectly smoothed swoop of bangs across her forehead that's starched with enough product that it could withstand a hurricane.

She's the most-sought-after event planner in the South and though I've paid her an exorbitant amount for the fund-raiser, I doubt she realizes that I've been mentally planning tonight for years.

"I was just . . ." I gesture at the photos. "Lost in memories."

She smiles. "I understand." Her eyes slip past me to the portrait over the mantel: Libby as a baby clutched in her mother's grasp while Cecil kneels with his arms around both. "You look like your mother."

It's an easy compliment to make and likely a hollow one. Even so, I allow a bit of a shy blush to dust my cheeks. "Thank you—that means a lot to hear." I glance back at the portrait. "There's not a day that goes by that I don't miss her."

"I'm sure she'd be quite proud of the woman you've become," Cynthia says. "Lord knows when I was your age I wasn't nearly as put together."

I laugh. "I find that hard to believe." Her lips twitch and I know I've won her over.

She holds up her clipboard, a line of neat blue check marks march down the side of the list. "We're almost through with the setup. Is there anything else you want to go over?"

I shake my head. "I defer to the experts on these things." I wave my hand around the room. In the past few hours while I've unpacked, they've moved most of the furniture out, replacing it with high top tables draped in starched white tablecloths. In the center of each is a square vase filled with flowers from various counties around the state. It's a nice touch. "This all looks great," I tell her.

"Thanks." She smiles and starts back for the kitchen.

"Oh, there was one last thing," I call after her. I grab a bottle of bourbon with a rounded bottom and a stopper in the shape of a horse and jockey from a nearby table. "I found this in my dad's study. It was one of his favorite labels and I think I remember reading somewhere that it's Mrs. Wells's favorite as well. I just wanted to make sure it made it to the bar in case she or any other guests wanted some."

Cynthia takes the bottle. "I'll personally make sure Mrs. Wells is offered a glass when she arrives."

With a nod of thanks I retreat upstairs to get ready. I take my time, making sure every detail is as it should be, my eyes sweeping back over my appearance, probing for any flaws.

After the rescue I'd had my chin sharpened and palate widened, my teeth veneered and my eyebrows reshaped. Thanks to bimonthly highlights and keratin treatments, my hair is shiny smooth, cascading to my shoulder blades in dark waves. With the help of tinted contacts, my eyes take on a darker brown tint that I then emphasize with purple-tinted mascara. Properly applied bronzer takes a bit of the roundness out of my cheekbones and highlight powder lengthens the appearance of my neck.

I watch myself smile, the corner of one side tilting higher, just like in all the photographs downstairs. Anything even remotely Frances has been steadfastly and systematically eradicated.

Everything about me is perfected and polished, and thoroughly, thoroughly Libby.

Though becoming her on the outside may have been a bit of a struggle in the beginning, it's now merely a set of routines and habits. I've been practicing for so long that most of it is secondhand. Convincing Shepherd of my identity was my first test. Tonight will be the second.

If I can pull it off—if I can convince Grey and his father that I'm Libby—then the rest of my plan will fall easily into place. And if I fail . . . I shake my head, refusing even the possibility.

Before heading downstairs, I reach for my purse and slip free an old, tightly folded piece of newspaper from my wallet. I open it carefully, smoothing down the edges, and stare at the old me.

According to her gravestone, Frances Amelia Mace died on March 21, 2011. She'd just turned fourteen the week before. The newspapers ran her photo along with all the other passengers who died on the *Persephone*.

I collected all the articles, hoarding every clip I could find— anything that mentioned Frances Mace. At night, when the rest of school was in bed asleep, I'd pull an old metal lockbox from under my bed and spread the yellowing pages across the floor.

A hundred Franceses all staring back at me. Perpetually frozen in time. Just a girl—nothing special about her. Only child. Midwestern roots. Awkward smile.

The picture wasn't the most flattering and I felt sorry for that. All over the world people would remember Frances as she existed in the class photo taken at the beginning of eighth grade: slightly blurry, one of her earrings tangled in her brown hair at that unfortunate stage of being grown out, braces peeking between chapped lips. Eyes hesitant, as though the man behind the camera had promised to count to three but snapped the photo on two.

Anyone glancing at that picture would know exactly what kind of girl Frances had been. Normal. Average. Typical. She'd had crushes on boys and flirted clumsily. The first time she'd held hands with a guy, she focused more on the sweat of her palm than the feel of his fingers laced with hers.

She'd spent hours texting and chatting with friends, dissecting conversations with guys for deeper meanings. At night, she'd daydreamed elaborate scenarios that would inevitably throw her and the boy of her dreams together—trapped in an elevator or an avalanche or on a deserted island.

There was nothing in her life she didn't approach with a fearful passion, one eye trained on those around her, always anticipating their potential judgment; the other eye trained on the wilds of her imagination. The unrestrained belief that nothing in life would ever truly be off-limits. That it was only a matter of time.

It hadn't seemed fair how quickly she'd been forgotten. For a few months her various social media accounts had displayed notes of shock and sorrow over her sudden death. People posted photos of her and shared their favorite memories. But eventually those had faded. Her friends had grown and changed, struck new allegiances in school. Moved on.

I envied them at times. Being able to forget Frances. I'd been unable to. In the early days after the *Persephone*, Frances's rage and pain became so overwhelming that daily life was impossible. Cecil took care of her then, in a remote European hospital with an army of nurses and specialists—therapists and drugs.

And then one day, I'd been standing in front of a mirror staring at a stranger. I wasn't yet Libby but I was no longer Frances. I hadn't gained back weight after the rescue, I no longer had the energy to brush my hair. Nightmares stole sleep at every opportunity.

All I could do was replay the attack on the *Persephone* endlessly. Trying to find the clues I'd missed, the ones that would have allowed me to save my parents. Hating myself. No—reviling myself and wishing I'd died out on the ocean instead of Libby.

Knowing I didn't deserve to have survived.

The same emotions rolled through me unceasing: rage, despair, horror. All with an undercurrent of helplessness. That was the one I could never escape: the helplessness.

And in that moment, staring at myself, despising myself, wishing myself dead, one word began glowing in the back of my mind. The only brightness in the black I'd plunged myself into.

*Truth.*

Another, darker word followed quickly after.

*Revenge.*

Whispering the words aloud had been like lancing an infected wound—the relief was immediate, the pressure finally relieved. The words were a box into which I could put all those crushing emotions. A way to store them for a while as I figured out how to recover.

Because suddenly I knew what to do. I saw a way forward. I decided that I would fight. I would use rage to push back the ragged edges of my grief. I would become Libby, I would recover my strength, I would bide my time, and I would plan.

Then one day, I would put those plans in action.

# EIGHT

I run into Shepherd in the foyer. He's wearing the same shorts and T-shirt from before, his feet bare. "The fund-raiser for Senator Wells starts soon," I point out.

He glances at me, his eyes quickly taking in my appearance. A muscle along his jaw tenses. "And?" he asks.

"And you're not ready."

He lifts his eyebrows. "Right. Because I'm not going."

"Why not? You're the one running the conservation and the whole point of hosting this thing is because the Senator supported Cecil's efforts along the coast."

Shepherd stares at me for a long moment. "So you call him Cecil now?"

My fingers twitch, wanting to ball into a fist with frustration at the stupid misstep. I let my gaze fall to the floor, searching for a quick explanation. "I guess it's easier to deal with the fact that he's gone if I call him Cecil instead of Dad." I add in a chin wobble and it's enough that Shepherd doesn't press the point.

"I'm not going to the reception because Senator Wells is a douche," he says instead. I cough to cover my surprised laugh and his eyes lose some of their hostility toward me, but none of the passion for the subject. "He pays lip service to environmentalism and conservation, but does nothing to back it up. If anything, he's a proponent of development. He's been pushing bills through congress to expand drilling on protected land and even convincing his crony friends to build on Caldwell."

"But don't you think that if Dad were still alive he'd be the one hosting—"

He cuts me off. "Cecil hated the Senator—hated it when the guy built down the island. So, no, Cecil wouldn't have done anything that involved Senator Wells."

The doorbell rings, interrupting. I realize that in the course of arguing we've stepped toward each other and are now uncomfortably close. We stand that way for a beat longer than necessary. I let him take in the familiar smell of Libby's shampoo, the soft scent of the rosewater sachet she hung in her closet. Even her deodorant is the same as it was four years ago.

Scent is one of the most powerful memory triggers and I know that right now Shepherd's mind is on fire with memories of Libby. And now he'll associate every single one of those memories with me: the young woman standing in front of him. Tying me in the present to the girl of his past.

He's the one to step away, his expression somewhat haunted. His eyes sweep my face, a silent question in them. He blinks, and it's gone. "You pierced your ears."

I'm taken aback by the unexpected statement. "Yes," I say,

my fingers unconsciously lifting to twist at Libby's mother's diamond earrings.

He nods. "I guess you got over your fear of needles, then."

I almost smile. It's been a long time since I've learned something new about Libby. But I can't have him dwelling on the inconsistency, so I give him something else to dwell on instead. I look at him pointedly. "I've gotten over a lot of things in the last four years."

I've been standing in the foyer greeting guests for what feels like an eternity. I'd banked on my presence to induce a fairly high turnout, knowing that many in the state would pay good money to see a reunion such as this. The three survivors of the *Persephone* disaster, meeting for the first time since the ship went down four years ago. It'll be the talk of the summer—already photographers from various newspapers stand poised, waiting.

Which is fine with me because every single aspect of this party is a ruse. Completely designed with one goal in mind. So while I wait for the unwitting players to arrive, I patiently shake hands, accepting condolences from strangers for Cecil's passing months before. Giving them the bitter-sad smile they're expecting in response, letting my eyes frost with carefully controlled tears.

And then the door opens. Everything in the world comes to a stop. Conversations fall away and it feels as though the air pressure in the room has dropped, every lung drawing breath at the same time. Holding. Watching. Waiting.

Senator Wells comes first, his presence larger than any television could capture. He wears a perfectly tailored suit, his "you can trust me" salt-and-pepper hair impeccably combed, and just the right amount of humble confidence furrows the ridge between his eyebrows.

I swallow thickly and square my shoulders as he approaches. He presses my hand between both of his. "I can't thank you enough for your generous support of my campaign." His words come out honey sweet, but if anyone else in the room could see his eyes they'd know the truth. That he'd rather be done with me, that our paths never cross again.

That he doesn't trust me. And he shouldn't.

But of course, the money from this fund-raiser is simply too much for him to pass up. Which is exactly what I'd been counting on. As the world turns and the sun rises and sets, politicians will always be in need of money. Senator Wells is no exception.

I smile, letting the corners of my lips wobble. "It's the least I could do for all the support you've given my father's conservation efforts."

Senator Wells tips his head to the side, frowning slightly. He knows I'm lying. What he doesn't know is why. "Though it's belated, please accept our condolences on his passing." He slips an arm around his wife and she nods as she takes my hand.

"It's a shame your father isn't here to see what a beautiful and gracious hostess you've become," she adds. The problem is that she's being entirely sincere. The back of my throat tightens unexpectedly. I know she means Cecil, but for a moment I can't stop thinking about my real father. The way he'd take my hands and pull my feet on top of his and dance me around the room on Christmas Eve.

I close my eyes against the dizzying memory. "My beautiful Frances," he'd say as we spun in circles.

It's been so long that I can't even remember his voice. All the different ways he'd say my name: to wake me up in the morning; to call me to dinner; to scold me; to cheer me on.

To tell me he loved me.

That, along with everything else, was taken from me on the *Persephone*.

*How did I think I could come back and not be affected?*

Mrs. Wells squeezes my hand and says, "I'm sure you miss him terribly."

I nod. Words impossible.

And then, while I'm still reeling, a scent so intimately familiar washes over me. It's as though I've been set on fire the way it causes my skin to burn. I open my eyes and he is there.

*Grey.*

He's wearing pressed khakis and a light pink button-down shirt that emphasizes the width of his shoulders and the narrowness of his hips. His hair's cut short, the bangs sweeping across his forehead already streaked lighter by the summer sun. I'd forgotten how improbably blue his eyes could be, how prominent his cheekbones and the slanted angle of his jaw.

I've imagined this moment so many times that it seems impossible it's never actually taken place before.

Ever since the *Persephone* sank, I've daydreamed this reunion a dozen different ways. At first I pictured him sopping wet, shirt plastered to his chest, as he swept into the room and didn't even hesitate before wrapping his arms around my waist and pulling me in for a kiss as necessary as air.

Then later, as I began to understand more what it meant that he'd lied about the *Persephone*, I imagined tracking him in the dead of night, slicing a blade across his throat before he could even say a word.

Over the past four years Grey has been both my daydream and my nightmare, my fantasy and my darkest desire. He's become my obsession—I've read every article with the slightest reference to him, tracked his high school sports teams, stalked him across every social media platform that exists.

I thought I was prepared for him.

I was wrong.

Standing in front of me, he simply occupies more space than I expected. It's one thing to see a picture of a boy full grown, but it never completely erased the way he's always been in my head; what his bony shoulders felt like cupped in my palms, the angle my head tilted to meet his lips.

It takes everything I have to keep my expression calm and neutral when everything inside me is strung tight enough to snap. I want to leap across the distance between us and claw my nails down his cheeks and demand answers. How did he survive? Why did he lie? Did he know it was going to happen?

What is he hiding and why?

A warm flush pools along my lower back, spreading out in all directions. I want to run. Hide. Take a moment to regroup, refocus. But I can't do any of these things and so I stand, feet rooted in place, and wait while his gaze sweeps over me.

Frances flexes under my skin. *See me!* she screams when Grey's eyes finally find their way to my own. A slight frown pinches the skin between his eyebrows and my breath comes faster—needing him to believe the disguise, but wishing that he'd remember me well enough to see through it. For a moment, we share the same stunned expression: something disquieted if not a little startled.

"Libby." The name escapes his lips on a breath of air, and behind me comes the collective movement of each guest straining forward to hear.

His voice triggers something inside me, a flood, hot like adrenaline. But there's a taste there as well, a slow contraction of my stomach. I can't help it, my eyes fall to his lips.

A memory from the cruise rises unbidden: the two of us together on deck, the night sky infinite as he kisses me for the first time. His forehead had been pressed against my own for what felt like an eternity. The distance between our lips minuscule, yet infinite. His fingers found their way to my temple, slowly sweeping my hair back behind my ear. Goose bumps trailed in the wake of his touch.

*Please, can I kiss you?* he'd asked, the question whisper smooth. I'd barely begun to nod when his mouth met mine.

It's hard to believe there was ever a time when the biggest questions in my life were as simple as this: *Please, can I kiss you?* My back stiffens and I force a well-practiced smile.

"Grey," I respond with a dip of my chin.

# NINE

Grey opens his mouth to say something but whatever it is is lost to the sound of his father loudly clearing his throat. Something shifts in Grey's expression, a controlled tightness taking over.

Before he can slip away into the crowd I lean toward him, placing the tips of my fingers against his bare wrist. Tension roars around me, a battle between the knowledge that he is one of the only people who truly knows what happened on the *Persephone* but is also someone I can never speak to about it.

Not yet, at least.

"Thank you for coming," I tell him. I let my eyes linger on his for just a moment longer, watching as his pupils dilate ever so slightly.

Then I turn to the next guest in line. A small frown flickers across Grey's face at my dismissal, confusion as though our meeting wasn't as he'd expected. The room hums with disappointment, silence giving way to rabid whispers.

Grey follows his parents through the foyer to the open living room. Every few feet someone stops his father to shake his hand. The Senator thanks them all by name, the consummate politician. Martha Wells plays the part of the Senator's wife perfectly, freshly starched and styled, jewels glittering at her throat and her heels impossibly steep.

It surprises me how well Grey fits in with them, how smooth his smile is as the other society wives flirt with him shamelessly. He responds easily, keeping them at bay while not exactly pushing them away. There's nothing of the awkwardness or hesitancy I remember from the cruise ship.

As I rotate through the reception I steal glances at him, envious of the confident ease with which he controls the room. Libby had been like that, the girl everyone else clamored to be around. I'd experienced it myself the first moment I'd met her on the *Persephone*.

*The captain's voice drones hollowly through the loud speaker as everyone on the ship files somewhat reluctantly into the dining room, the rain having forced the safety drill indoors.*

*"Let's go, little sailor," my father says, nudging me forward. He's actually wearing the glaringly orange life vest whereas most everyone else just carries theirs. "Where's your spirit of adventure?" he asks me, and he's grinning in that way that makes it obvious he knows he's stepped over the edge of embarrassment.*

*The room is crowded and warm, and to my dismay the average age of the occupants is well north of forty and probably solidly past fifty. As I'm trying to hide my disappointment, a girl squeezes next to me in line, knocking me slightly off balance.*

*I'm taken aback by her—she seems to be about my age with strikingly similar features. It's as though I looked into an aged mirror fogged by steam, except she's poised and polished and I'm . . . dull and frizzy. If we were in a magazine, I would be the "before" photo and she'd be the "after."*

*"Lamest way to start a cruise ever." She lets out a huff before shaking her life jacket. "Like we're ever going to need this stuff. And seriously, if I'd wanted to get rained on I could have just stayed home and stood in my shower fully dressed."*

*My first thought is that she can't be talking to me and I glance at her ears, searching for signs of earbuds or a hands-free headset. But then she holds out her hand to me, her grin earnest and lopsided. "I'm Libby."*

Libby's attention was like a spotlight that made anyone caught in its glare feel somehow *more than*. More interesting, more important, more special and pretty. I knew even then that I'd never be like her—I could try to mimic her walk, her expressions, her favorite phrases, and I'd never achieve what she had: the ability to make other people *want* to know you.

That realization had left me aching then, and still does now. Because no matter how hard I try to become Libby O'Martin, I will never be more than a shell of what she could have been.

When Grey finally steps toward the patio, I make my move, careful to get the timing right. We reach the open French door at the same time, our shoulders colliding. Before he realizes it's me he's run into, a smile begins to light up his face. It freezes the moment recognition hits. Awkwardness slams down around him.

As he begins to fumble out an apology I let my breath hitch, allow a bit of panic to seep into my eyes. I press a hand to my chest, talking over him. "I'm sorry," I say, stepping away. "It's just . . ." I wave generally toward the crowd of people inside and shake my head as if it's all too much.

Instantly he's concerned and begins to ask if I'm okay but I don't give him the chance to finish. I'm already halfway across the patio, trying to keep from breaking out into a run. When I reach the boardwalk I crash my toes against the bottom step, tripping forward and catching myself on the railing. I pull myself up and rush down the old wooden planks past the dunes to the beach.

And then it is there in front of me: the wash of ocean. It's the closest I've been to it since being rescued. Even now I feel some sort of tug, as though it had laid claim on my life four years ago and intends to collect.

"*Not now*," I whisper under my breath. *Not yet*, I add silently.

I force myself forward, pushing the fear under a layer of cold determination—focusing on the plan rather than the way the pulse of waves matches the beat of my heart.

The tears come freely when my feet hit the sand and I'm almost at the water's edge before I let myself crumple to my knees. In front of me, the ocean stretches out seamless against the sky and the taste of salt claws at my throat. I press my face into my hands, as though to block out the world.

Knowing this is how he'll find me and that he won't be able to resist offering comfort. Grey never could pass up a damsel in distress.

I hear his footsteps first, the gait uneven as he jogs through the soft sand after me. Even though I hear him call, "Libby," I don't turn. He slows as he comes near, but he doesn't stop until he's by my side.

This time when he says, "*Libby*," like a whisper, I tilt my head up toward him. He towers over me, his eyes scanning quickly across my face: the tear tracks, the openly exposed misery. The loneliness. Instantly he crouches, not caring that the damp sand soaks the cuffs of his perfectly ironed pants.

But he hesitates as he reaches for my shoulder. He starts to say something, ask if I'm okay, but whatever it was is swallowed when I fall against his chest, my arms trapped between us.

In this I give Frances rein, allowing her misery to seep through so that the tears and anguish are authentic. Over and over again I tell him I'm sorry, the words muffled against his shoulder and he just responds with "It's okay," as he keeps his arms awkward and loose around me.

It was one of the things that had drawn me so fiercely to Grey on the cruise ship: his compassion. Nothing triggers it so as much as a girl in tears. There's a part of me that hates that I've used this against him. That this is how I've laid my trap.

But there's another part of me that only cares that, after all these years, I'm finally in his arms again.

## TEN

I keep myself pressed against Grey a few moments longer before letting out a flustered laugh and pushing myself free of his arms. Keeping my head ducked, I bite my lip and squinch my eyes closed, as though I'm too embarrassed to face him.

"I'm sorry," I say, shaking my head. "I didn't realize how hard it was going to be to come back. All the memories of my dad and everyone talking about . . ." I trail off, letting the *Persephone* go unspoken.

"No, it's okay." His fingers flutter against my upper arm. Now that the tears have passed he's unsure of how to handle me. There's no protocol for this sort of situation—no guidebook for what to say when a girl you once met four years ago and left to die out on the ocean abruptly comes back into your life.

It was Frances he'd been close to on the cruise, not Libby. To him Libby had been more of a third wheel. It's not that he'd only tolerated her—he'd been more friendly than that. But it had always been clear that, given the option, he'd have rather had Frances to himself.

"It must be difficult being home after all this time," he murmurs. And the thing is, I know he's being earnest. That's just a part of who he is—or at least who he was. But being earnest isn't enough.

A streak of anger flashes under my spine. Because the *Persephone* took everything from me and nothing from him.

*Which is why I'm here*, I remind myself. To show him what it is to lose those you love.

I let one side of my mouth twitch up into a brief smile. A Libby trademark. "It sucks."

That gets a soft laugh. He eases back onto his feet, standing slowly. Giant wet patches circle his pants from where he knelt, but he doesn't seem to notice as he holds out a hand to help me up. We stand, side by side, staring back at the house. Even with the wind coming off the ocean at our backs, the sound of conversation and clinking glasses carries from the reception. Neither of us makes an effort to start toward the boardwalk.

Already, a stiffness begins developing between us again. I can almost hear the way his mind winds up, going through all the calculations of how to approach this situation.

How to approach me.

I don't want him overthinking. It will only cause him to pull away, put distance between us. And that's not part of the plan. I need more time with him first.

"I know most everyone is here just for the gossip." I gesture toward the house and pluck at the damp hem of my dress. "But I'm a little afraid of what will happen if we go back looking like this." The testy salt air has tousled my hair and I know my lower lip is swollen from biting back tears.

It looks like we've spent the past several moments rolling around in the sand together. A blush trails up his throat. He ducks his head and rubs his hand along the back of his neck as he lets out a nervous laugh.

It's a gesture so familiar that I almost can't breathe.

He must notice and think it's the prospect of rejoining the reception that has me uneasy because he asks, "Do you want to walk maybe, instead? Let things dry out a bit?"

I smile, grateful. "Yes, thank you." I slide off my sandals and he jogs toward the boardwalk and leaves them on the step along with his shoes and socks. When he rolls up the cuffs of his pants and shirt I notice that his legs are somehow already tan even though the summer season has barely begun.

A few clouds have drifted in over the course of the afternoon, the wind turning sharper. It's enough to have driven the few beachgoers inside, and Grey and I have most of the long stretch of sand to ourselves.

After a long pause in which Grey clearly struggles to find something to say that isn't about my prolonged absence from Caldwell, my father's death, or the *Persephone*, the conversation begins almost unbearably stilted. "You planning to stay in town for a while?" he asks.

"For the summer at least," I tell him. Which is the truth. "After that . . . ?" I shrug. "I'm still figuring it all out." Also the truth. Because I really *don't* know where I'll be or even who I'll be when fall comes. I could only plan so far ahead before the variables became so expansive I had to let go.

In reality, much of what happens next rests on Grey. How long it takes for him to let me in—how much force I need to apply before someone cracks and the truth comes spilling out.

"What about you?" I ask.

He keeps walking, hands shoved in his pockets and shoulders hunched. "Working on Dad's campaign. Then USC Honors in the fall."

"Not Stanford?" During the cruise he'd admitted to Frances how tired he was of his father's expectations. Everything was already planned for him: same boarding school; same summer camp; same college. He wanted something different and far away, like Stanford.

He stops, turning toward me with a frown. No doubt wondering how I'd know all of this—wondering how much Frances must have told me of their conversations.

But to ask would be to bring up the *Persephone*. And I know the moment he realizes this because he presses his lips together and resumes walking.

Softly, I set my fingertips against his forearm just below where he's rolled up the sleeves. The muscles tense under my touch as I turn him toward me. "This is either going to be a very long walk or a very short one if we try to avoid what we're both thinking."

Relief and wariness war in his eyes, which have turned the smoky color of the cloud-shadowed waves crashing to shore. His pulse thrums along his throat, but he says nothing.

"The *Persephone*," I murmur. I didn't even believe it was possible, but his expression becomes even more guarded, his jaw clenching. But still he remains silent.

I cross my arms and turn, looking out at the sea. The waves are now tipped with white, growing angrier as the gray sky on the horizon presses toward shore. I shiver, as much from the bite of the wind as the memory of the last time I stood with Grey as a storm approached.

We'd been kissing. His hand against the curve of my bare lower back, pulling me against him. It was the last perfect moment of my life before everything was shattered.

Something warm and soft falls across my shoulders, shrouding me in a familiar smell. It's Grey's shirt, and I turn to find him standing in a plain white undershirt that stretches tight across his chest, molding to his muscles.

"You were shivering," he says, as though I'd asked for an explanation.

If I knew nothing else about Greyson Wells, I'd assume he was the perfect guy. Good-looking, wealthy, charming. Caring. Nice.

But that's the problem. I've seen him lie—seen him stare straight at the cameras and tell the world that a rogue wave took out the *Persephone*. I know just how skilled he is at deception. How convincing.

For a while, he'd even made me second-guess my own memories from the night of the attack.

I realize now just how dangerous of a game I've begun. How easy it would be to forget who Grey really is and what he's done. I tilt my head back, looking up at him and making myself appear small and vulnerable. "I don't remember anything," I tell him.

There's a flash of confusion.

"About the *Persephone*," I explain. After a beat I add, "Nothing."

He steps back, raising his hand to the back of his neck and rubbing vigorously. "At all?"

I shake my head.

"How?" he asks.

I lift a shoulder. Tell him the perfectly crafted lie. "The doctors all have a different theory. Post-traumatic stress. Some argued I probably hit my head when the wave struck. Or that dehydration and malnutrition messed with things. Apparently maritime history is rife with stories of people lost at sea losing their minds. It's not uncommon."

He lets this sink in, walking toward the ocean until the tips of the waves slide around his toes. I stand slightly behind him, out of reach of the water, waiting.

A muscle twitches along his jaw as he clenches his teeth. "And Frances?"

# ELEVEN

Something tight squeezes my heart at the sound of my name on his lips. I look down at my hands, fingers twisted in the hem of his shirt. Libby's signet ring gleams in the dull light. "I remember a few things." My voice comes out broken; it's perhaps the most honest thing I've said to him so far.

"She didn't say anything, though?" He faces me, scrutinizing my reactions. "When you were on the lifeboat together? About what happened on the *Persephone* when she sank?"

Shaking my head I tell him, "They tried everything to try to fix my memory: hypnosis, therapy, drug treatments." I squeeze my eyes shut, taking a shuddering breath. "But I don't want to remember. Please." I feel the tears burning, forcing their way free. "Please don't make me remember." I swallow, thickly. "I can't," I add in a whisper, telling him what I know he wants to hear: that I'm not a threat. That whatever secrets he has can remain buried.

That he can afford to let down his guard around me.

His hands fall lightly on my shoulders, fingertips nudging me toward him. "I'm sorry," he murmurs, wrapping me against his chest. We stand like this for several moments, his racing heartbeat eventually slowing under my cheek.

Closing my eyes, with the sound of the waves as a backdrop, I can almost believe I'm back on the *Persephone*. Before anything went wrong. When my future was still a brightly coiled path of possibility.

"Trust me, you don't want to remember." He swallows several times. "It was awful," he adds, almost silently.

I pull my head back and look up at him. He's staring at the horizon, but his gaze is unfocused. I wonder whether, like me, his mind churns with images from that night. The terror. The confusion. The pain. It's obviously all still there, grinding under the surface. The truth of what happened, struggling for release.

The trick is in getting him to confess it all willingly. "You're right—I *don't* want to know and I won't ever ask you to remember any of it," I tell him.

I can lie as convincingly as he can.

Because I know that if I ask him now, he'll feed me the same lines he's fed everyone else. About the rogue wave. About the miraculous rescue.

He needs to trust me first.

He needs to *know* me.

His expression turns grateful, the wariness almost gone. And I know I've achieved my goal—that I've put him at ease.

"They'll probably start wondering where we are soon if

we don't get back." I turn and start toward the house. In the storm-darkened evening the lights around the patio and pool have come on, turning the O'Martin estate into a beacon. I point it out to Grey, adding, "Don't lighthouses usually signal danger?"

He chuckles. "Who's to say that's not accurate?"

I smile, allowing my shoulder to bump gently against his. This time, the walk in silence is amiable rather than awkward. But my steps slow as we leave the beach behind and make our way up the stairs to the boardwalk. Even with the turning weather the yard is strewn with people. Strangers. My stomach tightens and I honestly wonder what would happen if I just turned and started running. Never stopped.

If I could run fast enough and far enough that I could forget everything.

But it's never worked before.

There's only one path forward and I'm already far enough down it that the only option is to keep moving.

"I guess we have to go back in there, huh?" I ask. Grey's shirt whips out behind me in the wind, the hem popping and snapping like a flag.

"Unfortunately," Grey responds. He stands slightly behind me and I hear the way his voice shifts, a note of regret playing under the words as he adds, "I'm not sure familial duty ever ends."

As a Senator's son I'm sure much is expected of him. But there's bitterness and anger in the way he says it, as though the sentiment runs deeper. I make a mental note before turning and letting his shirt drop from my shoulders, holding it out to him. Once he's shrugged into it, I take my time slipping the buttons into place for him.

"Thank you," I tell him. He frowns, confused, and I smile. "For making this"—I wave a hand between us—"bearable." I lift one corner of my lips higher, the Libby trademark. "Maybe moving back home won't be so bad after all." His eyebrows rise in surprise, but before he can say anything his phone chirps in his pocket.

Almost apologetically, he slips it free and glances at the screen. He frowns. *My dad*, he mouths to me as he presses the phone to his ear. "Hey, Dad, what's—" He swallows the rest of the greeting and turns slightly away, listening. A look of concern flashes across his face. "Is she okay?" He glances back toward the house, clearly anxious.

"Good." After listening a moment more, he cringes. "Oh, um . . ." His eyes snap to mine. "No, I . . ." He takes another step away. His voice drops. "I left early—decided to walk home."

He glances at me again. "No, I'm not—I'm . . . I'm by myself." He rubs that spot behind his ear, shoulders pulled tight. It doesn't take a master sleuth to figure out the other side of the conversation. If Grey's lying, clearly he's doing something he doesn't want his father knowing about.

And I'm guessing that something is anything involving me.

The call ends abruptly and Grey inhales sharply. "Sorry about that," he says, sliding the phone back in his pocket.

"Everything okay?" I ask.

He lifts a shoulder, having a hard time meeting my eyes. "My mom wasn't feeling well so Dad took her home. He was just calling because he couldn't find me at the party and was worried."

I feign surprise. "Oh no, is your mom okay?"

"Probably just something she ate or a bug. Dad says she'll be fine. But, uh, I should be going." He takes a step backward and then another. There's a stretch of silence between us and I can see the way his mind churns, trying to figure out how to fill it.

I wait, knowing that it's in the silences where truth often comes.

But not tonight, apparently. He simply nods and then turns, jogging for home. And I smile, knowing it's not the last I'll see of him.

This is just the beginning.

## TWELVE

I'm up early the next morning, anticipation making it difficult to sleep in. After showering I drive into town. Caldwell is a collection of small islands, some of them protected by Cecil's conservation easements, but most dotted with high-end, expensive beach houses set on large lots. Though the town itself sits on the biggest island, it's still only a few blocks long. I pull into one of the many open parking spaces along the street and make my way into the specialty food store.

The thing about small towns is that everyone knows everyone else. And while I may be a stranger, Cecil wasn't. When I approach the manager, he greets me warmly, immediately expressing his regrets over my father's passing. I tell him I'm looking for a get-well gift for Mrs. Wells and he helps me fill a sweetgrass basket with some of her favorite items: 80-percent-cocoa dark chocolate; organic scuppernong grapes; and several vials of Refreshergy, the energy drink she takes every morning.

"Looks disgusting," I comment as the manager rings them up. He shrugs, claiming that the Senator's wife swears by them.

Once I'm back in the car, I flip open the glove compartment and pull out another Refreshergy vial, tucking it into the basket with the others. Except for the fact that the seal is broken, there's no way to tell the difference between them.

That done, I grab my cell phone and dial a number I'd memorized this morning. After two rings, a soft voice with a drawn accent answers, "Good mornin', Caldwell Island Country Club, how can I help you?"

"Yes, this is Mindy Gervistan and I work for Harrison Cheefer, Senator Wells's chief of staff?" I let just a touch of nervous energy come through in my voice. "I was just going over his calendar for the day and I have on here that the Senator's playing golf, but somehow I don't have the actual tee time. Do you mind letting me know when it is?"

"Of course," the woman says. There's a rustling of paper. "We have him and his son down for noon with their usual caddies."

"Oh, thank goodness," I gush, sounding relieved. "You're a lifesaver. Thank you!"

She chuckles as she says good-bye and I check the time before slipping the phone back into my purse. It's ten fifteen now, which means I've got at least an hour to kill. For a moment I think about heading toward the Caldwell Island Marina where the *Libby Two* is still docked, but I'm not quite sure I'm ready to handle that just yet. So I decide to wander my way back to the O'Martin estate— taking turns at random to familiarize myself with routes I'd only seen online. I drive past acres and acres of forest and marsh, all protected thanks to Cecil and managed by Shepherd. I smile, rolling down the windows and letting the fresh summer air play through my hair.

It's so different here along the coast, that I still haven't fully adjusted. I grew up in Ohio and my family had been solidly middle class, which meant access to the ocean was rare. And for years after the *Persephone*, the thought of living anywhere near the ocean terrified me.

I couldn't even stand the taste of salt on my food, much less face the prospect of a horizon that never ended. Which is why when Cecil had given me my choice of European boarding schools, I'd chosen one tucked deep in an alpine valley, far away from the sea, from my old life, from anyone who'd ever known anything about me or Libby.

But I've always known that eventually I'd have to conquer my distrust of the ocean. It's the only way I'd be able to get close enough to Grey and his father to implement my plan. Luckily, rage is a powerful emotion, strong enough not just to burn away pain but also to sear back the whispering tendrils of fear.

Back at the O'Martin estate I leave my car parked in the driveway before striking out on foot, the sweetgrass basket balanced in my arms. It's not a long walk to the Wellses' house—only a mile and a half—but for privacy reasons, most of the lots on this island remain shrouded with stunted pines that tangle the ocean breeze before it can make it to the road. I'm sweating by the time I turn into their driveway.

The Wells house is monstrous and modern—all sharp angles and slick panes of glass that do nothing but lash out against the natural curving beauty of the island coast. It clashes against the moss-draped oaks lining the long driveway, as though, like the family inside, it were determined to make the land bend to its will.

After ringing the bell I stand on the porch, waiting. Despite the fact that it's still early in the summer, my sundress sticks damply to my back and already the late morning hums with the thickness of humidity and cicadas.

I'm pleased that when Grey finally opens the door, his eyes widen in surprise.

"I was worried about your mom," I say, holding out the sweetgrass basket. "I don't want to intrude, especially if she's still not feeling well, but I did want to stop by and make sure she's okay. See if there's anything I can do."

He hesitates, trying to reconcile my presence, wondering whether to sort me into the enemy or the friend camp. My hope is that after our walk on the beach yesterday, I've at least earned a "to be determined" designation. Just to be sure, I let my chin drop a fraction, allowing one corner of my lip to kick up higher than the other in a self-conscious smile.

In response, he glances over my shoulder at the empty driveway and must figure out that I walked up here. His grip on the door loosens and he steps aside. Having been born and raised in South Carolina, he well knows that manners dictate you offer someone refreshments when they've gone out their way like I have.

I nod my head in thanks as I step inside. When Grey takes the basket from me, his eyes linger for a moment at where I'd been clutching it against my chest. As I expected, the air-conditioning is running at full blast, and the thin material of my sundress does little to hide that my skin instantly prickles into goose bumps.

I cross my arms, rubbing at the exposed skin to warm it. It's just enough of a natural response that I can tell Grey's not sure whether I caught him ogling or not. Flustered, he turns and leads me through the house.

"It's funny you showed up here," he remarks as we walk.

"How so?" I ask, taking the opportunity to scan my surroundings as I follow him. The inside of the house has about as much character as the outside: furniture in various shades of white with severely sharp angles; walls that sport grayish-toned abstract paintings; and a polished concrete floor that echoes our every footstep.

It's quieter than a church, less personal than a hotel suite.

"I'd been thinking about offering to show you around town." He steps aside to allow me to enter the kitchen first. It's enormous, the ceiling intricately vaulted and the entire far wall a row of French doors looking out toward the ocean. There's nothing at all homey about this room with its twelve-burner gas stove and row of gleaming Sub-Zero refrigerators. If anything, it's more designed to cater elaborate parties than family dinners.

"But clearly you don't need that anymore," he says, holding up the basket as evidence that I know my way around.

I lean against the marble-topped island and laugh. "Yeah, but I had to use the GPS to get to the store and relied on the clerk to let me know what your mother might like. Speaking of . . ." I pull free the extra bottle of Refreshergy and I pretend to slice my nail against the seal in order to uncap the lid. I sniff at the contents, bracing myself for the smell of rotting fish and honeysuckle. "What is this stuff?"

Grey sets the basket down and rolls his eyes. "Some organic crap my mom puts in her breakfast smoothies. One of her friends recommended it—convinced her it would somehow make her look younger and give her more energy."

I wrinkle my nose. "Have you tried it?"

"God, no," he says, shaking his head adamantly. "Though she swears by it. Drinks it religiously every morning before her swim."

"That's what the clerk at the store said." I place the vial back on the counter and riffle through the rest of the basket, holding up the contents and inspecting them as though I'd never seen any of it before. "I basically just asked him to grab anything he thought your mom would like."

"You really didn't need to do all of this," he tells me. "But I know my mother will be very touched you thought of her."

My smile turns rueful. Playful. "Well, I felt bad she fell ill at the fund-raiser. I figure poisoning the neighbors doesn't give the best first impression." There's something reckless and delicious in the admission of truth.

Grey's just started laughing when his father walks in, attention focused on a stack of letters in his hand. The sound chokes in Grey's throat.

Senator Wells glances up and the moment his eyes land on me, his expression tightens. Ever the consummate politician, he quickly shutters his true thoughts behind a slick smile.

"Miss O'Martin," he says with a slight tilt of his head. "We weren't expecting you." His words are perhaps sharper than he intends.

# THIRTEEN

Sensing the tension, Grey jumps in before I have a chance to. "She came to check on Mom."

Senator Wells keeps his attention focused on me. It's not surprising that he's found so much success in politics—power radiates from him.

"I was so sorry y'all had to leave early last night and I didn't have a chance to say good-bye in person." I feel Grey's eyes on me, his awareness that I've just lied to cover for him. "I also really wanted to thank you for continuing my dad's legacy with the conservation efforts. It means a lot to me that he's remembered that way."

Senator Wells's response is brisk. "Of course. I appreciate your support of my campaign. Now," he says, turning toward Grey, "if we don't want to miss our tee time we'd better be going." He walks toward a door that leads into the garage and, just like that, he dismisses us both.

Grey's eyes flick toward me, distressed by his father's rudeness. "I . . . uh . . ."

I lightly touch my fingers to the back of his hand, cutting off his floundering. "It was good to see you again," I tell him. I start toward a set of French doors that leads to the patio and the beach beyond. When I pry them open, a blast of hot sticky wind rolls against us.

"Ugh," I groan, rolling my eyes. "It's days like this that make me wonder why we don't all move to Maine." I'm just about to step outside when Grey stops me.

"We can drop you off on the way to the club." He glances toward the garage and the muscles around his eyes tighten with wariness.

I bite my lip. "You think your dad will be okay with that? I don't want to make you late." It's obvious to both of us his father would like nothing to do with me. Even though this is only something minor—a simple ride home—I'm asking Grey to choose between me and his father.

Though I doubt he sees it that way. And that's the whole point. Choosing me now makes it easier for him to choose me again in the future.

Grey lifts a shoulder as though it doesn't matter. "It'll be fine," he says, but tension still radiates off him. He motions toward the garage, and as we walk, I feel the barest glance of his fingers against the back of my dress, ushering me forward. It's a casual gesture, even a common one in the South, but with Grey there's a familiar intimacy to it that causes my breath to catch.

Because my body remembers so strongly the feel of him and reacts accordingly: heat flushing, throat tightening, stomach squeezing. I ball my hands into tight fists, swallowing over and over again to bring myself under control, so that my expression is neutral again by the time we step into the garage.

Unsurprisingly, it's huge—at least five bays wide and stuffed with a variety of gleaming cars. Grey's father already sits in a sleek black convertible, engine purring softly, and Grey leads me to it.

"I told Libby we'd give her a ride home," he explains as he opens the passenger door for me. He doesn't give his father time to object, but instead flips the backseat forward, preparing to climb in.

I put my hand on his shoulder, stopping him. "That backseat is tiny," I protest. "Your legs would never fit."

He's about to argue when his father interrupts, snapping, "Greyson, we'll be late to the club." And that solves that.

The car is low and sporty and I'm intentionally ungainly as I contort myself into the backseat. The hem of my dress rides up my thigh, high enough to reveal a small sliver of lace edging along my underwear. Hastily, I tug it back down but it's clear from the way Grey's ears blush red that he noticed.

Once we're all settled, the Senator pulls the car out of the garage with a jerk. He drives angrily, engine revving once he hits the main road. The way I've positioned myself in the back, I have a clear view of his eyes in the rearview mirror. I pretend not to notice how he flicks his gaze back to me, over and over.

He's calculating, trying to figure something out about me. I keep a smile plastered to my face, refusing to give him anything, and focus on my cell phone.

The drive is short and uncomfortably silent. Grey's fingers dig into the sides of his leather seat, bracing himself as his father takes the circular drive in front of my house too fast.

Grey gets out first, holding out a hand to help me from the backseat. I'm well aware of how my dress gapes open when I bend over trying to maneuver myself free. But my foot catches on the seat belt, and I pitch to the side, dropping my purse into the footwell. The contents spill everywhere.

"You okay?" Grey asks, reaching toward me.

I nod, my cheeks heating with embarrassment. "Sorry," I mumble. The Senator lets out an exasperated sigh as I drop to my knees and scurry to shovel my belongings together. With a glance I confirm that the call on my phone is still connected before shoving it farther under the passenger seat.

Once out of the car I thank the Senator for the ride before turning to Grey. It's clear he wants to say something but isn't sure what. I save him the effort. "Thank you," I tell him softly. I keep my voice low, as though intending only Grey to hear me while knowing very well the Senator is listening in.

"I was glad to see you again after our abrupt good night . . ." I drop my eyes a moment and smile, one side tilted higher than the other and it has the desired effect, eliciting a brief flicker of hungering interest.

And then his father barks at him that they'll be late and the moment is broken. Grey's barely able to shut the door before his father takes off down the driveway, engine revving. He turns to wave, but his father grabs at his shoulder, pulling him back around to face forward. Even though the car's too far away to hear what they're saying, it's clear the Senator's berating him.

# FOURTEEN

I walk straight through the house and into the kitchen where evidence from the reception the evening before still clutters the countertops. Chafing dishes stacked next to crates of glasses waiting to be collected by the catering company; the remains of the bar arranged neatly on the island.

Careful to avoid clinking them together, I sift through the liquor bottles until I find the one I'm looking for: a squat round bottle with a cork stopper in the shape of a galloping horse and jockey. Mrs. Wells's favorite kind of bourbon.

Uncapping it, I pour the remains down the sink, running the water in an attempt to mask the musky odor. Had anyone else become ill at the party last night, I'd have just blamed it on a bad batch of seafood. It's not like that's the kind of thing anyone would be able to check. It's doubtful that anyone would put together that those who became sick all drank the same kind of bourbon.

But even so, there's no reason to tempt fate by keeping the evidence around. Once the bottle's empty, I rinse it out and toss it into the recycling bin with the rest of the empties and head out to the pool.

The sun's arcing high overhead, and along the horizon over the mainland dark clouds sit, heavy and promising. A high wind kicks from the ocean, pushing against the storm, and it's still too early in the day to know which side will prevail.

I settle onto one of the lounge chairs, digging my toes between the rope slats as I pull my phone from my purse. It's a clone of the one I "accidentally" left in the Wellses' car when I dropped my purse and it shows one missed call—from myself thirteen minutes ago.

My voice mail is set to record for a full twenty minutes—enough time for Grey and his father to drive to the country club. Already, impatience nips and I tilt my head back, waiting. Trying not to dwell on the ghost of Grey's touch against the small of my back. Because thinking about that makes me think of other things too.

Like the sound he made, deep in his throat, the first time he kissed me on the *Persephone*. Like the way his fingers twisted in my hair as he pulled me closer. Like the way his eyes shone when he looked at me, as though I were all that mattered.

The Frances part of me frolics through these memories, pulling them tight around her, and with a growl, I wrench free of them. Thankfully, my phone chirps that I have a new voice mail and that promptly ends the internal struggle.

As I hold the phone to my ear and press play, I smile. A real one—not the crooked grin that belonged to Libby or the sweetly shy one that belonged to Frances—one more monstrous. Cold. A smile born of this new hybrid creature I've become—with razor edges and calculating intentions.

The message begins with the sound of tires crunching over the cracked oyster shell driveway. And then comes the clunk of my purse dropping and me apologizing to the Senator. There's the sound of me shuffling to gather everything back together, and then Grey says good-bye, the Senator growls that they'll be late, the car door slams.

At first there's nothing but the sound of popping shells as the car retreats down the driveway. Then the tires hit the black-top with a vibrating hum and I can hear their muffled voices.

Senator Wells, his voice tight: ". . . with her last night. You told me you'd left to walk home and now I learn that you two were together? You lied to me!"

"It's not like that," Grey protests.

There's a squeal of brakes and then it's just the sound of the engine, vibrating against the phone. I frown—I know the route to the country club and there aren't any lights. There's no reason for them to have stopped for this long unless the Senator chose to.

"You will tell me exactly what happened between you two." His voice is venomous.

"Dad, it wasn't that big—" Grey's response is cut off by the sound of a *thump* and a sharp inhale. For a moment there's only breathing.

I close my eyes, picturing the car pulled to the side of the road, shaded by stunted oaks and untouched by the breeze. The air would feel heavier, more claustrophobic. Someone shifts, the sound of leather squeaking. "I don't think I need to tell you how serious this is," Senator Wells says.

When he answers, Grey's voice is more subdued. "Libby and I went for a walk together during the reception. She told me she doesn't remember anything about what happened."

"You just happened to talk about the attack?"

I freeze at the Senator's use of the word *attack*. It's the first time I've heard anyone else actually refer to it as an attack and there's something fiercely validating about it. My fingers tremble as I press them to my lips, relief and rage warring in my stomach.

"It wasn't like that, Dad," Grey insists. "It's just—I mean, of course it was going to come up. How could it not?"

"Was it you or was it her who brought it up?" the Senator demands.

"It was . . ." Grey hesitates. "I don't . . . I'm not—" He's cut off.

There's movement and then Grey hisses in pain. "Do I need to remind you how much is at risk here?" the Senator growls.

"It was—I think she brought it up," Grey gasps. "But it wasn't like what you think. I swear! She didn't ask anything at all. It was just obvious it was something everyone was thinking about and *she was right*."

"What were her exact words?"

Grey talks fast, his voice laced with pain. "That she didn't remember anything. It was all blocked out. She'd tried doctors and therapy and medicines and nothing worked, and she liked it that way. She's doesn't *want* to remember."

I almost sense a note of regret in his last statement. As though he wished I *did* want to remember. That maybe he wanted someone else to talk to about what really happened.

And I wonder for a moment, could it be that easy? That I only have to ask and he'll spill it all?

My pulse pounds at the possibility but then I shake my head. If it were that easy, the truth wouldn't have stayed buried that long.

"She didn't ask me anything about how the *Persephone* went down," Grey insists. "Not one thing." There's a pause, more shifting, and then Grey exhales slowly in relief. Whatever pain the Senator had been inflicting seems to have stopped. "And she promised she never would," he adds.

"I don't care. I've told you before—she's dangerous."

There's a long moment of silence before Grey finally sighs. "I know, Dad."

"I'm not sure that you really do. This isn't something I control anymore," the Senator spits.

I sit bolt upright in my chair, pulse pounding. *Control? Anymore?* I press the phone harder against my ear.

"I can only protect you so much," Senator Wells continues. I'm surprised to hear a slight hitch in his voice, making his statement more of a plea than a threat.

"Maybe I don't need your protection," Grey snaps back.

There's a long pause. "Do you really believe that?"

Another stretch of silence as I wait for Grey's answer. And then a long exhale ending with a "No."

The car pulls back onto the road and I check the phone to see how much time is left on the voice mail. Not a lot. Maybe not even enough for them to get to the country club.

I swing my legs off the side of the lounge, knee bouncing anxiously as I wait for them to say more. "Come on," I whisper, as though this conversation were taking place now and not over twenty minutes ago.

"I don't want you going near her, Grey."

My jaw clenches. At least I'd been expecting this response and have built it into my plan. The Senator may order Grey to keep his distance, but our paths will most certainly cross again—I've guaranteed it.

Grey doesn't answer, at least not verbally, but the Senator persists. "She's dangerous."

"No, she's not," he counters. "She's just a girl with shit luck."

The unexpected defense on my behalf draws me up short, causing my breath to catch. *Just a girl*, I think. My eyes flutter closed as I swallow. If only that were the case. Life would be so much simpler if it were true.

"She's a loose end," the Senator barks. "There's no reason for her to have come back here—"

"It's her *home*," Grey argues. "Where else would you expect her to go?"

"And *now* of all times," the Senator continues.

Grey snorts. "You weren't complaining last night when her reception raised a shit ton of money for your campaign."

"Why is she here?" the Senator roars, loud enough that it startles even me. "What does she want?"

## FIFTEEN

In the silence that follows, the turn signal begins ticking and the car slows. There's a *thump* when the Senator's car crosses over a speed bump along the entrance to the club.

"Listen to me, Grey," the Senator says, voice low. "This is bigger than you. It's bigger than me."

Grey sighs and it sounds tired and sad. "I know, Dad."

The car hits another speed bump.

The Senator continues. "I can see no reason why the two of you need ever associate in the future. What's in the past is in the past. Leave it there."

"You're the one who made the *Persephone* the cornerstone of your campaign," Grey objects.

The car pulls to a halt. There's a muffled conversation and the Senator tells someone—probably the valet—to wait.

"Look." The Senator's voice has lost its sharp edge. "I just don't want to see you go through it all again." For the first time, he sounds like a father, like he actually cares about his son. "We've worked so hard to get to where we are. I don't want her bringing it all back up—we almost lost you the first time and—"

There's a loud beep: the voice mail ending. My breath catches, totally unprepared. I stare at my phone, willing it to give me more even though I know it's an impossible request.

Jumping to my feet, I pace around the pool, trying to sort out the jumble of thoughts racing through my head. It felt like the Senator had confessed, but as I think back through the fragments of the conversation, I realize there's nothing definitive.

Nothing proving it. The Senator only talked about how this was something he couldn't control anymore. About how he could only protect Grey so much. About how this was something bigger.

*He'd used the word* attack.

But even that wouldn't be enough evidence to bring him down. He'd find a way to brush it off—to claim he meant the rogue wave attacking the ship. And people would believe him.

However, the Senator *had* made one thing abundantly clear: I was dangerous. Because the Senator was afraid that I might uncover the truth. And for that to be a real fear, that means not only is there a truth to uncover, but that it is something within my reach.

Suddenly, it is all too much. I crouch, digging my fists against my forehead and squeezing my eyes shut. *It's all true.* A sob presses against my teeth, and I bite my lips to keep it contained.

For four years I've clung to the memory of the *Persephone.* I've relived the attack over and over again. But as time passed, the memories began to erode around the edges until a small voice began to ask, "What if you're wrong?"

And now I realize that a part of me had *hoped* I was wrong. Hoped that I'd dig and dig and dig and, in the end, Grey would come out clean. Because then it would be okay for a small part of me to still pine after him.

To believe in him.

The Senator's last statement echoes softly in my head. *We almost lost you the first time.* Frowning, I head inside and up to my room where I pull a suitcase out from under my bed. Tucked inside is a fireproof briefcase and I enter the combination to pop it open.

Several well-worn notebooks are stacked inside, and I sort through them until I find the right one. It has an orange cover with GREYSON WELLS printed in small letters across the top. The dog-eared pages are filled with cramped handwriting— various shades of ink, my emotions at the time evident in how messy or neat the writing is.

It's everything I ever learned or knew about Grey; page after page of details no matter how minute. What I remember from the cruise, what I found online or learned by asking the right questions of the right people, even what I'd seen with my own eyes.

Over the past four years I've become an expert on Grey. An expert on everyone in the Wells family. I have the same kind of notebook on each one of them—it's how I knew Mrs. Wells drinks that horrid Refreshergy supplement every morning in her smoothie and what her favorite brand of bourbon is. It's how I knew that Senator Wells's chief of staff is named Harrison Cheefer, whose secretary is Mindy Gervistan, and that during the summer he golfs at the club at least once a week.

I flip to the back of Grey's notebook where I sketched a meticulous timeline of his life—before and after the *Persephone*. It's stuffed with things like attendance at sailing camps, scholastic awards won, matriculation at posh boarding schools.

But there's a gap. For almost a year after the *Persephone*, there's nothing at all. At first he'd done a few interviews—told his story to CNN and to *Good Morning America*. Answered questions for Brian Williams and Diane Sawyer. But those were all in the days before I was rescued.

From the date of my rescue, Grey's entire timeline goes blank. Sure, there are still mentions of him in a slew of articles, but nothing with any new quotes. It's like he ceased to exist: He didn't attend school; he didn't go to camp; he dropped out of all extracurricular activities. No sailing. No lacrosse.

I pull out the Senator's notebook and compare the timelines. He was still active during that time, but less so. There weren't nearly as many fund-raisers as he usually threw and he missed more votes in the Senate than he attended.

Mrs. Wells's timeline is similar—there were still the tennis matches with her club team, but she slipped in her ranking.

Grey eventually broke his silence—at a hearing on Capitol Hill as part of an investigation into what happened with the *Persephone* and whether such tragedies could be avoided in the future. It was a year to the day after her sinking—no doubt some staffer found the timing to be poignant.

The Senator had testified first and was exactly what I'd expected—smooth-talkingly arrogant. Haughty and confident in his position above the law. More than anything he'd been grandstanding, enjoying time in the national spotlight and laying the foundation for a future presidential bid.

But I hadn't expected the same from Grey. Because that wasn't the kind of boy I'd met on the *Persephone*. Grey had been nothing like his father, even back then.

Somehow, that had all changed. At the time of the hearing, Grey was sixteen, yet appeared totally undaunted by the cameras and rows of microphones. He'd been magnificent. Tanned, robust, assured. His voice cracked in all the right places, his recounting of the night so sincere it brought tears to more than one viewer's eyes.

Watching it had cut away any last hope I had of his innocence. Not that I believed he'd been somehow involved in the attack, but it was obvious that he was intentionally covering up the truth. I hated him then, the consummate actor. No hint of hesitation behind his lies. Nothing left of the guy I'd considered myself in love with.

After that it became difficult to be charitable toward Grey. Instead, I clung to the lifeline of revenge, painting Senator Wells as enemy number one and Greyson as a close second, deserving of every bad thought and intention I could hurl their way.

I'd written off this year-long gap as his father's fear that Grey would trip up and confuse the narrative. The less he talked, the less anyone could investigate.

But now, a small part of me wonders whether he struggled like I did. Maybe he hadn't spent the year being trained in the art of media manipulation, but instead had spent the year trying to put himself back together.

The Senator's words echo in my head—*we almost lost you*—and the Frances part of me begs to feel a minute *ping* of sympathy for Grey.

I don't allow it. Instead, I lie back on my bedroom floor and throw my arms wide. Outside, thunder booms against the windows, wind tossing the clouds like sea foam. I recall something else the Senator said: *We've worked so hard to get to where we are.*

I close my eyes and smile. How much more delicious will it be, then, to tear it all apart?

## SIXTEEN

That evening, I'm reheating leftovers from the fund-raiser when Shepherd strolls into the kitchen from the patio. He's obviously been out in the ocean: His chest is bare, a beach towel hangs low around his hips, and water drizzles down his sun-darkened skin. It's difficult not to stare.

When he sees me, his steps falter.

"Hey," he says.

"Hey," I say back.

"You sticking around town for a while?" he asks, expression guarded. "Or are you headed out now that the fund-raiser's over?"

I shrug as though I haven't thought about it. "I'd planned on staying for the summer at least. Not sure after that. I wanted a break from school."

He comes closer, glancing around at the open food containers. But says nothing.

"You hungry?" I ask.

He shakes his head. "Nah, I'm headed out with some friends tonight."

I nod. "Oh."

"You want to come?" he adds, almost as an afterthought.

"No," I respond automatically. I'd assumed he'd invited me just to be polite, but at the disappointment that flickers across his face I wonder if it was more than that.

My first instinct is to scramble to offer an excuse but I swallow it down. I don't realize I'm twisting the ring on my finger until I notice Shepherd staring.

His eyes lift to meet mine and for a moment I catch a glimpse of raw emotion. Rage and pain but more than anything else—need.

It feels somehow like a punishment.

If only he knew that no one can punish me worse than I can punish myself.

To prove it to him I lift my chin slightly. "Have fun," I tell him dismissively.

Like a switch, he shuts his emotions away and shrugs. "Night, then."

The moment he leaves the room I let out a long breath. Shepherd has always been a threat. The one variable I couldn't nail down before coming here was his feelings toward Libby. Had he moved on? Did he still care?

Would he look too closely for the girl he lost?

It's that last question that makes him dangerous. Because he's the only one left who may know Libby better than I do. And that's why I must keep him at a distance. Even though it's the last thing Libby would have ever wanted.

I stare at Mrs. O'Martin's lifeless body sprawled across the floor of the hallway. Her chest is ragged and raw. Her blood runs down my arms and across the lovely clothes Libby'd let me borrow.

There's movement, and when I look up, a man's standing at the end of the hallway, where it branches off like a crossroads. I have the same jolt of wrong when I see him that I did when he kicked down the door to my family's stateroom. I'd expected a thug—a movie villain with a sneer in a scarred face. But the man staring down the hall at me looks like he should be wearing a business suit. He looks normal. And his face is bare—no mask—which means he doesn't expect anyone to survive to identify him.

It all happens in a split second, though it feels like forever, every second burning itself deep. He raises the gun and I slam the door shut before Libby sees what's left of her mother. I run, followed by the concussion of gunshots and splintering wood as the armed man shoots at the door.

Libby's in the master bedroom and she yells at me to hurry. I kick that door closed too as she tears open the window seat and rips free an emergency life raft in a large plastic egg and two life vests. "Here," she says, shoving one in my hands as she yanks the other over her head. I pull mine on and struggle with the straps. All I can see is the blood now coating my front. I think there might even be bits of flesh as well. Libby's mother's body caking my arms.

I think of my own father's head shattering. The blood blooming on my mother's chest.

"Frances!" Libby screams in my face and that's all it takes to bring me back. She struggles with the doors out to the balcony. I fall to my knees, straining against the dead bolt at the base of the door. Finally it pulls free.

Behind us the man keeps shooting, another coming in behind him.

Libby stumbles onto the balcony and heaves the plastic egg out into the darkness. But I hesitate, just for a heartbeat, out of instinct and a fear of heights. Outside the noise is the same but different. The night is full of rain and fire, screams and gunfire, but the wind picks it all up and tosses it around into a jumbled confusion.

Libby's lifting a leg over the railing when she looks back at me, still on one knee, just rising to follow after her. She leans toward me, her hands out. "Come on, Frances!" she shouts.

I reach for her, and she grabs my wrists and pulls, hauling me up and toward her. My hip slams against the Plexiglas baluster. There's this infinitesimal sliver of time in which I catch her eyes and the sphere of the moment almost expands as if we could've paused and just said to each other, "Okay," and breathed. But then it's gone.

"Go!" she screams. "Jump!"

She already has one leg over the railing, and I follow, gasping at what's about to happen as I teeter over the black emptiness below. Libby must sense my terror of heights, and before I can think about what I need to do, she shoves me, hard.

I tumble through the air, the night spinning.

Coming awake is like that first moment I reached the surface after jumping from the *Persephone* and almost drowning. I'm so desperate for air that it's difficult to breathe and I find myself gasping, choking. It's only then that I feel hands on my shoulders and realize someone is trying to tell me it's okay.

I strain to jerk free but I'm trapped and I open my eyes to find a man leaning over me. His face is thrown in shadow by the light in the hallway and I don't know who he is or where I am. In a panic I claw at his arms but he doesn't budge. He uses one hand to trap both of my wrists, pinning them gently against my chest while he places his other hand on my cheek, pushing me to look at him.

His eyes are like water as he stares at me and repeats the words softly but insistently, "It's okay. You're safe."

For a moment, this is all there is. Me trying to breathe as my blood screams through my body and this guy telling me I'm going to be okay. That I'm safe. I focus on him as though he's a lifeline.

*Shepherd*, I tell myself, as my mind slows enough for rational thought to trickle in. He's wearing thin cotton pajama bottoms and nothing else. There's concern in his eyes and something more—worry. Fear.

I feel the way his palm slides against my cheek and I realize I've been crying. My throat throbs, raw and pained. I relax, sinking into the bed, and he loosens his grip.

"You were screaming in your sleep," he explains. He's close enough that I feel his words brush over my face and he stays that way a moment longer before easing back on the bed, putting distance between us.

"I'm sorry. I was . . ." I'm about to say that I was dreaming but that's not really true. I don't dream anymore. I remember. Over and over again, every time I fall asleep I'm trapped back in the ocean.

My hands tremble and he must notice because he's still holding my wrists against my chest. Belatedly, he releases me and immediately I miss the warmth of his touch. The comfort of it.

It's easy to understand how Libby could have been so in love with him.

Just then, the storm that threatened throughout the evening finally crashes to shore, a fierce pummeling of wind and rain blowing wide the French doors I'd left cracked before going to bed. Before I can even free myself from the covers, Shepherd leaps up and dashes around the bed. The muscles along his arms strain as he struggles to force the doors shut while I race to throw the lock.

He turns to face me, damp from the rain, droplets of water sliding down his bare chest. The lights flicker once, twice, and then they blow, leaving us in darkness punctuated by the reflection of lightning against the storm-soaked night.

I start toward the bathroom to find a towel but his words stop me. "Why, Libby?" He's panting slightly from the effort of fighting against the doors. "Why didn't you ever write back?"

# SEVENTEEN

I've been expecting the question and have an answer ready. Something about the therapists' requirements that I not focus on the past, that I embrace the future. But when I try to tell him this, I realize that I can't. I begin twisting Libby's ring around my finger.

He'd written e-mails, letters, texts. He'd called. There'd been such pain in his words that eventually turned to desperation and anger. He didn't understand then and clearly still doesn't.

His face as he waits for my answer is anxious, both afraid and pleading. I'd hoped that after four years he'd have let Libby go but I should have known better.

All I can do is say, "I'm sorry."

My response is so clearly not the answer he'd been expecting and frustration burns hot in his eyes. I can feel his scrutiny, sense him trying to gather the pieces of who I am now and compare them against who I was then.

Outside, the wind shrieks around the *boom* of thunder. He

waits for me to say something more. To explain myself better. But there's nothing I can offer him.

He steps forward, crowding against me. "What happened to you?" he asks, almost a whisper. Now that he's confronted me, he's not going to back down. I can't avoid him in person like I could a letter or e-mail.

I sigh and step around him to sit on the edge of the bed. It should be easier to lie in the dark, without having to fear your expression giving your inner thoughts away.

But it turns out that darkness is where truth truly thrives. Confession comes easier when you don't have to directly face the visible censure of your confessor. I press my fingers against my eyes and Shepherd waits—what's a few extra minutes after years of patience?

I give him the truth: "You kept wanting me to be the same girl I was when I left for the cruise, and I wasn't." I pull my legs up, wrap my arms around my knees, and hug them to my chest. "You still want me to be her and I'm not."

*I never will be*, I add silently. Libby is dead and Frances is buried so deep inside that sometimes I think I've lost her forever.

Shepherd leans back against the door, lightning illuminating him like a shadow. "I just wanted to know that you were okay. You couldn't even tell me that much. And Cecil . . ." He runs a hand over his head in frustration, dislodging droplets of water that trail in rivulets down his fingers. "He was just . . . different afterward."

Something about the way he says it makes my throat tighten. "How so?"

Shrugging, he pushes from the door and walks across my room, almost aimless. "He was just"—he struggles to find the right word and settles on—"gone. I mean, I understand why. When the coast guard gave up the search for you and Barbara, he was devastated and refused to believe it. Of course he was going to try and find y'all on his own. But then after you were rescued and he became a widower—all those months in Switzerland taking care of you."

He paces back across the room, agitated. "The thing is— you're his daughter. Of course he's going to move heaven and earth for you. I'd have done the same thing but—" He bites back whatever he was going to say next.

"Luis was already away in law school then. And I had boarding school. Sure, Cecil had an army of staff to keep everything running when I was home for breaks. But . . ." He presses his palm against the glass of the door, the tips of his fingers tapping lightly.

A sick feeling grows in my stomach as I wait for him to continue.

"You know, Luis used to always tell me, 'Remember where you come from,' every time he thought I was becoming too white. He was sixteen when our parents died—he could remember what they were like. But I was only six. When Cecil and Barbara took us in they became the only parents I knew."

He turns sideways, his head dropped and eyes closed. "As far as I was concerned, I lost my mother when the *Persephone* went down. And Luis was gone and I understood because he was still the kid who'd lost his parents a decade before. But then you were gone too. And so was Cecil. And where did that leave me?"

Thunder rolls across the ocean, lightning streaking along his profile, illuminating his anguish. In all the years since I'd become Libby, I've only ever thought about Shepherd in terms of him being a threat. Of everyone, he's the one most likely to uncover the ruse, to see straight through to the heart of the truth.

I've avoided him, spurned him, because it's the only way to protect myself. I hadn't considered how much his life also changed the night the *Persephone* was attacked. What it must have been like to lose your foster mother to disaster, only to have your foster father abandon you by choice.

It makes my heart ache, not just for Shepherd, but for Cecil too. Because I know that Cecil loved Shepherd. But not enough to tell him the truth. Not enough to stay around for him. To comfort him in those months after.

"I'm sorry." Which I know is wholly inadequate for the reality that I—a stranger then—took what was his.

When he faces me, his expression has hardened into something more indifferent, but anger still hums beneath the surface. I can't blame him—if there's anyone who understands the power of rage to beat back sorrow, it's me.

"You know when it would have been really nice to hear that?" he asks. "Four years ago."

He starts toward the door. I know I should let him leave— it's smarter to keep distance between us—but I don't. Because he deserves more than he's gotten.

"He thought of you as a son," I tell him. Shepherd stops,

his back drawing straight. "He loved you," I add. "He talked about you all the time."

"I'd have preferred if he actually talked *to* me rather than about me." He pauses and then looks at me over his shoulder. "You're right that I wanted you to be the same girl you were before the cruise. She was someone who smiled, who didn't hold back. She actually gave a shit.

"But you . . ." His eyes rake over me. I wait for him to finish, but he merely shakes his head and leaves the room, saying nothing more.

When I know he's gone—when the sound of his steps recedes down the stairs and into the distance—I finally draw in a wheezing gasp. Tears burn at my throat and no matter how much I swallow, I can't clear them away. Everything inside me feels off, shifted in some way I can't put right again.

I'm not responsible for Shepherd and his hurt feelings. It was never my job to save him or protect him. He's a stranger to me—an obstacle, just another notebook under the bed filled with facts and details that I've memorized in order to further my own designs.

Yet somehow his condescension slithers past all my defenses and makes me feel less than. For so long I've been a role—Libby's life a mask I've grown accustomed to. Anything anyone has ever said against me easily brushed away because they're not judging the real me, they're judging this girl I'm pretending to be.

I've allowed myself to imagine that if Libby could see what I've built of her life—of the intricate plans I've concocted—that she'd be proud. But now, seeing the expression on Shepherd's face, hearing the pain in his voice, I realize that Libby would despise me.

The thought causes a panicked kind of shame to blare through me, my skin flushing hot. I ball my fists against my knees, forcing the self-doubt to the darkest corners of my mind, letting the hot light of anger burn it away.

In the end, it doesn't matter what Libby would think about what I've done or what I'm doing. Because here's the truth about Libby: On that life raft, she gave up.

And I didn't. And I refuse to give up now.

## EIGHTEEN

It's barely dawn and already the air's thicker than soup. It's too early for anyone else to be out on the beach, so I have the wide swath of tide-drenched sand to myself during my early-morning jog. The back of my mind counts the rhythm of my footfalls, three on the inhale and two on the exhale. Over and over as I race toward a horizon I'll never reach.

This stretch of coast is eight miles long and my planned route takes me past Senator Wells's house toward the tip of the island. Far enough that my legs burn and my side cramps, but not enough that I forget.

There's no distance far enough for that.

But still, if I push hard enough, I can't think beyond the next step, the next breath, and for now, that's enough. Because I don't want to think about Shepherd standing in my room, rain-soaked and angry.

I don't want to think about him at all.

When I pass the Senator's house on the front half of my loop, several of the downstairs lights are on, as I'd expected.

The nice thing about those in public office is that they generally like to talk about themselves, and for some reason, the media likes to report on the most mundane of facts.

Like *Magnolia Magazine*, which ran a detailed profile of the Senator's home life with a sidebar article about his wife:

*Martha Wells lives an enviable life: heiress to an aluminum fortune and married to one of the most powerful politicians on Capitol Hill. She's on the board of several charities, volunteers weekly with Hands Across the Carolinas, and still finds time to prepare home-cooked meals for her family. What's her secret? "I love being outside whenever possible and keep fit by swimming three miles in the ocean every morning during the summer," she tells us. When asked how she finds the energy for such a busy life, she credits Refreshergy liquid protein. "I add a bottle to my smoothie every morning—I couldn't imagine starting my day without it!" But what about finding time for romance? "My husband likes to start and end his day quietly. He's usually already on the back patio reading the paper when I head out for my swim, and afterward, we'll talk about our schedules and touch base. Then in the evening, before bed, we like to sit in the library with a glass of Blanton's bourbon and catch up. He's always put his family first."*

These kinds of profiles are a stalker's dream come true. I've spent a lot of time studying maps and satellite photos of Caldwell, timing my training runs and route so that I've just started back when Mrs. Wells walks toward the ocean to start her morning swim.

I increase my pace, making sure I reach the Wells house while she's still swimming. I stand at the base of the boardwalk, watching her while I catch my breath. Her strokes are long and even, the bright yellow of her bathing cap bobbing through the swells as she cuts parallel to the shore.

Satisfied, I start toward the house. It's situated on one of the largest lots on the island, a sharp-edged box clashing against gnarled old trees. The boardwalk from the beach spills onto an elaborate flagstone patio that sweeps around the edges of an infinity pool flanked by a hot-and-cold tub.

On the other side there's a wide porch filled with rattan chairs and tables. This is where I find Senator Wells, coffee by his side and a newspaper held in front of him.

My running shoes are crusted with sand and grate against the flagstones, alerting him to my approach. He flicks down the corner of his paper and frowns. His eyes scan me top to bottom, considering me.

I'm not wearing much: a jog bra and my smallest pair of running shorts, both soaked through with sweat. I'm almost as bare as if I were wearing a bikini and I'm well aware of the amount of flesh this puts on display.

"Miss O'Martin," he says, standing. "This is a surprise." His tone is enough to convey that it is an unpleasant one.

I smile, keeping my tone light and respectful. "Good morning, sir." Glancing toward the ocean, I add, "Glad to see that it looks like your wife is feeling better."

The Senator begins folding his paper precisely, using his nails to sharply crease the folds. "Yes." He says nothing more.

I force my hatred of this man to the back of my mind. I can't allow any hint of that revulsion to show through. "Anyway, I lost my phone yesterday and looked everywhere at home for it, but it didn't turn up. I'm wondering if maybe it fell out in your car when I dropped my purse? Do you mind if I check?"

Sighing, he sets his paper on the table. "Of course not." He gestures toward a set of French doors that lead into the kitchen. Ever the Southern gentleman, he allows me to enter first and when we reach the garage he flicks on the row of overhead lights.

"Should be unlocked," he says.

"Thank you—I'm so sorry for taking up your time like this." I make my way to the other side of the black convertible and drop to my knees so I can fish around in the backseat footwell. My phone's exactly where I left it, wedged under the passenger seat.

I stand, empty-handed. "I couldn't find it. Do you mind calling the number? Maybe I'm just not seeing it."

He doesn't hide his annoyance as he pulls his phone from his pocket. I rattle off the number and a few moments later an upbeat ring sounds from the car. Feigning surprise, I jump to retrieve it.

"Found it," I call, holding it up. "You don't know what a relief it is to have it back." I start toward the kitchen but he's standing in the doorway, blocking the way. There's something about the set of his mouth that sets me on edge. I tilt my head to the side. "Um . . . everything okay?"

His eyes narrow, but not necessarily in anger, more like he's studying me. "You've been away for several years and so I'm not sure how aware you've been of the goings-on back home," he says.

I lift an eyebrow, evidencing my uncertainty.

He steps farther into the garage, narrowing the distance between us. I don't bother hiding my hesitation, knowing that his intent is to intimidate me. "I wasn't sure if I should even bring it up," he continues. "I like the past *staying* in the past." He hits the last words with emphasis. There can be no missing his meaning.

I cross my arms over my chest, cupping my elbows in my palms and allowing my shoulders to hunch so that I take up less physical space. It makes me appear vulnerable and weak.

"Since your return, there's just been a little more interaction between our families than I'm comfortable with." He takes another step closer, forcing me to look up at him. Trying to assert his dominance and control. "And I would like it to end."

I have to give him credit, it didn't occur to me he'd approach the issue so directly. I'd been expecting subterfuge— conversations like the one I overheard yesterday where he warned Grey away from me. A part of me wants to smile that he thinks it could be so easy.

That I haven't designed a dozen ways to further entwine myself with Grey. That I haven't already put several of them in motion.

But I keep those thoughts from my expression because I need the Senator to think of me as weak. Easily intimidated. Controllable.

And I need Grey to think of me as a victim of his father's ire.

I once read about this interrogation tactic in which you break the person's will in steps so small that they don't even realize it's happening. Here's how it works: Imagine a suspect sitting in a police station, refusing to talk. Ask them something about the crime, they're going to stay silent.

But, instead, ask them if they'd like a glass of water and they're likely to answer. Because not answering a simple question like that seems unreasonable—it's a question unconnected to the reason they're at the police station, so what's the harm?

Except now they've broken their vow not to speak. So getting them to break it again isn't as difficult. It's no longer about whether the suspect is going to talk or not, it's about what information the suspect will be willing to share. Suddenly, the playing field has shifted.

It's like this: Ask someone to run a marathon, they're likely to say no. But ask them to take one step and they usually will. Because taking that one step is no big deal. Then ask them to take another step and same thing. And once they've taken a dozen steps they're invested.

You can get them through an entire marathon that way.

And that's my goal with Grey. Foment dissent between him and his father, create small situations for Grey to rebel against his father's wishes. To tell his father no. So that when it comes time for me to ask him to betray his father—to come clean about the truth behind the *Persephone*—it will be as simple as asking him to take just another small step forward.

As if on cue, Grey shuffles into the kitchen, a hand over his mouth to stifle a yawn. And with all the players in place, it's time for me to take the stage. If the Senator wants me to crumble under his authority, then that's what I'll do.

I bite my lip, hard enough that my eyes water. My breath catches in my throat as I stammer, "I-I'm sorry, I was just looking for my phone . . ." I swallow, jittery with panic that he could be accusing me of something that could get me in trouble. "And, really, I lose it all the time."

Tears skim my eyes. I move past him quickly and turn so that I'm walking backward into the kitchen. Not looking where I'm going. "I'm sorry—I would never—" My heel catches the lip in the doorway and I trip, dropping my phone. It skitters across the kitchen floor.

Right toward Grey. He bends to pick it up, his expression crashing into a frown when he sees my expression: scared, vulnerable, intimidated. Tears begin spilling over, and my hand trembles as I swipe my phone from him.

"Thank you, I . . ." I turn back to where the Senator stands in the doorway to the garage. For a split second his gaze is murderous and it sends a sharp chill down my spine. But I've known from the beginning there are no rules to this game.

"I'm sorry, I'll go." I stumble over the words, voice cracking as I rush to the doors leading out to the patio and the beach beyond.

"Libby." Grey starts toward me but I hold up both hands, almost panicked in my insistence he not follow me.

"No—please, just no." And then I'm out onto the patio and racing toward home.

Through the open doors behind me I hear the argument already starting. Grey's voice raised as he asks his father what the hell happened. Once I hit the beach and I'm alone, I allow myself to smile.

## NINETEEN

There's no better feeling than the deliciousness of a well-crafted plan executed perfectly. I spend the day picturing Grey's expression in the kitchen this morning. His delighted surprise at seeing me, morphing into confusion and, in the end, rage at his father.

But it's the emotion that came in between that causes my stomach to flip: that brief moment of possessiveness. It was raw and fleeting, the flicker that he would defend me against whatever it was that had caused my distress. That I was somehow his to protect. This is what confuses me the most—to him I should be practically a stranger and certainly not his responsibility. Not yet at least.

There's no indication that he suspects my true identity or that he doesn't take me at face value. He's as fooled as the rest of them. And yet, it's as though something in him responds to that part of Frances still left inside me. As though there is some sort of subconscious recognition.

This both elates and terrifies me.

When evening falls, I change into my swimsuit and head to the pool, hoping that floating will bring calm to the thoughts spinning so hectically through my head. With my ears underwater, the sound of my breathing becomes amplified, dominant, and I slowly relax, letting the rhythm of it unmoor my thoughts.

As much as I'd hated the ocean after the *Persephone*, I'd found myself more and more drawn to pools—my fascination with bodies of water unquenchable. At least with pools I have a sense of safety with knowing the boundaries, of seeing the bottom. The ability to thrust my head underwater and know that I cannot be lost.

Adrift on the ocean I'd been at her mercy. Floating in a pool I'm wholly in control.

Overhead, the sky morphs from blue to pink, and just when it begins creeping dark, I catch movement from the corner of my eye. It jerks me out of my meditative state and I splash upright.

Grey stands at the base of the boardwalk, expression hesitant and apologetic. He's dressed casually: khaki shorts slung low on his hips and a white button-down shirt with the sleeves rolled to his elbows. His hair is ruffled from the walk along the beach, his feet bare. "Sorry to startle you," he says. "I don't want to interrupt." He half turns back to indicate he'll leave.

"No, please." I wave him forward. "Come on in." And then I realize how that invitation sounds given the context. "I mean, not *in* as in the pool." But then that sounds rude. "I mean, unless you want to. Go swimming, that is. In which case you can totally come in. I just meant . . ."

He laughs, thankfully cutting off my rambling. "I know what you mean," he reassures me. His shoulders relax a bit, my apparent awkwardness having done the trick of easing the tension.

I smile gratefully and kick toward the side of the pool as he crosses the patio. There are no chairs nearby and for a moment he stands while I tread water, staring up at him. It's full twilight, the sun sunken behind the mainland and stars peppering the sky above the ocean.

I'd turned off the patio lights before coming out here and somehow it makes the distance between us seem greater than it is—his expression more difficult to read. "May I?" he asks, gesturing to side of the pool.

"Of course," I tell him and he sits, easing his feet and legs into the water next to me. I dip my head back under the surface, ostensibly to clear the hair out of my face, but more because I know the movement puts my body on display and gives me an edge of power.

I want Grey to look at me. I want him thrown off balance, distracted.

It's too dark to tell whether his ears are tinged pink but he clears his throat, his focus shifting to where his feet swirl lazily in the water. His smile slips a little, replaced with the same serious expression as before. "You seemed upset this morning and I just wanted to make sure you were okay," he says.

"Oh." I pause, reaching to cling to the wall beside him. "Yeah, I'm okay." But I don't say it with a lot of conviction.

With a wet finger I draw damp circles on the concrete.

Grey watches, forehead furrowed in contemplation. "Did my father"—he hesitates—"say anything? That . . . upset you?"

"No." I twist my lips, ensuring that the uncertainty of my tone undermines the response. I focus on my circles for a moment, rewetting my finger again and again. "He asked me to keep my distance from you."

His fingers flex where he's gripping the side of the pool and he drops his chin to his chest, jaw clenching. He takes several deep breaths, each one strained with anger.

I push off the wall and float sideways until I'm only inches in front of him. Pretending to be tentative, I touch one of my hands to his shin, my body slowly drifting closer. "It's okay," I tell him softly.

He looks down at me and I don't know if it's my continued momentum or him moving, but his foot brushes across my lower abdomen and I find myself between his legs.

Inside me, Frances jolts, sending electricity searing through my veins. I have the sudden urge to rest my cheek against his leg, to let the edge of my lips press against the soft flesh inside his knee.

To see if he tastes the same as he did four years ago.

I'm almost dizzy at the force of my own resistance.

But either he doesn't notice, or he doesn't care. "It's not okay," he says, and there's strained frustration—the kind that makes it sound like this is a familiar emotion between Grey and his father. The kind I intend to exploit to turn one against the other.

"Look, he's your dad and he has a really high-profile job.

It's smart for him to be cautious—and maybe even a little paranoid," I offer.

"He still shouldn't have said anything." He clenches his teeth as another wave of anger rolls through him. I feel it in the way his muscles contract, rippling under my touch, causing me to bob slightly in the water.

"He's just worried about you." I shift my hands from his shins to his knees. Even though four years have passed there's a familiarity to the feel of him. "He wants the past to stay in the past," I add.

Grey closes his eyes, exhaling in resignation. "Of course he does." He says it so softly I'm not even sure he realizes he spoke aloud. Or that he intended me to hear it.

"Hey." I squeeze his thighs to get his attention. "Look at me." He does and I swallow at the heat rippling through my abdomen. At the part inside me that recognizes him on a level I can't control.

*Grey is the enemy,* I remind myself. *He's a liar and a cheat.*

"If that's what you want as well—just tell me. And I'll stay away." I lean my temple against his knee. His skin's warm, his heartbeat tripping under my touch proving that he's unsettled by my nearness.

I bite at my lower lip before continuing. "I just . . . You know, it's nice to be with someone who's been through the same thing. Even if I don't remember any of it—it's nice to be around someone who isn't always thinking of me as 'that girl who survived that cruise ship disaster.'"

His legs tighten ever so slightly, his calves brushing against my sides, toes wrapping toward my back. Ripples break away from the movement, brushing around us, shushing against the wall of the pool. The night is full of crashing waves and screaming cicadas, but all I hear is the uneven rhythm of his breathing.

"That's not how I think of you," he says, almost a whisper. "I don't want you to stay away." There's meaning and intent to it and the part of me that once saw him as my hero—the Frances part of me—screams with old memories of unmet yearning. She roars forward, surging with desire. Blood pounds ferociously through my veins as I press my fingers harder against the edge of Grey's thighs.

Nothing but tension crackles between us, the kind that's been pent up for years, circling and circling with no release. I'd assumed time had dulled the intensity of any emotions between us. But if anything, I feel them more acutely now.

It scares me how quickly the pull to him sizzles along my nerves, dimming out any kind of rational hesitation. Flashes of him come to mind: his hand skimming the edge of my shoulder blade; his lips pressed against the hollow in my throat; his hips pressed hard against my own.

My breath escapes in a puff and it's like a call-and-response. The blackness of his pupils almost swallow his eyes whole and he's already leaning toward me when there's an explosion of brightness. The outside lights ringing the pool blare to life, section by section.

# TWENTY

The lights catch me by surprise, and I flinch as though I've somehow been caught doing something wrong. On instinct I push away from Grey and he must feel the same because he rocks back on his hands, sucking in a tight breath and putting distance between us.

I glance at the house and find Shepherd's shadow on the other side of the French doors leading into the kitchen. Right where the outdoor light switches are. I can't see his expression, but then he flicks on the pool light, casting my body in hues of red and blue, making clear his intention.

When I turn back toward Grey, he's standing. Water trails down his legs, puddling at his feet. "I should go." His eyes flick back to the house where Shepherd still hovers inside, watching. It's easy to read the question on Grey's face: He's wondering what the relationship between Shepherd and me is and why Shepherd felt compelled to interrupt our conversation.

It's also easy to recognize how unsettled he is, how he doesn't know where to take things from here. How to bridge the gap between such an intimate moment shared in the dark to the brightness of reality.

There's no reason for him to know I've already figured that out. That it's been set in motion for days. And so when he only tells me, "Good night," before turning back to the beach, I'm not concerned that he doesn't say anything about seeing me again.

But there's a deeper part, the Frances part still stalking under my skin, that's left unsatisfied. That misses the feeling of Grey's legs bracing around me. With a huff of frustration, I dive underwater, letting the cool pressure of it drive away the staining heat of unmet desire. I stay deep until my lungs burn, and then I force myself to stay under even longer until I'm almost choking.

I want to punish my body for reacting to Grey—to starve it of what it needs until every part of me understands what is at stake here. I am alive purely by chance. This life that I lead is not mine—it is borrowed. Every heartbeat, even the air I breathe, is borrowed.

My weakness toward Grey only confirms what I've known for years: Frances is too weak. Her heart too easily turned toward forgiveness and understanding.

Lungs bucking and desperate, I hold this body hostage until Frances retreats. Until everything is aligned inside me with one desperate goal: survival. Only then do I burst to the surface, gasping.

Unsurprisingly, Shepherd stands, waiting. "Impressive," he says, one eyebrow raised. At first I think he means the length of time I can hold my breath but then he adds, "Girls down here have been throwing themselves at Greyson Wells summer after summer." He grabs a towel from a table and holds it open for me. "Not one of them has sustained his attention the way you have."

Moving toward the steps, I take my time reaching up and pulling my hair off my shoulders, twisting it to get the water out. And then, just to tease him a little more, I tilt my head to the side and jump a few times to dislodge water from my ear. My bikini covers enough, but not that much, and Shepherd's hands tighten ever so slightly around the towel.

I step forward, taking it from him. "Perhaps they weren't using the right bait." I wrap the towel around my waist, folding the top over to keep it snug at my hips. Shepherd takes in every movement, and though it's just a flash, a frown crosses his features.

"Maybe not," he says, looking me over one last time before turning back to the house, leaving me feeling as though I've somehow missed something important.

After showering that night, I slip a photo free of its hidden pocket in my wallet and prop it against the mirror. The edges are worn to the point of being frayed, the color smudged in the bottom-right corner. But the two girls with arms draped across each other's shoulders, their chins jutting out as they smile and their noses pink from the sun, are the same as they have always been. Trapped in time, a snapshot taken with Grey's new cell phone by the pool on the *Persephone* and e-mailed to all of us the day before the attack.

Slowly, I sink onto the cushioned stool, leaning forward

until my own reflection hovers just to the edge of the photo. As though I am a ghostly third to their duo. My eyes flicker across the picture, picking out the similarities and differences, comparing them with my own reflection.

It's a ritual of mine. A reminder of who I used to be. Who I am now. At the time, other passengers on the cruise had joked about our likeness. We'd been constantly asked whether we were sisters and every time it secretly delighted me. Because the very idea that I could be mistaken for Libby was beyond flattering. Despite the uncanny similarities, it had seemed impossible that I could ever be mistaken for her.

Now it sometimes feels that I have only ever been her. That Frances was an imaginary friend lost to wind and distance long ago.

Sometimes I wonder what would have happened if I'd refused Cecil's offer. If I hadn't so readily jumped at the opportunity to escape my life, as though that would somehow allow me to escape from the pain of everything I'd lost. I'd step out of the shell of one girl who'd become an orphan and into the shell of another girl who still had a father.

Libby hadn't seen her parents murdered. She hadn't felt the desperate awakening of what it truly meant to be alone in the world. To have no home. Nothing to anchor her.

Pretending to be Libby allowed me to pretend that everything Frances experienced belonged to someone else. And for years it seemed like Frances was okay with this decision. What was left of her settled deep inside me, curled and protected against the world. Letting the facade of Libby take over, protect her.

But now, being in this home that never belonged to her, slipping into this life that was never rightfully hers, Frances is beginning to wake up. I can feel her stretching under my skin. Her heart beats inside of mine, the rhythm of it now off as though she's no longer content letting me set the pace.

As though she's contemplating revolt.

I see hints of her now, in the mirror. A flicker of her eyes shifting behind my carefully crafted Libby mask. She's hungry, I can tell. And she's angry. She's raw emotion, unhealed from the past and if there's one thing I know for sure, it's that emotions have no place in any of this.

It's funny, most people think that revenge is a passionate affair, driven by rage and pain. But it can't be. Feelings such as those make you weak. They overwrite thought and cause reckless impulses that lead to poor decisions.

If anything, revenge is the *absence* of emotion. It's pure, calculated thought stripped bare of entangling emotions. It's cold, deliberate action.

Frances was always the emotional one which makes her weak. Given the chance she would let her feelings sway her thoughts. She would second-guess. Hesitate.

Libby is none of those things. At least not the Libby I've become. She's crafted and honed for this one purpose, forged by misery and rage, until every raw edge was seared away.

Until she could feel nothing. Nothing at all. There are no soft corners to Libby, no weaknesses. She is the perfect armor against the world.

And the perfect cage for keeping Frances safe and protected.

# TWENTY-ONE

My run the next morning is uneventful and when I pass the Wellses' house, it takes everything I have to keep my gaze straight ahead. I can feel the Senator's eyes on me, watching, and I wonder if he knows that Grey came to see me last night.

It doesn't particularly matter to me or my plans if he does. I've maneuvered Grey into enough situations where he's had to disobey his father that I'm not concerned he'll suddenly cave and do as his daddy says. As I'd expected, the hardest rebellions were the early ones—lying to his father about being with me on the beach that first night, going against his father's wishes and offering me a ride home—and it's simply gotten easier every time since.

I arrive back at the house sweaty and out of breath, and head straight to the kitchen for water. My steps falter when I find Shepherd standing in front of the sink. He's wearing faded jeans with a ragged hem and an old T-shirt with the words, "We never know the worth of water till the well is dry" printed across the back. He stands with one bare foot tucked behind the other as he cleans the blender carafe.

I wonder if I can just barrel through and avoid the awkwardness of talking to him. But then he glances over his shoulder at me, the rising sun highlights his face, making his eyes glisten like the tips of waves. "Morning," he says, smiling. As though the tension of the past two nights never existed.

"Um, good morning," I respond. I wait for him to say something more, to bring up last night or even the night before. But he just continues with cleaning dishes, casual as can be.

"I hope I didn't wake you," I say, going to the cabinet and pulling down a glass. I fill it with water from the fridge and gulp it down too fast. Rivulets spill around my lips, trailing down my neck, but I don't stop. I can't. Ever since my time adrift in the ocean I've become greedy about water.

"I'm not one for sleeping much once the sun's up," Shepherd says, grabbing a dish towel to dry the carafe and his hands before wiping off the counter. "Besides," he continues, folding the towel and hanging it from the oven door, "I realized that I haven't made it particularly easy for you to come home." He lifts a shoulder. "Sometimes it's easy to forget that the past four years were probably just as difficult for you."

It's not at all what I expected to hear and I frown, trying to fit this new information into my carefully constructed plans.

"Smoothie?" he asks, pushing a frosted mug across the counter toward me.

The gesture surprises me. "Oh, um . . ." My instinct is to decline. But then he leans back against the sink, a second mug clasped between his hands.

"I'm not going anywhere, Libby," he says. "If we're going to live in the same house, we can at least be civil to each other."

I hesitate a moment longer before slowly nodding my head. He could be useful, I remind myself. Somewhere down the road I may need his help. "Okay, yeah. I'd like that." I take the offered smoothie, ignoring the slight burn of the frosted glass against my fingertips.

He lifts his mug. "Cheers."

"Cheers," I echo, taking a gulp. The flavors are bright and cold, sending goose bumps flaring across my skin. "Mmm, yum."

He lets out a breathy laugh, as though relieved, but keeps his eyes on his mug, his thumb tracing around the frosted rim. "Yeah," he says, shaking his head.

There's a beat of awkward silence and I take another sip. "Well, I'm going to head up and take a shower," I eventually say. I start for the door, but he whips out a hand, wrapping it tightly around my wrist. Keeping me from leaving.

"What—" I start to protest.

He cuts me off. "Who *are* you?"

I frown, angry at the way my heart begins to race. "What are you talking about?"

He steps closer. "Who are you?" he demands, louder.

"You know who I am," I snap, rolling my eyes. "What the hell's gotten into you?" I struggle against his grip but it tightens enough to be painful. Pulling me closer.

His eyes scour my face. "You're not Libby. Who are you?"

He says it with such certainty that I know—*I know*—he's figured it out. That I'm not Libby. I try to figure out where I messed up, what I did to tip him off. But it doesn't matter. His knowing who I am isn't part of the plan. It could ruin everything I've been so carefully constructing.

I need to get away from him. "This isn't funny," I warn, trying to pry his fingers from my arm. He spins me around, shoving my back against the sink.

A deep, welling panic spikes through my gut.

"Tell. Me. Who. You. Are."

"Let go of me," I bite out between clenched teeth. But even *I* can hear the uncertain fear in my voice.

*He knows.*

He leans closer, his chest a wall crowding me against the counter. Trapping me. "Tell me," he growls, "who you are."

"*Libby*," I whisper. Because I don't know how to be anyone else. Not anymore.

He shakes his head. Angry. His fingers tighten, cutting through muscle to bone. "Libby has a scar along the back of her knee from when she was five and fell climbing a chain-link fence."

"Scars fade—I used Vitamin E oil on it," I argue, refusing to cede anything.

His hands shift, grabbing the counter to either side of my hips, caging me in. "Libby's left eye has a streak of green across the outer edge."

"People's eyes change as they grow up. And don't forget I spent a week blinded by the sun in the ocean. There was permanent damage."

He leans closer. "Libby's bottom teeth were crooked."

"I got them fixed."

"Libby's left pinkie toe is bent from when she broke it jumping from a tree swing in the neighbor's yard."

My breath flutters. "Things change, Shepherd." I lick my lips. "*I* changed."

"No!" he roars, slamming his palm against the counter next to me. The vibration of it shudders through me. "You aren't *her*!"

"Why can't you just believe me?" I shout back, desperate.

"Because I loved her! I adored her! I noticed *everything* about her!"

Sensing a weakness, I turn this around on him. "Oh, that's why you don't want me to be Libby? Because you can't face the fact that I don't love you?" I laugh, a mocking bark that's cold and cruel. "Is it easier for you to believe I'm someone else than to believe I don't love you anymore?"

He presses his lips together, the muscles along his jaw clenching as he draws several deep, shuddering breaths. He's livid and his hands grip at the counter on either side of me, fingers like claws.

There's exhaustion and resignation in his voice when he finally says, "You tied your towel wrong."

The statement is so preposterous it catches me off guard. My eyes fly to meet his and I almost flinch at the accusation in them. "What?"

He leans away from me slightly, giving me space. "You didn't care when I put the dish towel back after cleaning up a spill just now. You sleep with your windows open. You got your ears pierced." Misery is visible on him now, in the way he holds himself so rigid as though he can somehow fight off the truth.

I roll my eyes, but he just lowers his voice, continuing. "That's what you don't get. I have to admit, you're pretty brilliant at pretending to be her. That smile, slightly crooked. The way she twists her ring when she's flustered." He shakes his head. "But you missed the stupid things that no one ever thinks about. That no one would ever notice if they weren't hopelessly in love."

"Like how someone ties a towel?" I ask, incredulous.

"Libby was allergic to wild blackberries," he says softly. I look at him blankly. He picks up my mug from the counter. "What do you think I put in your smoothie this morning?" He lets it fall, not caring when it smashes against the floor.

My mind scrambles. How could I not have known about that—how had Cecil never told me? I desperately try to turn it back on him again. "You fed me something I'm allergic to? You could have killed me!" I spit at him.

He stares at me, breathing fast. And for a moment I think I have him. The tension leaves his shoulders. "I'd have never put Libby in any danger," he says, almost incredulous at the very suggestion. "Wild blackberries made Libby sneeze. We figured it out one day while out catching crabs in the creek."

I scoff but he leans closer, each word precise and ordered. "I've been testing you for days."

His eyes are a storm, violently tumultuous. And I can so

clearly see the truth of it: *He knows*. This isn't him grasping at straws. This isn't him chasing a hunch.

He knows that I'm not Libby.

It becomes difficult to breathe.

"And you've failed every one."

## TWENTY-TWO

When Shepherd's fingers brush my cheeks, they're damp with my tears. He pulls my chin until I'm facing him. It's like drowning all over again. Those moments after jumping from the *Persephone* when the world went dizzy and all there was was falling and then sinking, sinking, sinking so deep into the ocean that I thought it would drag me down forever.

*"I know you're not Libby,"* he whispers. *"Who are you?"*

There's no surface I can swim toward anymore. And there's nothing left in me to fight against the surge of water.

For the first time, I wonder if this is how Libby felt out on the raft when she decided to give up. If she experienced this same kind of lightness. That it could be over. There could be an end. If only I let go.

I run my tongue over my lips, but it does nothing to ease the dryness. "I'm Frances," I whisper. "Frances Mace." The name once so familiar, now so foreign.

And even though he must understand what this means, he still asks the question. "And Libby?"

"She died on the life raft."

He turns his face away, but not before I catch a glimpse of the anguish. I glance down at the mug broken at my feet, giving him this moment. Suddenly his hands on my shoulders aren't keeping me pinned to the counter, but are keeping him standing.

"*I'm sorry*," I whisper. But how can that ever be enough?

He says only one word: "Why?"

When I don't answer fast enough, he lifts his head, expression cold. "Why are you here? Why are you . . ." He pushes away from me so that he can scan me top to bottom. "Why are you her?"

"I can explain," I tell him, hands up as though to physically fend him off. He stares, waiting. I cross my arms over my chest, fighting back a shiver. Trying to find the right words to make him understand.

With a sigh, I tell him the truth. "The *Persephone* wasn't struck by a rogue wave. She was attacked. Armed men boarded her, killed everyone on board, and sank her."

His jaw clenches, anger brewing in his eyes. And then he barks out a scornful laugh. "This is ridiculous," he says, shaking his head. He starts for the door. But I can't let him leave, not without him understanding.

"Wait!" I chase after him, grabbing at his arm.

He whirls on me. "Don't touch me!" Warning is written all over his expression.

"I can explain! Please," I beg.

"You're pathetic," he bites back, continuing toward the garage.

I flinch, the barb striking deep. Hating that this man now knows my deepest secret. "For Libby!" I call after him. His shoulders bristle. "Please, just give me a chance to explain—for her."

When he turns to me his eyes are murderous and I force myself to meet them head-on. His resolve doesn't waver. "If you really cared about her—" I start.

He draws a sharp breath. "Don't you *ever* question my feelings for Libby," he snarls, jabbing a finger toward me.

I use his emotions to my advantage. "Then just listen to me. I know you don't trust me. But please, just give me this."

We stand, both drawn so tight we're almost quivering. The air conditioner hums, cold air blanketing across my sweat-dampened clothes. Shepherd's gaze flickers down and then aside. Then he nods, once.

I let out a relieved breath. "Thank you." He responds by clenching his jaw. I try to think about the best way to explain—how to make him understand. "There's something in my room you should see."

He says nothing as I lead him upstairs. When we reach my room he hesitates at the threshold.

For the first time, it feels like I've lost control of everything. Up until this point, I've played this game of revenge like chess, pushing the players around the game board, knowing how to move each one to impact the others. The endgame always firmly in sight.

But now, Shepherd's changed the rules. Suddenly he can move the pieces around as well and it throws everything into jeopardy.

I've lost the ability to control him.

The only thing I have left is the truth.

I fall to my knees and reach under the bed to pull out the fireproof briefcase. My fingers dance over the lock, such a familiar pattern of numbers and movements. And then it's open, revealing stacks of notebooks and albums, some of them bursting at the seams with yellowed newspaper clippings. Years of meticulous research. Documentation. Planning.

"It's all here," I say, gesturing. He doesn't move from his place in the doorway.

I push to my feet, starting toward the bathroom. "I'll shower," I tell him. "Give you time to look through it all. Then we'll talk." He says nothing in response.

Once in the bathroom I pull off my sodden jogging clothes. And then I just stand there, staring at myself in the mirror. I search for signs of Frances, trying to recognize myself again.

But I'm not sure there's anything of her left. Certainly not enough that Grey could see it. I've spent so long holding the pieces of Libby around me that I'm not sure I'm even capable of letting go.

My eyes fill with tears, blurring the image in front of me. No longer looking at the individual features, just seeing the whole—those things that Frances and Libby always shared. Oval face. Dark hair. Brown eyes. Wide forehead.

What's left of either of us? Unsettled, I twist the O'Martin signet ring on my finger. Libby's old habit, now mine. I pull the ring free, holding it up between my reflected selves.

It was the first thing of hers Cecil gave me. A seal between us that I'd accepted his proposition. I glance at my bare hand, the skin at the base of my finger indented, a paler white. A ghost of the ring.

A reminder that even if I chose to, I could never be free of Libby. She is entangled in me, now and forever.

## TWENTY-THREE

I stay in the shower until the water runs cold and even then I don't get out until my teeth chatter and I can no longer feel my toes. I take my time brushing my hair, putting on lotion, postponing the inevitable. Finally, I tug yesterday's clothes from the hamper and dress.

When I open the bathroom door I find Shepherd standing on the balcony, staring out at the bright ocean. A light breeze teases at his hair, tugs at the hem of his shirt. Behind him, the notebooks are scattered across my bed and a few yellowed newspaper articles have drifted to the floor.

I bend, picking one up. It's a picture of Frances. The one from her yearbook.

I swallow.

From *my* yearbook.

"All this time and she's been dead." He doesn't bother turning to look at me, just continues staring out into the empty horizon. "For years I'd hoped . . ." His voice cracks and he swallows the rest of the sentence.

But I know what he was going to say. He'd hoped that he and Libby could be together again. That maybe he could remind her of their history together, of the way they'd fallen in love.

He'd been holding on to a girl who no longer existed. And now he hadn't just lost her, but the dream of her. Of them together.

Sometimes I think that's the hardest part to recover from. Not the loss of someone, but the loss of the possibility of them.

"And this . . ." He turns and stalks to the bed where he grabs one of the notebooks at random and flings it at me. I flinch, throwing up my hands to catch it as it smacks against my chest. I don't have to look at it to know the pages are filled with details about Grey. Just thinking his name causes a heat to swell inside me, battling against the terrified numbness of having been unmasked.

"All these details—so dry and cold." He reaches for another one and I recognize it instantly as his. He starts reading. "'Shepherd's parents both worked for Cecil—his mother, Mariana, first as a maid and then as a personal assistant. His father, Manuel, as his estate manager. Both Mariana and Manuel were killed in a car accident when Shepherd was six (Luis was sixteen). The only family that could take Shepherd and Luis in lived in Mexico and Cecil offered to act as their guardian so they could continue living in the States.'"

"Stop," I tell him. He does, tossing the notebook at me so that I fumble to catch it.

He's already moved on to another. This one is Libby's. "'If she wears a watch (which she only does when school is in session), she puts it on her right wrist. She detests anything between her toes and refuses to wear flip-flops. From around ages nine to eleven she had a plant in her room that Shepherd nicknamed the suicide plant because—'"

"Please, stop," I whisper.

He throws this notebook at me as well, reaching for another. "'According to several interviews Martha Wells takes one vial of Refreshergy every morning before her swim. That she drinks it with a smoothie will impact metabolism of the toxin but since it's stable unless mixed with sodium chloride, the cramps won't hit until she's in the ocean.'"

I lunge toward him and rip it out of his hands. "Enough!" I shout at him.

But he surges against me, coming so close that not even air separates us. "What the hell is wrong with you?" he shouts. "You planned to poison an innocent woman!"

"It's not a lethal dose," I counter.

His eyes go wide. "Do you even listen to yourself? 'Not a lethal dose'? That's not an acceptable response!"

He's right. I know he is and I hate it. I hate the condemnation in his voice. Even more than that, I hate the disappointment. Because disappointment only comes when you expect something of someone. And no one has expected anything of me in years.

Except to be Libby. That's the only thing anyone has wanted from me since the moment I was pulled from the ocean. Even then I knew it was an impossible task. I would always fall short.

Even the fake me is a disappointment.

Cecil never said so directly, but I could see it in his eyes. He tried to love me. He was always kind and generous and I truly believe he cared for me.

But at the end of the day I was not his daughter. I was neither Frances Mace nor Libby O'Martin.

I was simply lost. As adrift in this new life as I'd been in the *Persephone*'s life raft.

The only thing that has ever truly been mine—that belongs to neither Frances nor Libby but to this new hybrid creature I've become—is this: my quest for truth and revenge.

And I will not allow Shepherd to take that from me. I will not allow him to condemn me for seeking the truth.

I lift my chin, squaring my jaw. Ready to face anything he throws my way.

He shakes his head, horrified. "Everything—all of this. Is it some sort of messed-up game to you?"

"You don't understand," I scoff.

"There's nothing to understand!" He waves his hands at me, as if I were some sort of specimen he's afraid to even come into contact with. "This—you—it's out of control!"

I raise a finger, pointing it at him. "I am *not* out of control. If you've learned anything from reading through my notebooks, it's how meticulously I've planned it all out."

He turns and starts pacing, his fingers laced behind his head. I can't hear the words he's mumbling, but it's pretty obvious it's about me being crazy.

I begin gathering the notebooks that dropped to the floor, setting them on the bed with the others and arranging them in order. Every sense is trained on Shepherd—listening to the stuttering shuffle of his feet, the harsh way he inhales and holds it.

"You can't mess with people's lives like this, *Frances*," he finally says.

Hearing my name—the real one—sends my pulse racing. Half in fear, half in thrill. I clench my fists, nails digging into my skin. "They messed with mine." I hate how petulant that sounds, but it's the truth.

He lets out a long breath, moving close enough that the heat of him radiates against my back. "You have to let that go." His words are a gentle plea. And it makes me wonder what stake he has in all of this. Why he even cares.

I close my eyes, thinking how easy it would be to sway back against Shepherd and let his arms circle around me, bearing me up. It wouldn't be that difficult to let it all go—I could take Libby's money and run. Disappear and let the Wells family live out their lives in whatever peace they've been able to find.

But then I think of Libby. Not how she'd been when I met her—vibrant and full of life. Mischievous and brilliant. But how she was at the end, as she gave up.

And how desperately I wanted to give up as well.

That's why I can't just walk away.

# TWENTY-FOUR

I turn and walk out on the balcony. The wind from the ocean plays through the damp ends of my hair, flinging tiny drops of water down my back. Out on the life raft I'd sworn to myself that if I survived I'd never take water for granted again. It's amazing how little time passed before I broke that promise. How quickly I'd grown accustomed to turning on a faucet without second thought.

"Do you know what happens to a person's body when they're cast adrift without food or water?" I glance over my shoulder to where Shepherd leans against the balcony door. He says nothing, his jaw rigid.

"The rule of thumb is that a body can only go three minutes without air, three days without water, and three weeks without food." I explain. "Libby and I were adrift for *seven days*."

I let that hang in the air a moment before continuing. "It's not the hunger that's the problem—not really. I mean, it's there, feeling like your body's eating you from the inside out. But the thirst." I shake my head, wetting my lips just because

I can. Such a simple gesture, one I'd have cut off a limb to be able to do when out on that ocean.

"At first, your tongue starts sticking to the roof of your mouth. To your teeth. It's like there isn't enough room in your mouth for it anymore. And the taste." I tighten my grip on the iron railing. "It's foul—sticky and thick and wrong. It feels like there's something solid stuck in your throat and all you can do is swallow incessantly but it makes no difference."

Shepherd is still silent, but I can tell from the tension in the air that he's listening. "Everything hurts—your head, your neck. Your ears. The inside of your nose. It's unbearable and all you want to do is scream but you can't because your voice cracks and it feels like your throat bleeds from the effort." I'm on a roll now, half my mind standing here on the balcony with Shepherd and the other half back on that raft.

"Eventually, your lips split from the dryness. Your skin no longer sweats, and through it all the sun is relentless. Burning you so bad you start to blister. That's when you start hearing things. Seeing things."

I glance back at Shepherd. His eyes betray his mixture of revulsion and curiosity. It's obvious he knows he shouldn't want to hear this, that the horror is too great, yet he can't stop himself from listening.

These are the kind of details that never made it to the papers. That aren't even in the notebooks piled on my bed. These are the things I've kept only to myself, the memory of them sealed into my veins like blood.

"We were lucky—it rained on the second day. We were able to drink fresh water." I lift a shoulder. "But the process just began all over again. The cotton mouth, the pain. Your head feels like it's too big because your skin starts to shrink. We snapped at each other—argued. Because of the pain and because our brains weren't working right and nothing made much sense.

"By the sixth morning, our tongues were rocks—practically solid, like they were some kind of foreign object in our mouths. We were mummifying in front of each other's eyes."

"Frances—" Shepherd steps beside me, a hand held up, asking me to stop.

But I'm in no mood to show mercy.

I turn toward Shepherd, hands balled to fists at my sides as the familiar comfort of rage billows over me like a blanket. "You wanted to know why I need revenge against Senator Wells and Grey? Why I can't let this go?" I jab a finger against his chest. "Well, this is the reason.

"There was always salt water in the boat and at first we could bail it out but eventually we were too weak. Both of us had sores everywhere and the salt was like acid. Libby had a rash up her arms and at night she'd scratch at it, like she wanted to tear her skin from her bones.

"You start to see things. You think you hear ships and planes. But it's always just your brain playing tricks. And, God, you want to believe *so badly*." My voice cracks and I cross my arms over my chest, hands gripping my shoulders as I fold in on myself under the weight of memory.

"The blood sweats started on the seventh morning." Shepherd winces, but stays silent. "There was a storm out on the horizon and I kept thinking that if it would just come closer . . ."

When I blink my eyes I'm back on the raft, watching the clouds boil into the sky. So close. So close. Sheets of rain fell in the distance, gray curtains of water just out of reach. "I thought for sure that eventually the rain would hit us."

I pause, listening to the ocean crashing against the sand just beyond the dunes. And I think about the sound the waves made against the walls of the lifeboat. A hushing sort of whisper that I'd eventually found comforting.

It had become, for me, the reckoning of death.

"I couldn't take it. I started drinking seawater several days in." Shepherd lifts his eyebrows in surprise. "I know. Libby begged me not to but . . ." I shrug. The pain had been too much for me and I was so envious of Libby's ability to endure it.

I'd felt so weak willed. As if *I* were the one giving up.

"Because of that, it was always worse for Libby. She was more dehydrated and at every stage, she was worse off than me. But that seventh afternoon I woke up and she was lying against the other side of the raft. There were red streaks down her cheeks and at first I didn't understand. I thought she was dead but then . . ." My voice cracks. This is something I've never told anyone before. Not written down. It's a memory that's belonged only to me.

To both Frances and Libby.

It seems almost cruel to be sharing it. To push these images into another person's mind. The weight of them is crippling.

"As I watched, a drop of blood welled in the corner of her eye and spilled over. It looked like she was crying. And I knew. Right then, I knew."

Shepherd inhales sharp, his fingers gripping at the railing so tight that the skin strains across his knuckles.

"She couldn't speak at that point. It was too much of an effort." Her lips had become almost nonexistent, eyelids split, skin leather tight, and cheekbones impaling her from the inside out. "But she mouthed the words and I understood.

"She said, 'I'm sorry.' By the time I got to her, by the time I grabbed her hand, she'd given up." I swallow. "And I was so jealous because I wanted to be the one to die. And I was mad she was going to give up and leave me alone. So I turned my back on her. Even as she was dying."

My memory of the moment is so vivid, so bright and colorized. "I don't know how much time passed before I turned to check on her. That's when I saw the boat—it was headed right for us. I grabbed Libby—told her we were saved. She was still breathing—just barely—and I told her to hold on. Just a little while longer."

I shake my head, the next bit coming out in a whisper. "But it was too late. I tried, but I couldn't keep her alive long enough. And I've always wondered . . ." I have to pause, and Shepherd waits, silent, for me to continue.

"If I hadn't turned my back on her. If I hadn't been so mad at her, I would have seen the boat earlier. Libby might have lived." My voice cracks. "I let her die."

## TWENTY-FIVE

At first, Shepherd's touch on my shoulder is hesitant but then he's pulling me against him, tucking my head under his chin. It's the first time since being rescued I've let someone hold me while I cried.

But I don't allow myself to draw too much comfort from it. Because if there's anything I've learned from my time adrift, it's that you can't depend on anyone. They will all abandon you in the end.

"You can't blame yourself, Frances," he murmurs.

That name on his lips jolts me, wrenching me from the past. I push away, dashing the tears from my eyes and shaking my head to clear it. "You're right," I tell him, walking back inside. I shuffle through the stack of notebooks on the bed until I find the one I'm looking for. Flipping it open, I thrust it at him. "I blame *them*."

I point to the photo of Grey and his father, taken moments after they'd been rescued. It ran in half the newspapers—the powerful Senator and his golden-boy child who survived.

He starts to laugh. But when I don't join in, the sound dies out and his eyes go wide. "Wait, you can't be serious."

"That isn't what someone looks like when they've been cast adrift for three days."

"Maybe, but—"

I cut him off before he can say more. "How about this. Tomorrow you go lie on one of the rafts in the pool and stay there for a few days. And then we can compare. You think your skin will look that good—no open sores?" I point at the picture. "No third-degree burns from the sun? For God's sake, even their lips aren't cracked from dehydration!"

"What you're saying is . . ." He struggles for the word. *Ridiculous. Impossible. Absurd. Crazy.* I hear all the possible choices in my head—I've thought them all before.

"What I'm saying is there were three hundred twenty-seven people on that cruise ship and three hundred twenty-three of them were murdered. Libby and I only escaped through dumb luck. But Grey and his father"—I shake my head—"that wasn't luck."

I take a step forward. "What I'm saying is they lied. You laughed earlier when I told you, but it's the truth. There was no rogue wave, the *Persephone* was taken down by armed men."

"Do you have proof?" he asks.

"That's why I'm here," I bite back.

He lets out a long breath and paces across the room thinking. "Okay, then why not go to the cops?"

I shake my head. "Don't you think I've already considered that? My word against a well-respected sitting Senator of the United States and his son? There isn't enough proof. Remember when that Malaysian Airlines plane went missing a while back? The whole world mobilized to look for it because the disappearance was unexplained. But what would have happened if the plane had just flown into a storm and a few days later they'd found two survivors—a Senator and his teenaged son? If the Senator blamed it all on the storm, who would second-guess that?"

When he says nothing, I answer for him. "No one. And even if they'd found another survivor a week later who said it was hijacked, who'd have believed her? They'd say she went mad from dehydration and starvation. Sure a few conspiracy theorists might grab hold, but nothing would come of it. And you can forget even the loons listening if she came out with that story four years later."

At my argument, Shepherd's expression shifts from utter disbelief to measured uncertainty. With a sigh I sit on the edge of the bed and run my thumb over the ghost of Libby's ring still visible at the base of my finger. "Look, I watched those men kill my parents and Libby's mom. I watched Libby die and it was not an easy death."

I press my palms against my eyes, wishing I could erase the searing images. "I tried to move on. I tried to have a normal life. But how could I? There's not a night I don't have nightmares. There's not a moment that I forget the sound of those bullets or the look on my mother's face when those men pulled the trigger."

I open my mouth to say more, but know that if I do, my voice will waver and crack. And so I sit silently a moment, forcing the memories back.

The bed shifts as Shepherd sits beside me. Not close enough to touch, but close enough that I can feel the heat radiating off him. I drop my hands to my lap, staring at the sliver of empty space between the edge of my knee and his.

"I used to think that I just needed to understand," I tell him. "That if I could find out the truth, that would be enough. And the truth still matters to me, don't get me wrong." I press my lips together and shake my head.

"But that's not enough anymore. There were 5,783 minutes between the moment when Grey and his father were rescued and when Libby's father found us—5,783 minutes of agony. Of thirst and hunger and desperation. Every second drove us closer to death. That's 5,783 minutes where the coast guard could have found us. If they'd kept looking. But they weren't, because Grey and his father lied about what happened on the *Persephone*."

"You can't know that for sure," Shepherd interjects.

"Our chances of getting rescued earlier would have been a whole lot higher with the coast guard still looking," I point out. He says nothing, conceding the point.

"Here's the thing, Cecil always hoped I'd make something out of Libby's life. And for a long time that's what I wanted too—to make him proud. To prove myself worthy of having survived.

"But I can't do that anymore. I can't move on until this is settled. And to do that I had to come back. I had to confront Grey and his father—shake loose the truth."

I turn to face him, trying to make him understand. "At best Grey and his father lied because they were scared. And at worst they lied because they were somehow involved. Either way they lied and I intend to find out why. You can hate me if you want. You can blame me for all of this, for keeping the truth from you. You can help me, or you can leave." I keep my voice cold, resolved. "But the one thing you can't do is stop me."

## TWENTY-SIX

The next morning my legs feel a little sluggish, but I still force myself out on my usual run. I can't afford to miss it. I've just reached the tip of the island and turned back when I see Mrs. Wells in the distance, making her way slowly across the boardwalk to the beach. As she does every morning, she pauses when her feet first hit the sand, and stretches.

There's a little table where she drops her towel and then she takes her time stuffing her hair into a bright yellow swim cap. The Wellses are nothing if not wed to their routines.

I keep my pacing even, watching her as I jog closer. From this far away I can't see any of the details—her bathing suit is nothing more than a brush of black against pale skin, her goggles mirrored reflections over her eyes. It's low tide and she takes her time walking toward the water. She enters it haltingly, pausing when it hits her knees and using her hands as cups to splash the rest of her body.

The storms over the past few days have churned the ocean some, but this morning the waves have calmed. The whitecaps are muted and dulled, more rolling hills than cutting cliffs.

She makes her way deeper, her arms spread wide with her palms hovering against the surface, swishing her fingers back and forth. When she dives under it's an elegant movement, the curve of her body graceful and slick. She kicks a few yards farther out and then turns parallel to the beach, swimming up the coast toward me.

I increase my pace, pushing myself harder as I watch her. Waiting to see if today's Refreshergy is the one that I poisoned.

Her strokes are crisp and even, elbow pulling high out of the water by her ribs before stretching forward. She's done this every summer morning for years—decades. So often she probably doesn't even think about it anymore. Like me with running, she probably lets her body fall into its pattern, untethering her mind to drift free.

Which is why when the first cramp hits her, it must come as such a surprise. The muscles spasming first in her gut, twisting so hard it's like she's ripping in half. She wouldn't be prepared for it, her thoughts would already be too far away. By the time she reels them in, forces them to focus, it's too late. It's hit in her other muscles: calves and hamstrings knotting impossibly tight, back cramping.

I see the moment it happens. The way her arm crumples as she reaches forward. The yellow curve of her head jerking from the water. She's splashing and panic. Pain and terror.

Unlike Mrs. Wells, I'm prepared. I've run through this all in my head too many times to count. Racing down the beach as fast as I can, I rip my cell phone from my armband and punch in 911. It rings only once and the moment the dispatcher picks up, I start reciting.

"Send someone quick!" I shout, modulating my voice so that it has enough panic to be sincere, but not so much that it is incoherent. "I think she's drowning!"

"Okay, ma'am, calm down," the dispatcher says in a soothing voice. "What's the address?"

I glance toward the Senator's house. "Oh God, I don't know. Um . . ." I pull the phone away from my mouth and scream, "HELP!" as loud as possible, hoping someone might hear.

Out in the ocean, Mrs. Wells continues to thrash, barely keeping her head above water.

"Ma'am—"

"It's the beach in front of—it's the Senator's house. Senator Wells's house." I'm gasping now, from sprinting.

"I'm sending a rescue crew but can you—"

"She's—oh my God, I think it's the Senator's wife!" She's about twenty yards from shore, gasping, crying—trying to scream but unable to get enough air. Her head goes under, stays under. Bobs to the surface again.

More panic creeps into my voice, making it high-pitched and scratchy. "They'll be too late. I have to help her!"

"Ma'am—"

"Tell them it's the Senator's house! Tell them to hurry!"

And then I fling the phone up the beach, not even bothering to turn it off, and race toward the water's edge. My heart seizes at the shock of entering the ocean for the first time since the *Persephone*. The tide grips at me greedily, and I have to force myself not to turn back to the safety of dry land. Foam splashes over my feet, clinging to my thighs as I run out as far as I can, leaping over the waves before eventually diving in.

The flood of salt causes me to gag, but I push it all aside to focus on reaching Mrs. Wells. The water around her is a churning white. She's beyond panic now. Beyond any kind of thought at all. This is pure survival mode. I've studied enough about drowning victims to know that the most dangerous thing you can do in a rescue is let them get ahold of you.

They'll push you under in a heartbeat if it will allow them to get their own head above the surface. By the time I'm within reach, she's weakened enough that every time she slips under, it takes longer for her to surge up again.

I maneuver behind her, one knee raised and ready to kick her away if she tries to turn and grab me. My plan all along has been to save her. Drag her to the beach while the media swarms, lauding me as a hero. Making it so that the Senator is in my debt. So that he cannot keep me from Grey.

So that Grey himself feels indebted to me.

The next thing I'm supposed to do is slip my arms beneath hers and lean back, pulling her to the surface on top of me. She's within reach. I'm perfectly positioned.

Yet I hesitate. Thinking for one brief moment that perhaps the best thing for Grey and his father is for them to lose someone they love desperately. So that they understand the pain of it. The absolute hollowness.

It would serve them right. Whether they had a role to play in the sinking of the *Persephone* or not, it seems so unfair that they escaped with their family intact when I did not.

When I didn't even escape with my own self intact.

In this moment I am the most powerful force in Grey's and his father's life. More powerful than even the sea itself. Their lives are mine to control, their futures mine to dictate.

Mrs. Wells's hand breaks the surface, but she is unable to pull her head above water. Still, I don't move to rescue her.

*Could I really let her die?* I ask myself.

The most alarming realization is the sudden and sure answer: *yes*.

I could absolutely let her die.

## TWENTY-SEVEN

But letting Mrs. Wells drown is not part of the plan. So I reach my hands under her shoulders and pull her to the surface. Her chest spasms as she flails, gurgling sounds choking her throat.

"You're going to be okay," I tell her. "Hang on for me—just hang on!" I start kicking for shore, using the momentum of the waves to push us closer. "We're almost there," I promise.

The moment my feet hit bottom I grab her wrists and haul her up to the beach, not even bothering to drag her completely free from the waves before turning her to her side. She retches, salt water gushing from her mouth and foaming around her nose.

The wheezing sound afterward is desperate and panicked as she claws at the sand. I hold her head, hovering over her. "You're okay," I tell her again and again. She coughs, gasping and choking, retching.

But she's breathing. Her eyes open, lucidity slowly returning. Her body lies limp, exhausted, shuddering as she coughs and gasps. The sound of sirens grows louder and in the distance a news chopper roars into sight.

I shift, sitting back on my heels and pulling her so that her back rests against my thighs, her head tucked against my stomach. I reach for one of the water bottles still attached to my belt and uncap it. Lifting it to her lips I encourage her to drink. She does, much of its thick liquid dribbling down her chin, but enough making it into her body to neutralize the toxin she'd ingested earlier.

"Mom!" I hear the scream and glance over my shoulder. Grey comes racing from the house, sprinting down the boardwalk. The Senator's not far behind, shouting, "Martha!"

Grey crashes to his knees next to me, eyes wild and panicked. "Mom." He reaches for her and then hesitates, not sure what to do. She tries to smile, tears streaming down her face.

"She's okay," I tell him. "She was swimming and—"

Just then the Senator arrives. "Martha!" He grips her shoulders. "Martha, are you okay?" She nods weakly, but when she tries to speak her voice is nothing but rasp.

I scoot back, giving him access to her. "I called nine-one-one—the ambulance is on its way," I tell him. But his focus is entirely on his wife. His gaze sweeps her body, searching for injury. Other than a cut down her calf from where I must have pulled her across a sharp shell, there's nothing. Satisfied, he cups her face and leans down until his forehead presses against hers. "*Thank God, you're okay,*" he whispers. His eyes are closed, eyelashes damp. He takes her hand and presses her palm against his cheek.

It's a tender moment, totally incongruous with anything I

would expect of him, and I shift, looking away, uncomfortable.

Just as the paramedics come storming onto the beach the news helicopter banks overhead, keeping enough distance that it doesn't kick up sand, but close enough that I feel the spin of its rotors thumping through me like a heartbeat. I'm not surprised it arrived so quickly; almost any station has someone monitoring the police radio bands. While the news of someone drowning would be motivation enough to investigate, it's the location that got them here quickly.

That's why I made sure to mention the Senator's house as a landmark.

The paramedics waste no time, kneeling next to Mrs. Wells and taking her vitals. Neighbors look on, crowded along their boardwalks, holding up phones and cameras, documenting it all. In the distance, sirens rage as several four-by-fours race down the beach toward us, lights blazing.

When the lead paramedic asks Mrs. Wells what happened, she points to me. There's a split second when my heart jolts, terror that she actually knows the truth—that I was the one to do this to her.

But then she rasps out, "Saved me."

Eyes wide, I sputter an explanation. "She was swimming just fine and then—I don't know." My answer comes out rushed, almost choked. As though I still can't believe it all. "She started flailing and it was obvious something was wrong. That's when I called nine-one-one. But I couldn't just watch—not when she needed help."

The paramedics return their focus to Mrs. Wells, loading her onto a backboard. As they start toward the house, a reporter with a camerawoman in tow races toward them.

The Senator pushes them away with a growl. "Greyson," he barks over his shoulder, "take the car and follow."

As though he hadn't heard the command, Grey stands by the water, frozen. He's staring down at the sand where his mother lay only a moment ago. There's a dark patch of red, scarlet rivulets being pulled into the ocean by the seeping water.

"Grey," I say softly, moving toward him. My teeth chatter as the spike of adrenaline leaches from my system. I touch trembling fingers to his arm, lightly. "She's going to be okay."

He looks up at me and his eyes churn deeper than the storm-cast sea. There's something both fierce and lost about his expression, and I swallow, caught off guard. "Libby," he begins, "I—"

And then he lunges toward me, wrapping me in his arms. "*Thank you—*" he whispers in my ear.

He's cut off by his father. "Greyson!" he roars. "Let's go!"

Grey blinks, pulling back and shaking his head. There's a damp spot on his shirt from my drenched jog bra, but he doesn't notice. "I'm sorry." He points toward his father, apologetic, and I nod.

"Go," I tell him, crossing my arms across my chest in an attempt to keep warm. "Of course."

For a few steps he jogs backward, still looking at me, as though there's something more he's trying to say. And then in one fluid motion he tugs his shirt over his head and tosses it to me. When I pull it on, it clings against the dampness of my skin and bra. But it's warm and it smells like Grey.

He smiles, fingers twitching in a wave, before he turns and dodges around the camerawoman as he chases after his father.

It's obvious from the self-satisfied gleam in the reporter's eyes that she captured every second of the exchange between Grey and me. Just as I'd hoped.

## TWENTY-EIGHT

The police quickly realize that interviewing me on the beach is impossible with all of the people hovering around. What began as a trickle has turned into a flood—not just reporters, but neighbors and townsfolk drawn to the scene, cameras and cell phones at the ready.

So instead the cops lead me up to a table on the Senator's patio. There are three of them—two male officers sweating in their uniforms and a female officer in plainclothes. She pulls out a chair for me but I hesitate before sitting.

"Um, is it okay if I use the bathroom before we talk?" I rub at my forearm where some of Mrs. Wells's blood still stains my skin. "I just need a second to—" My breathing's a bit ragged, my chin trembling as though I'm overwhelmed.

The female cop nods. "Sure thing. Take your time."

I mumble thanks and hurriedly make my way toward the kitchen door. The housekeeper's the one to answer my knock, wisps of grey hair escaping the tight bun at the nape of her neck and a scowl on her face. When she realizes that I'm not a reporter or a cop, she grabs my shoulders, her eyes glistening with tears. "You are such a brave, brave angel."

She pulls me in for a hug and I'm too surprised to resist. "Thank goodness you were out on that beach this morning! Just thinking about what might have happened with Martha . . ." She inhales sharply.

I say nothing and when she eventually relaxes her grip, I look down at my feet, feigning embarrassment at the attention. "I just did what anyone else would do," I mumble. *Except for the bit about poisoning her*, I add silently.

She smiles. "I like to think so. Now, can I get you something? Water? Tea?"

I shake my head, shy. "I think the officers might like something, though—they've got to be burning up out there. I was just hoping to maybe use the restroom? Wash some of this salt off?"

"Of course, honey, let me show you." She leads me down the hallway, giving my shoulder another squeeze before returning to the kitchen. I turn on the water and splash a few handfuls on my face. When I'm sure the housekeeper is distracted with the task of taking drinks out to the officers, I slip out of the bathroom, leaving the water running and closing the door behind me.

Holding my breath, I dash down the hallway and into the home office I'd caught a glimpse of when I was here the other morning. Though the furniture shares the same clean, sparse lines as the rest of the house, this room feels a little more lived-in. There are actual books on the shelves along with photos of the Senator with various Important People.

Papers are stacked haphazardly across the glass-topped desk and I hurriedly shuffle through them. I have no idea what I'm looking for—it's doubtful the Senator would just happen to have a confession lying about. Unsurprisingly, all I find are drafts of various senate bills, correspondence with fund-raisers, and financial documents.

I tug on the drawers, riffling through the usual office clutter of pens and paper clips, flipping through file folders neatly labeled with things like PAC, USCFR, and DMTR. Nothing stands out.

I'd known the likelihood of finding anything was small, yet I can't help the kernel of disappointment sitting heavy in my gut. I do a quick tour of the room, scanning the shelves just in case I missed anything. My eyes fall on a photo of Grey and his father, standing on the deck of the coast guard ship that rescued them.

They have their arms around each other. Only the Senator is smiling.

A flash of anger rips through me. I imagine the Senator at the hospital right now, by his wife's bed. I wonder whether he's afraid, whether he's come even close to understanding how narrowly he avoided losing her today.

I hope so. He deserves that fear. He deserves to know how easily and quickly you can lose the ones you love.

There's the sound of the kitchen door opening and closing—likely the housekeeper taking drinks out to the officers. I use the opportunity to slip back into the bathroom, wash some of the blood and sand off my arms, and turn off the faucet. I'm not overly concerned about getting caught somewhere I shouldn't be—saving Mrs. Wells's life will give me quite a bit of leeway.

But there's no reason to arouse suspicions this early in the game.

Outside the two male officers stand when I approach, one of them pulling back a chair for me. I tuck myself into it, pulling Grey's damp shirt tight around me. Overhead news helicopters bank and the female officer waits for them to pass before introducing herself as Detective Morales. It's almost impossible to tell her age—her long black hair is pulled up in a ponytail and her face is smooth and unlined. Instead of the dark blue uniform, she's wearing khaki pants and a polo shirt with a badge stitched over the pocket. She shakes my hand with a wide, friendly smile. "Feeling better?" she asks.

I nod. "Thanks."

"So, Miss O'Martin," she says. "This is just a formality—any time the police respond to a distress call we need to fill out a report. You're not in trouble here, okay?"

I nod, my expression uncertain.

"How old are you?" she asks.

"I just turned eighteen," I tell her.

She nods. "Do you have a parent you want to call? They're welcome to be here with you if you'd prefer."

It's a simple question, and other than the fact that Caldwell is a small community, there's really no reason for her to know that my father died earlier this year and I'm technically an orphan.

But I can tell in the set of her expression that she already knows this about me. It may be imperceptible to most people, but when someone's looking for information they don't already know, there's an anticipation that causes their pupils to dilate.

Hers don't.

That's the moment I understand how she's been so success-ful at her job: She has the easy kind of manner that makes you instantly want to be her friend. It's not until you look closely that you notice the shrewdness in her eyes.

This is a woman who misses nothing and it puts me on guard.

I clear my throat, lifting my knees up to my chest and pulling the shirt over them so that I look small and vulnerable. "Both of my parents are dead," I tell her. The other two officers at the table shift, uncomfortable at the trembling emotion in my voice. They're both middle-aged men with wedding rings and the kinds of bags under their eyes that indicate sleepless nights caring for young children. I've immediately gained their sympathy.

That's one of the benefits of being an orphan: instant sym-pathy.

"I'm sorry for your loss, Miss O'Martin," Detective Morales murmurs.

"Thank you. And, please, call me Libby," I tell her, adding a hesitant smile.

"Okay, Libby. Can you walk us through what happened this morning?"

As I begin recounting the story, she leaves it to the officer on her left to take notes. It's a smart tactic—maintaining the appearance that she and I are just having a conversation so that I'll let down my guard.

It doesn't take long for me to go through it all. When I'm done, Morales asks a few questions, just to make sure she's got the details right. "Are you close with the Wells family?" She looks so earnest asking the question that I doubt even the two officers with her realize she knows the answer.

I wrap my arms around my shins, hugging them tightly. It makes me look even more childlike. The two male officers shift, again. "Grey"—I clear my throat—"um, we were on the *Persephone* together."

The two men draw sharp breaths and Morales leans forward. "Oh, honey," she says. "I should have remembered that. I'm so sorry."

I lift one side of my mouth, a trembling smile. "It's okay."

She tilts her head to the side. "Did you and Grey keep in touch afterward?"

"No." I shake my head.

"You'll have to tell me how you've been able to pull that off," she says with a laugh. "There are a few people in Caldwell I'd love to avoid running into. That's the problem with small towns."

Another excellent tactic: wrapping a serious question in a joke. I don't respond.

There's still sand crusted along the side of my leg and I run my finger against it, slowly dislodging it. She knows as well as I do that most people despise silence, that the easiest way to get someone to talk is to say nothing, sit back until they rush to fill the empty space.

It's Morales who cracks first and I have to bite back a small smile of success. "Well, I guess that explains the media." She gestures toward the reporters flocking the beach. "Not that a prominent Senator's wife almost drowning wouldn't be news. But when the rescuer turns out to be the only person other than the victim's family who survived one of the biggest disasters in recent memory . . ." She shakes her head, her eyes still on me. "That makes for good TV."

Something about her expression causes my heart to race. The way she's scrutinizing my reaction. There's absolutely no reason for her to be suspicious of me. As far as she knows, I'm just a teenage girl—an orphan—who happened to be in the right place at the right time to save someone's life.

But telling myself that doesn't stop adrenaline flooding my system. Nor does it stop a warning in my gut. "My dad always used to say that truth is stranger than fiction," I tell her.

"Mark Twain quote," Morales says, smiling and standing. "Let me give you a ride home. Keep you away from the media storm a little while longer."

The housekeeper leads us through the kitchen to the front door. Morales takes the lead, me trailing behind. I watch the way she's able to take in her surroundings so subtly, without drawing attention to the fact she's cataloging everything. Once we get outside, I bet that if I quizzed her on how many glass globes were arranged on the silver platter on the living room coffee table, she'd have the answer.

It makes me wonder what she's noticed about me that I don't want her to. What have I given away without realizing it?

## TWENTY-NINE

The end of the Wellses' driveway is cluttered with news vans, most of them parked haphazardly off the side of the road. When the reporters catch sight of the cop car, they rush it, cameras at the ready. Officers push them back, forcing a gap large enough for Morales to ease through, her foot heavy on the brake.

I glance out the window, long enough for most of them to get a good shot of my face to run on the evening news. My expression is one of surprise, a bit of "deer in headlights" mixed with a healthy dose of "youthful innocence." I want them to think of me as the everyday girl who just happened to rescue a prominent politician's wife.

I want them to love me. Everything is so much easier if you have the media on your side.

A few of the reporters shout questions but it's all a muffled blur and then we're through the throng and accelerating down the road. "You'll have to watch out for them—they can be vultures," she says, flicking her eyes toward the rearview mirror.

"Aggressive as hell and rarely care much for the law. Or common decency for that matter."

"I know," I say, still staring out the side window at the scrub trees skimming past.

"Right," she says. "I guess this wouldn't be the first time you've been the center of media attention." She pauses a moment. "Though I guess you're pretty good at avoiding them. I don't remember seeing any pictures of you after the *Persephone*."

On the surface her question sounds like idle curiosity, but I detect an undercurrent to it. One that's constantly pushing and pulling at the edges of my story, searching for weakness. What I can't figure out is why. Whether her inherent skepticism is part of the job description or whether there's something about me in particular that's piqued her suspicion.

"My dad took me to Europe. He thought it would be easier for me to recover if I didn't have to worry about the attention."

"Lucky you," she says, and I have to clench my teeth together to keep from snorting in response.

As we near the O'Martin estate, there's a smaller camp of reporters, and judging from the vans following along behind us, it's about to grow. "Guess they've ID'd you already," she grunts, not bothering to slow this time before turning into my driveway. "I'll see if we can get an officer down here to keep them in line."

She pulls around to the front of the house and puts the car in park. Turning toward me she says, "Be sure to keep your doors locked and it might be a good idea to cover your windows.

They really have no shame with what they'll photograph and sell." She fishes in her pocket and holds out a card. "This has my direct number and cell on it. Don't hesitate to use it."

"Thank you," I tell her, taking it.

Before I've even stepped out of the car, the front door opens and Shepherd rushes out, anxious. "Are you okay?" he asks.

"I'm fine," I mumble.

A loud dinging sounds from the cop car as Morales unlatches her seat belt and climbs out, leaving it running. "Mr. Sheep, nice to see you again. Though I guess it's probably a good thing it's been a while, huh?" She smiles, almost teasing.

Shepherd laughs, jogging down the front stairs toward the car. He reaches across the roof, shaking Morales's hand. "She okay?" he asks her, nodding his head back at me.

"Yes," I tell him from my place on the porch. But he ignores me. I watch as they fall into an easy conversation and frown, wondering how they know each other.

"She's a new local hero," Morales tells him. "Saved Senator Wells's wife from drowning."

"I saw that on the news—noticed there were a lot of helicopters floating around and turned on the TV just in time."

She glances back toward the road. "You've already got media circling. As I told Libby, I'll send an officer out to make sure none of the reporters get any ideas." She looks back to Shepherd. "But you have my number, so call if you need anything."

He grins, hand rubbing over his head. "Yeah, will do."

She starts to get back into the car but pauses. "You seem

like you're doing well, Mr. Sheep. I'm glad to see it." She says this earnestly but Shepherd only laughs and waves in response before climbing the steps to the porch.

"'Mr. Sheep'?" I ask him, eyebrows raised.

He shrugs. "She thought it was funny my last name was Oveja and everyone calls me Shepherd." He waits for me to get it and when I don't he adds, "Shepherd Sheep."

I remember Libby telling me the story of how Shepherd had gotten the nickname. Not long after Cecil became his guardian, one of the maids had remarked, "That boy follows you around like a puppy."

"A German shepherd," Libby had said with a giggle. And the name had stuck.

"How do you know Morales?"

His expression shifts into something more serious, clouded. "We've had some dealings in the past."

Before I ask more, Morales rolls down her window. "You did good, Libby," she calls out to me. "Not a lot of girls your age can keep a level head like that. Even fewer would take the risk of putting themselves in danger to help someone else out." She hesitates. "I'm sure if your parents were alive, they'd be really proud."

I'm barely able to bite back a cringe at the mention of my parents before I can force a smile to my lips. "Thank you," I respond. But I'm pretty sure Morales didn't miss my initial reaction.

She pulls away, waving, and I start into the house. Shepherd takes in my expression—my lips pressed tight, my eyes beginning to burn with tears—and frowns. "Frances?" he asks cautiously.

His using my real name is what makes it unbearable. "Don't," I say. Pushing past him I sprint up to my room and into the bathroom. I flip the knobs on the shower, not bothering to take off my clothes before stepping under the frigid spray. It's the only place I ever allow myself to really cry.

I hear the sound of Mrs. Wells's panic as water choked her lungs. The way her body fought for life. All because of me.

Morales's words run an endless circuit through my mind, pummeling incessantly against the barrier I've erected between my old life and new. Between Frances and Libby. All I can think about is my parents, now nothing more than silt at the bottom of the ocean.

They would never be proud of what I've become.

## THIRTY

After my shower, I come downstairs to find Shepherd in the kitchen, knife flashing as he chops an onion. The TV above the refrigerator is turned to a news station where reporters continue to drone on about the rescue this morning. The latest update is that Martha Wells is stable but will stay in the hospital overnight for observation.

Shepherd doesn't seem to be paying attention to it, nor does he realize I'm here. When the reporter mentions the *Persephone*, his shoulders tense, the knife going still as he looks up at the TV.

A news clip from several years ago begins to play. One so familiar I have it memorized. I bite my lip as the camera zooms in on the deck of a large coast guard ship, focusing on a small group making its way down the gangplank.

The Senator leads the pack and then there's Grey. The way he'd been years ago, with the same hungry, haunted look in his eyes that I'd seen in mine when I first glanced in the mirror after being rescued.

It's the first time I've watched the clip since seeing him again and I'm struck most not by all the ways he's changed since then, but by the ways he's still the same. There's a flicker of uneasiness that still hovers about him. It's tucked behind a veneer of confidence and bravado, but if anyone is an expert in masks, it's me.

I suck in a deep breath, loud enough that Shepherd turns. When he realizes it's me, he drops the knife and fumbles for the remote, silencing the TV.

"I'm sorry," he says, shaking his head at himself. "I shouldn't have been watching—"

I shrug. "No worries."

There's an awkward pause as Shepherd stares at the silent TV still showing the old news clip with Grey and his father. We watch a moment while the Senator answers questions, his mouth moving, saying nothing.

"It's strange," Shepherd finally says, cutting off the television entirely. "Seeing that now—knowing what you told me about everything. He just lies so blatantly. Both of them."

"I know." I slip onto a stool across the kitchen island. "So you believe me now?"

He studies me a moment. "I don't *not* believe you," he finally says. Which I guess is good enough for the time being.

He picks up his knife and returns to chopping his onion, but his forehead still furrows in thought. Finally, his hand stills and he looks up at me. "Can I ask you something?"

I nod, bracing myself.

"How do you do it?" His eyes rove across my face, examining me as one might a forgery of a painting or sculpture—critically, searching out the flaws. As though in his eyes I'm now an object rather than a person.

"How are you *her*?" he adds.

It's not a question I really know how to answer, so I grab a banana from the fruit bowl and begin to peel it slowly.

"I mean, knowing who you are now, I'm surprised I didn't figure it out earlier," he continues. "It just seems so obvious. But then you walk into a room and the first thing I think is, *Libby*."

The way he says it sounds like both a compliment and an insult.

I shrug again, focused on my banana. Trying to mentally stop the flush of chagrined heat creeping up the back of my neck. "I've been Libby for four years," I tell him.

"Is everything about you her now?" It's as though he's discovered some sort of new species and is intent on studying it. "I mean, what's Frances like?"

My hands still, the dangling banana peel trembling slightly. I force myself to take the bite even though my stomach has turned sour.

What am I supposed to tell him? That there is no such being as Frances? That she died out on that life raft four years ago?

Except that I feel her still here, pushing against me.

"Who Frances is doesn't matter," I finally tell him.

This seems to take him aback. "That can't really be true."

I twist my lips bitterly. "Well, take it up with the Senator and Grey. They're the ones who killed her."

He's quiet, lost to his own thoughts, as he pulls a bag of green peppers from the refrigerator and begins to clean them over the sink. I carefully fold my discarded banana peel and stand to throw it away.

He doesn't even turn to look at me when he says, "I'll help you with the Senator and Grey."

I freeze, my foot pressed against the trash can. With a sigh, he pushes from the sink and faces me. Water drips from his fingers, collecting in tiny pools on the floor. "I'm still pissed at you and I'm not okay with what you've done. For the past four years I've thought about Libby, wondering if she's okay, and what I did wrong." He shakes his head. "You've put me through hell, frankly."

I drop my eyes. "I'm sorry." He needs me to say it and so I do. Even though I don't wholeheartedly believe it.

"But regardless of everything you've done," he continues, "the truth is that Libby didn't deserve to die." He draws a shaky breath. "And she certainly didn't deserve to die like that," he says, voice rough around the edges with tears he'll never let fall in front of me.

"Libby deserves to have the truth. And if I can help her get it, I will."

I nod. "Thank you."

"But one thing," he adds. I tense, waiting. "I don't want anyone else getting hurt."

I frown, not understanding.

"No more poisoning people."

I roll my eyes. "It's not like she was in any real danger—"

He steps forward, cutting me off. "I'm serious. I won't be involved in anyone getting killed. I may know you're really Frances Mace, but to the rest of the world you're Elizabeth

O'Martin and I won't allow you to do anything that would make others think poorly of her."

This causes my skin to burn with indignation. "They killed a ship of innocent people," I spit.

He holds up his hands, fending off my rage. "That may be so. And you can be as reckless as you want with your own life. But not with mine or Libby's or anyone else's. Not until we're sure they deserve it."

"That's not the plan," I tell him.

"Then change the plan." His words are shot through with steel. "Or make sure you have a plan to deal with the cops because I won't hesitate to call Morales."

My first instinct is to fight, but it's obvious Shepherd has no intention of backing down. And perhaps the reality is, I don't need him to. Not yet. So I tuck my anger away and let the tension ease from my shoulders. "Okay," I tell him.

He watches me a moment and then nods, picking up his knife and starting in on a pile of carrots. For a moment I watch the way his fingers curl expertly against each one, knife moving in perfect precision.

"Can I help?" I ask, hoping to diffuse the tension.

He pauses before answering and for a moment I think he's about to tell me no. "Yeah," he says instead. "Sure."

I pull the peppers from the sink and begin cleaning out the seeds. "What are you making?"

"Libby's favorite." He says it aggressively, like a test.

I smile, remembering the Italian-themed dinner on the cruise. "Spaghetti sauce."

Shepherd nods.

"Even though she hated pasta," I add.

His lips twitch. "She'd just order bowls of sauce."

"And somehow she made it seem eccentric rather than weird."

He laughs. "That was Libby."

For a while, the silence between Shepherd and me isn't exactly strained. But it's not particularly comfortable either. I can feel just how aware of my every movement he is. How he compares everything about me to the Libby he knew. Cataloging the similarities and differences.

Wondering about it all.

It's like there's a ghost of her in the room shadowing me and for the first time after Cecil's death, I'm not the only one who can see her. "Libby kept a lot of journals," I finally offer. "She wrote about everything. Which you probably know . . ." My voice trails off.

His knife pauses, hovering just against the skin of a ripe tomato before resuming its precise slicing. He says nothing, but also doesn't stop me as I continue.

"You asked how I was able to become her," I explain. "A lot of it came from those days we spent together on the life raft. You'd be amazed at the amount of ground you cover when you think you're going to die. And of course a lot came from Cecil. Though obviously he didn't know about the wild blackberries," I add ruefully.

"But most of it is from her journals." I think back to reading through them for the first time. How invasive it felt. I remembered wondering at the time what had happened to my own journals, crowded in a crate under my bed at home in Ohio.

Who'd been the one to go through our house, collect our things? Did that crate still exist somewhere? The entire encapsulation of Frances Mace, inscribed in a few dozen diaries. The only place she still lived on.

It's the same for Libby, I guess. I'm just this shell of her—a badly formed replica.

"Was it hard becoming her?" he finally asks.

I ponder the question. Growing up middle class in Ohio— the daughter of a teacher and local banker. Clothes bought off the sale rack without concern about label or what was in fashion. Dinners as a family around the kitchen table, Sunday mornings at church, Tuesday afternoons at Brownies. It was just such a different life.

Not that I've glamorized it with the passing of time. I had few friendships, though the ones I did have were deep and fierce. I felt awkward and uncoordinated most of the time. Puberty hadn't been particularly good to me.

I'd assumed that was just the way of things for a girl still getting used to being a teenager. Certainly all of my friends faced the same issues.

But then Cecil had come along and I learned that there was little in life that couldn't be smoothed down with the introduction of true wealth of the kind Cecil possessed.

"Some things were hard," I tell him. "Learning to override my own likes and dislikes with hers, remembering the way she talked, adopting her mannerisms."

It's why I had to stay away, out of the spotlight for so long. People's memories of Libby had to fade so that they could be overwritten. Enough time had to pass that any aberrant tastes, mannerisms, or habits could be ascribed to "that's just what happens as kids grow up." Any changes in my appearance could be the passing nature of time—eyes can shift color slightly, a new haircut can frame the face differently, features can meld and change as a girl's body matures.

"Other things were easier," I admit. "Libby had everything." He snorts and I blush. "At least that's what it felt like to me. She wasn't Frances Mace," I tell him. "That's what really made it easy to become her."

He glances at me, surprised. "Do you really hate who you used to be so much?"

I let out a rueful laugh. "It's not hate. I was fine with my life before. But that's the thing—after the *Persephone* that life didn't exist either. Frances as she'd been before—that was no longer an option for me. My choice was a gaping black hole of uncertainty or Libby."

I lift a shoulder, as though the decision were meaningless. "I chose Libby."

"You know, not everything is black-and-white like that. Either/or."

"But some things are," I counter. "Alive or dead. Here or not. Libby or no one."

He looks like he wants to argue, but he doesn't. Instead he resumes his chopping, and I do the same, preparing the rest of the meal in silence.

## THIRTY-ONE

Later that night, I wake with a start, gasping for air. I'd been dreaming about those last days on the life raft, when Libby was dying and I'd screamed at her over and over again to just hold on. For one more minute. And for another after that.

In the darkness of my bedroom, my heart roars, and for a confused moment, I wonder whether I'm still dreaming because I hear someone shouting Libby's name. And then I realize it's coming from outside.

It takes me longer than it should to remember: *Oh, wait, that's me. I'm Libby.* And then I scramble from the bed. When I throw open the French doors and step out onto the balcony, the sound of scuffling intensifies.

"Libby!" the voice yells again, somewhat blurry sounding, followed by a grunt. I look down to find Grey trying to push his way toward the house, Shepherd shoving him back. Grey twists, rolling out of his grasp and points to my balcony. "There she is!" He waves wildly.

Shepherd looks up at me over his shoulder, his exasperation very evident. With one hand he makes a tipping motion over his mouth and I realize immediately what he's trying to say.

Apparently, so does Grey because as I start across the room toward the stairs I hear him argue, "I'm not drunk," followed by more grunts. Then there's a loud *splash* and I take off running.

I make it outside to the patio just as Shepherd hauls himself up out of the pool. His T-shirt and shorts are both drenched and plastered against his body. Water runs in rivulets down his face, catching at his jaw. "I'm calling Morales," he growls.

"Wait—don't!" I grab his arm. "I'll take care of it."

He glances down at my hand, his muscles bunching under my touch. "How?"

"I'll walk him home—give him time to sober up a little. He's underage, calling the cops will just make things worse."

Behind him, Grey slips trying to climb up the ladder and splashes back under.

Shepherd rolls his eyes. "I don't know that I want you walking the beach with him alone at night. I'll change and go with you." He starts to pull away but I hold him tight.

"I'll be fine," I tell him.

"He's dangerous, *Libby*."

I bristle at the way he emphasizes the name. "I said I'll take care of it." I keep my voice even.

Shepherd lets out a long breath. "Whatever." He throws his hands up and stalks toward the house.

When I turn to the pool I find Grey sitting on the top step, staring into the water. Where he'd been boisterous just moments before, now he seems contemplative and even a bit morose.

"Come on," I tell him gently, nudging him with the side of my leg. "Let's get you home."

He squints up at me. For a long moment he just stares. Enough so that I nudge him with my leg again, hoping to get him moving.

"You look so much like her—like Frances—sometimes," he murmurs.

Everything inside of me freezes. Painfully so. My senses flare to life, remnants from a time long past when humans were nothing but prey. The night comes alive all at once. The sharp ionized smell of the pool water. The striation of the ocean breeze as it sifts through my cotton nightgown. The *plonking* sound of water dripping from Grey's fingertips, falling to the patio.

I search my brain for some sort of light retort, something that will cover the panic thundering through my veins. "Beer goggles are a wonderful thing, my friend," I tell him, reaching to grab his elbow and pull him up. "I once had an entire pub of drunkards in Wales convinced I was the Duchess of Cambridge," I add, steering Grey toward the boardwalk.

"Bourbon, not beer," he corrects. "The finest I could swipe from Dad's library."

I move quickly to change the subject. "How's your mother?"

His head falls back against his shoulders. "Still being observed by a team of highly qualified doctors." He sighs. "I just couldn't stay at that hospital anymore. With all the beeping and the machines and reporters and cameras . . ." He frowns.

"It was too much like after the *Persephone*. Hence the bourbon."

There's nothing I can really say to this except, "I hope she'll be okay."

When we hit the beach, I turn to start toward his house, but he keeps going, straight toward the water.

"Oh no," I say, jogging after him. "I think you've had enough swimming tonight."

Ignoring me, he keeps walking until the waves reach his knees and then he stops. He just stands there, staring toward the horizon. The fabric of his wet button-down shirt molds along his shoulders and back, following the ridges and dips of muscles. His shorts sit low on his waist, heavy with water.

I take a few steps after him, holding up the hem of my nightgown with one hand so it won't get wet. "Come on," I tell him, trying to pull him toward shore. But he resists.

"I've never experienced that kind of darkness again." His voice is soft, both wondrous and sad at the same time. "Do you remember it? Being adrift and how black everything was?"

My mouth goes dry and I clench the hem of my nightgown into a ball in my fist. "Yes," I admit. "But there were stars too." They were almost blinding the way they filled the sky.

"Not that second night," he says.

Beneath my feet the sand shifts, pulled out by the tide. There's a seductive lulling to it that makes it seem like time and consequences no longer exist. "The storm."

From the corner of my eye I see him nod.

"It took so long to rain," I continue. "Gathering all day until the hope of it became this kind of physical pain."

Neither of us looks at the other.

I never realized how much pressure this story had built inside me. The *Persephone* has guided almost every waking moment of my life, hovering like a dark beast clinging to my shoulders. What a release it is to finally let the words escape. To share them with someone who knows and understands.

"You were rescued the next day," I add.

"You still had five days left."

I drop the hem of my nightgown and it floats around my knees for a moment before sinking under. It's a relief to cross my arms over my chest. To dig my fingers into the muscles until I feel bone.

"*How much do you remember, Libby?*" he whispers.

"Nothing." I say it automatically. My lips numb. The lying too easy.

He turns to me, grabs my arms, and pulls until I'm facing him. "But you remember the darkness. And the storm." There's a violent need to his voice that causes my breath to catch. "You *do* remember."

He must sense my alarm because he immediately lets go, his face twisted in anguish. His breathing shakes as he shoves a hand through his hair, trying to regain control.

"Let's go," I tell him, starting for the shore. But his next words stop me.

"I just can't stop thinking about Frances."

# THIRTY-TWO

I shouldn't ask. I know I shouldn't. I don't need to know. Frances isn't important to my plan. But at her name on Grey's lips, the girl inside me roars to life, kicking and screaming. Needing to hear what this boy has to say about her.

Reminding me that I'm the one who stole her life and she at least deserves this.

And so I turn back. Arms tightly crossed. Nightgown hem drifting like a translucent jellyfish around my shins. I don't have to say anything for Grey to continue.

"Frances was just so . . ." He presses his lips together, at a loss for words. "Everything. She was everything."

My heart squeezes, pain and euphoria fighting inside me.

"You know what's funny?" He lets out a small laugh. "You were actually the one I noticed first. Even back then you had this"—he waves a hand through the air—"flash about you. Frances kind of disappeared behind that."

I press my fingers to my forehead, letting out a breath of air as though I've been punched in the gut. It's true, even *I'd* seen that back then. But that doesn't make it easier to hear.

He pauses, suddenly realizing what he's insinuated about me. About Libby. "Not that I thought you tried to outshine her on purpose," he backpedals.

"No," I murmur. "I loved Frances." And whether these are the words of Libby or of Frances I do not know. But I do know that they are somehow true either way.

I tell myself that I should go back inside. That I don't need to be hearing this. But then Grey adds, "*Me too*," in words so soft they almost don't exist, and I know that I will stay. That I am desperate for his every word.

"I'm pretty sure Frances figured out pretty quickly that I was interested in you," he says, another whisper of a laugh. "I was trying to find a way to get closer to you by the pool. You were oblivious, of course. And I was this awkward kid."

The memories crawl up my throat and I have to bite my lip to keep them from spilling out. Grey wore this red-and-blue bathing suit, and I couldn't stop staring at the line of skin just above the lip of his waistband. It was only visible when he stretched and something about glimpsing it felt so intensely intimate to me. So wrong in a deliciously right way.

"I tried getting in line behind you at the bar but a lady spilled her soda all over me and I had to help her clean it up. I tried to get a deck chair next to y'all but this huge family claimed them all first. There was *nothing* I could do." He shakes his head, re-membering. "I don't know at what point Frances noticed me."

*From the beginning*, I want to tell him.

"But she started giving me this look. And you'd think I'd

have gotten embarrassed because here was this girl watching me strike out with her friend again and again, but it was almost like she was rooting for me."

*Because there was no way I ever thought I stood a chance. Not against Libby.*

He grins, his mind so deep in the memory I doubt he even remembers I'm standing here. "And then I realized that I didn't even care about you anymore. I was just doing whatever it took for Frances to give me that look again. God, I probably spent hours going after you just so Frances would smile at me."

My knees go weak and it takes every effort to remain standing as the sand shifts beneath me. *Hours.* All that time it killed me to watch Grey going after Libby, wishing it were me.

All that time I wondered whether I was just the consolation prize once he finally got it through his head that Libby wasn't interested.

It was me he was after all along.

"And then you got up to do something . . ." He frowns.

"Get a towel," I fill in for him. Because I remember the exact moment Libby walked across the deck to the towel stand, intending to hit on the guy who worked there.

*Grey looked across the deck at me then.*

"And Frances pointed, letting me know where you'd gone. But I wasn't interested in you."

*He came straight toward me, eyes never looking anywhere else. And I was dying.*

"I took the chair next to her." He laughs. "Your seat, actually."

*And he introduced himself.*

"I was so nervous all of the sudden. That she'd think I was some kind of freak because she'd seen me strike out so much."

*I thought he was going to ask me about Libby. Get her name. Wait for her to come back so he could talk to her.*

"And then I realized that I didn't know how to ask her out. We were on a ship!" He laughs. "There was nowhere to go, nothing to do."

*So we just started talking.*

"So we just started talking. You were caught up somewhere else and it was just Frances and me."

*For almost an hour. Just us.*

"If she'd have let me, I'd have spent every second from then on with her."

*I was afraid he'd get tired of me. Figure out how boring I was compared to Libby.*

He pauses and I realize that my breaths are coming in pants.

"And I was . . . God," He presses his palms against his forehead. "I think I was already falling in love." His voice cracks.

He looks over at me then. And under the stars, in the darkness there's a part of me that screams for him to see me. *Really* see me. To look past the trappings of Libby that I've wrapped around myself and see Frances.

He'd done it once before—seen past Libby's glamour to find Frances hiding in the shadows. He should be able to do it again.

My chin trembles and I bite my cheeks. The longer he says nothing, the more hope thickens inside me. Like the day cast adrift waiting for rain to come. The painful anticipation of it.

Because if anyone ever loved Frances, if anyone could rescue her and pull her back to the surface after drowning for all these years, it's Greyson Wells.

And I would walk away from it all right now if he asked me. All the carefully laid plans, the perfectly arranged pieces nudged into place. I'd rip free this Libby mask and cast it back into the ocean where she died all those years ago.

Grey leans closer and the girl inside my head screams that all he has to do is look. How can he be this close and not see? With the sound of the waves and the smell of the salt water—just as it was the first time on the *Persephone*.

His eyes twitch, and I see him mentally asking the question. His breath pauses. Because he knows—something in him remembers this.

Me.

Us.

"*I just need someone else who remembers her,*" he whispers.

*Yes!* the girl inside me screams. *I'm right here!*

And then he blinks. Wiping it all away. The doubt and hesitation. Replacing it with pain and memories.

Frances hovers, just under my skin, shattering again. Like the moment Libby gave up—leaving me alone with nothing but the ocean.

I swallow, again and again, as tears burn at my throat.

"How did she die?" Grey finally asks.

"Painfully." I hurl the word, dagger sharp, because I'm angry. And hurt. That even *he's* fooled by my act. This is as far as I've ever allowed Frances to surface, yet still she's invisible to the one person who should know better.

If Grey can't see it, then there really is nothing left of who I used to be. It's a staggeringly painful realization. And I understand, then, how Libby could have given up in that raft.

Because I can feel Frances letting go inside me. Slipping under. Letting the weight of memories fill her lungs.

Grey's face crumbles. "Oh God." He presses a hand over his eyes as he doubles over, falling to his knees in the surf.

For a moment I stand over him, watching the way that he's broken.

Knowing that I'm broken in the same way.

My stomach roils at what I say next—at my capacity for cruelty. At my need to hurt him.

But it's the only way I know to save myself. Truth and revenge, my only lifelines.

I let myself slip until I'm kneeling next to him, the waves dancing around my ribs. I place my arms around him. Comforting him.

"There's nothing you could have done." I say the words softly, knowing the aching brutality of them.

Because there *was* something he could have done to save her. He could have told the truth.

And he must know this. If he hadn't lied about the rogue wave, they would have kept searching. They would have found us before Libby died.

He slams a fist against the surface, again and again. "No! There was something! I could have told them . . ."

And it's like the moment the storm clouds broke on that third day—the first drops of water that hit against our upturned faces.

Just as then, I hold my breath waiting. For the deluge of truth.

But he shakes his head, growling. Choking it all back.

"What could you have told them, Grey?" I prod.

He looks at me, and it's as if he's asking me to hold something inside of him together that I can't reach. He pushes to his feet, stumbling against the incoming tide. I stand, start after him. "I'll walk you home," I offer, but he holds up a hand, keeping me at bay.

"No." His eyes rake across my body. The water's turned my nightgown sheer and it clings to me, making me appear almost naked. He clenches his jaw. "You should get inside." And then he turns and runs. Leaving me standing alone in the darkness.

For a long time I don't move, staring out into the blackness of the infinite ocean. Wondering what would happen if I just started walking and never stopped. If I'd ever be able to find my parents. If I could crawl inside the wreckage of the sunken *Persephone* where I belong.

How is it that I survived and Libby didn't? How was I somehow deemed worthy and she was not? I think about Grey and how reckless I've been with these stolen years. All of this time and the truth is still buried. Those responsible have never paid.

But *I* have. Every day, every minute and second, I've born the brunt of the *Persephone*. It is my purpose. My definition. In many ways, it is my savior. The very thing that should have killed me has kept me alive with a singular goal.

And every time my heart screams for Grey, that resolve wavers. He's meant to be a means to an end but instead he has somehow become my greatest weakness.

I'd expected the near death of his mother to make him

want to reach out. Trauma always has a way of accelerating relationships, creating intimacy where none existed before. Just look at me and Libby. That week together on the life raft we shared *everything*.

That's one of the reasons I'd put Grey's mother at risk and then saved her—to throw him and me together. To make him feel indebted to me. But I hadn't expected it to work on me as well. I hadn't intended that it would cause me to want to cling to him.

*If he'd asked I would have told him the truth tonight.* This certainty is appalling to me. Even more than that, it is unacceptable.

How could I even think of turning my back on the hundreds of dead—my own parents—for the promise of a soft kiss? For the chance at a sympathetic ear? For a heart that beats at the same volume as my own?

Especially when it's been proven that those kisses are lies.

Everything about Grey is a lie.

Inside, Frances objects. *Grey hurts too*, she insists.

"Good," I whisper to the ocean. He should hurt.

They all should.

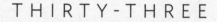

# THIRTY-THREE

*I* press myself against the cold metal wall of the dumbwaiter, my hand clamped so tightly over my mouth that my fingers dig into my cheeks. Even so, a high-pitched whine climbs its way up the back of my throat, coated in acid. I know without question that if they hear me, I am dead.

I'm dead either way. The thought is like white noise, filling my head and drowning out my ability to think. There's a scream. A quick succession of gunfire. Then shadows move along the far wall. On to the next room.

If anyone tries to run, they're taken care of by the men stationed at the emergency exits at either end of the hallway. A trail of bodies leads to their feet. The entire ship is locked down: the elevators, the stairwells.

They just didn't think about the dumbwaiter. But I had. I'd been thinking about it since our third day at sea when Libby dared me to ride it between floors and I'd been too chicken. When the gunfire erupted, my parents screamed at me to hide.

*I'd climbed in here. Knees crammed to my chin. Staring out through the two-way mirror of the door as armed men slowly. Slowly. And yet too, too fast make their way to my family's stateroom across the hall.*

*I can't push the button for the dumbwaiter to move. They might hear it. I'm too terrified to even turn my head. What if they can hear the whisper of my hair against my shoulders?*

*When they throw open the door to our room, I try to close my eyes. But I can't. They're crouched together, my parents. Dad with his arms around Mom as if that could shield her.*

*Mom's lips move. It doesn't matter. The man with the gun doesn't bother to listen. The sound of those bullets erases everything about me. It stops time, the absolute impossibility of the moment deafening. If I had lungs. Or a throat. Or if there were such a thing as air, I would scream.*

*But none of those things exist anymore. All of them shattered along with my mother's heart. My father's skull.*

I wake to absolute silence, even my heart hesitating in its beat. Everything in my room is perfectly still. Except for the air. There's a whisper of it across my cheeks and it feels out of place. I listen for the hum of the air conditioner, but it's off at the moment.

I slide my eyes from window to window but they're all closed. The only movement the slight swing of the cord to the blinds blocking the balcony doors. My pulse returns in a rush, filling my ears, and I gasp as though I haven't taken a breath in hours.

My body still retains that sleep heaviness, making me feel,

for a moment, that I have no limbs. I push slowly until I'm sitting, my senses straining. Then I slip from the bed, move to the balcony. Use the tips of my fingers to push apart the cracked doors.

The moon spills across the dunes, giving them the appearance of snow-dusted hills. Feather-tipped sea oats bend against the breeze, their narrow leaves fluttering. There's nothing out of place.

And yet . . . I shake my head and step back, heading to the bathroom. The light is bright against my eyes and I squint as I turn the faucet, cup handfuls of water, and drink.

Nightmares from the *Persephone* always leave me thirsty. But there is never enough water in the world to quench it.

## THIRTY-FOUR

The next morning the news stations are awash with video of Senator Wells on the way into the hospital to visit his wife before she's discharged in the afternoon. I take advantage of the opportunity and head over to Grey's hoping to catch him home alone. When I reach the end of his driveway, reporters rush toward the car. Photographers lean over the hood pressing close and snapping photos. The police push them back, creating a tunnel just narrow enough for me to eke through.

The Wellses' housekeeper opens the door, a harried look on her face, and I can only imagine how many times she's had to turn away reporters who somehow snuck their way past the cops. But as soon as she sees that it's me she takes my hands in hers and pulls me inside.

"If it isn't my angel," she tells me. She wraps me in a tight hug that smells of linen and lemons. There's a moment when I'm reminded of my mom, of the way her body felt—both soft and strong—when she held me.

An unexpected lump catches the back of my throat.

"I couldn't even sleep last night—just kept thinking about what would have happened if you hadn't reacted so bravely and calmly . . ." She shakes her head, unwilling to finish the statement. When she steps back I have a hard time meeting her eyes. She's so genuine in her affection and regard for me that I feel a bit embarrassed.

If she knew the truth about me, she'd shove me out of this house and slam the door on my back.

"Grey," she calls up over her shoulder. "Your friend is here!" She winks at me. "He was working out earlier—he should be down in a minute. If you need anything, I'll be in the kitchen."

She reaches forward, cupping her hand on my cheek. "A true angel." She smiles at me again before retreating down the hallway. It's exactly the kind of reception I'd been hoping to elicit. By saving Mrs. Wells from drowning I've bought myself access to the Senator's home and family.

And I've brought the media to bear to ensure that I keep that access. Right now I'm seen as a hero—there's no way the Senator can push me away without facing blowback.

As before, the house is frigidly cold, the air-conditioning cranked at full blast, and I rub my hands over my arms, trying not to shiver. Finally Grey appears, jogging down the concrete staircase. He's wearing running shorts and a T-shirt, his hair tousled and damp. Sweat still snakes down his face and he uses the hem of his shirt to wipe at it, giving me a flash of smoothly toned abs.

As he approaches, I can't tell if his cheeks are red from work-ing out or if he's blushing because of last night. "I hope I'm not interrupting," I tell him, clearing my throat. "I realized that I don't have your number or I'd have called first."

He smiles self-consciously. "Yeah, I realized that last night, which is why I decided to show up in person." Dropping his gaze, he launches into an apology. "And about that . . ." He cringes. "Look, I was in really bad shape. With the hospital and all the reporters. I should have just gone to bed. But I was home alone and I couldn't stop thinking about . . . and I just . . . I wanted to stop remembering it all. I know it's wrong and that's not really the kind of person I am—"

I reach out to reassure him, my fingers gliding over the slick skin of his arm. "Hey, it's okay," I tell him.

"I really hope I didn't embarrass myself. Scratch that—I know I embarrassed myself, I just hope not too badly. I don't really remember that much after taking that dunk in your pool . . ." He trails off, rubbing the spot behind his ear. The tell that he's lying.

I have to swallow back the part of me that doesn't want him to brush off last night so easily. The part of me that could spend every night under the stars listening to him talk about Frances and how much he might have loved her.

But that's a dream from a different life. One that no longer exists.

This—what's between us now—is all just another step in the plan.

Forcing a smile I tell him, "It was nothing." The words are like acid across my tongue, painful but necessary. And so I flavor the statement with a bit of truth. "I'm glad I could be there for you." Our eyes catch and hold, and I'm the one to look away first.

"Anyway," I continue, "I just wanted to come by to make sure you're okay. Not just after last night but with . . ." I wave my hands vaguely toward the driveway and the outside world. "Everything going on."

I shuffle my feet, as though uncomfortable at the strained formality of having this conversation standing in the foyer. "But I don't want to interrupt, so I can go—"

"Don't," he says so quickly that our words tangle together. I look at him, my eyes widening slightly.

He clears his throat, cheeks flushing. "How about lunch?"

I bite my cheek. "I saw on the news that your mother's coming home today and I really don't want to be in your way. Plus I'm pretty sure your dad wouldn't want me here, so it's probably better if I just—" I turn toward the door and he reaches for me, fingers tugging lightly on mine.

For some reason the touch jolts me, causing my heart to race.

"Let me take you out," he says. "We can go up to Charleston and disappear in the crowd of tourists. Get away from all of this crap for a while." He pulls me toward him, just a tiny bit closer. "You have to feel it as much as I do—the claustrophobia of everything."

I nod. "But your mom," I protest.

His hand slips from mine. "Honestly"—he twists his mouth, bitter—"I'll just be in the way. Please," he adds. There's something about the way he looks at me that causes my stomach to jumble and breath to catch. It's the way he used to look at Frances—with a devouring need.

For a moment, I consider actually turning him down even though it would wreak havoc on my carefully laid plans. I'm supposed to be spending time with him, supposed to be making him fall for me.

But I'm not supposed to fall for him in return.

It had never occurred to me doing so could be a danger. Greyson Wells has been the object of my fury for so long. The linchpin to my revenge schemes. Except that the Greyson Wells in my head—the cruel, callous boy who lied about the *Persephone*, the perfect golden child of a powerful Senator—isn't the one standing in front of me. This boy is tortured and miserable. He's as broken as I am.

Even though I know it's dangerous, I smile at Grey. "I'd love to spend the day with you," I tell him as I lie to myself that it doesn't matter whether I acquiesce because it's in the plan or because I simply want to spend more time with him.

"Excellent!" He starts back up the stairs. "I just have to shower first, if you don't mind. Should only take about ten minutes." He glances over his shoulder and realizes I'm not following him.

"You can come up," he says, laughing. I'd been hoping to get close enough to Grey to gain access to his room, but I hadn't expected it to come so easily. All those convoluted plans and all I really had to do was stammer and blush.

## THIRTY-FIVE

Grey's room isn't at all what I'd expected. Not that I'd had a lot of expectations. Even though I'd spent countless hours thinking of Grey, scheming over him, daydreaming about him, I'd never spent much time considering his surroundings.

The rest of the house is so bare and cold I'd figured it would be the same here. But that's not what I find. Instead, Grey's room is a riot of color—the walls may be a sparse white but they're covered with vibrant photographs in ornately gilded frames—every one of them of the ocean.

The one above the bed dominates them all, stretching horizontally across the entire wall. It's of a giant wave, the tip curling white, and its placement makes it seem as though anyone lying underneath would be in imminent danger of drowning.

I'm mesmerized, sucking in a breath as I walk slowly toward it. Behind me I hear Grey clear his throat and shuffle his feet, uncomfortable. "My parents weren't very keen on that one," he says. "Or any of them really."

I nod, still drawn in by the intense beauty of such destructive power.

I wonder whether it's there to remind him—every night—of the lies he told. Whether he's hoped that he can stare at this image enough to erase the truth of what really happened on the *Persephone*.

"You'd think something that large—that powerful—I'd remember," I say softly, deciding to push him. When he doesn't respond, I glance over my shoulder.

His fingers rub at the spot behind his ear. "Right?"

I hold his gaze just a moment longer than is comfortable, and then shift my attention to the other photos crowding the walls. They're of all different sizes—the sea in every state imaginable: calm, torrid, languorous. And then of course, on the far wall is a large window with a view out toward the beach and the true ocean beyond.

"It's almost like being adrift," I murmur, pulling my arms across my chest.

He clears his throat again. "Let me just shower," he says, moving toward his bathroom. "I won't be long."

And then he's gone, the bathroom door closing solidly between us. But not solid enough that I don't hear the shuffle of him undressing, his damp shirt falling to the floor. Or the soft sound of the faucets turning, the rush of water through the pipes in the walls.

Or the sound of him stepping beneath the shower spray. The water gathering heavily on his shoulders, trailing down his arms to fall from his elbows and splash against the tiled floor.

Never have I been so acutely aware of the rhythm water

makes when showering. How different movements cause the water to fall in different, familiar patterns.

It makes it seem as though there's no door between us at all. The sound of water gathering, cascading, trailing along the planes, ridges, and hollows of his naked body feels more intimate than if he were standing in front of me wearing nothing at all.

I realize I'm holding my breath as I strain to listen. The tension radiating from me almost palpable enough to taste. *You could open the door*, Frances whispers. *Find your way through the steam, not even bothering to remove your clothes before stepping in with him.*

*His hands could slide along where your thin shirt molds against your hips. His fingers could find the hem, slowly gather it, inching higher.*

It's such a vivid image that I gasp, shaking my head to dislodge the thought. Almost forcefully, I make myself step away from the bathroom door, already chiding myself for wasting time.

This is too good of an opportunity to squander. As quickly and quietly as possible, I make a pass through his room, searching all the obvious spots, though for what I'm not sure. I'm just hoping that if there's something here, I'll know it when I see it.

I pull each drawer from his dresser, carefully pushing aside neatly folded shirts and shorts to search underneath. His scent envelops me, causing my stomach to flip, reminding me that he's only a few feet away. It only gets worse when I search his bed, sliding hands under his mattress.

Trying not to think about him lying tangled in the sheets at night.

From the bathroom I hear water splashing loudly against tiles, him washing his hair.

My eyes lift to the giant wave curling over his bed. I wonder whether he has nightmares like I do. Whether he thinks about the attack. After our rescue, I'd fled as far from the ocean as I could.

But Grey had brought it closer. Into his room. Practically into his bed. Why?

I lean forward, trailing my fingertips along the churning mass of water. It's beautiful in its own way, this force that simply exists. That would cause no destruction if we weren't the ones getting in its way.

And then, on a whim, I curl my nails under the edge of the thick frame, lifting it from the wall. Because isn't that where the criminal always hides the valuables? Behind me the water cuts off in the bathroom. There's a beat of silence and then the shower door opening.

Swallowing, I press my head against the wall, eyes scanning behind the picture. My breath catches in my throat. There's an envelope taped to the back of the frame, near the top.

From the bathroom comes the sound of Grey toweling off and I know I have only seconds left. I reach for the envelope but my arms aren't long enough. Which is perhaps a good thing because even if I could grab it, it looks too big to hide in the pocket of my shorts.

"Damn," I growl under my breath.

Footsteps approach the bathroom door. With my heart racing, I carefully let the frame fall back against the wall and practically leap across the room.

When he opens the door, I'm leaning against the window admiring the view of the ocean. Blood rushes through my veins, my breathing rapid and shallow.

But when I glance at him, it's obvious he doesn't notice. In fact, he has a difficult time meeting my eyes as crimson flushes his cheeks. I take in the damp towel slung low around his hips. It makes me think of the *Persephone*—how enraptured I was by that band of skin just above the waist of his swim trunks.

If I ever needed true evidence of how much things have changed, here it is. Whereas before his body showed the gangly promise of adulthood, now that promise has been realized. His torso is a wide expanse of muscles, each dip and curve defined by shadows.

I clear my throat, trying to pull my eyes away from a bead of water as it trails along the side of his neck. Trying not to think about where it will end up after its long slide down his chest and abdomen.

"I'll, uh, let you get dressed," I tell him, headed across the room to the hallway. He nods his thanks. As I pass by him, I feel a crackle of tension between us. A slow heat begins its way into my cheeks, mirroring the flush in Grey's, and I realize that I hadn't been the only one acutely aware of his nakedness in the shower.

After I close his bedroom door behind me, I pace toward the stairs, collapsing onto the top step. My mind whirls, trying to push thoughts of Grey's bare chest out of the way so I can focus on what really matters.

The envelope taped to the back of the wave photograph could mean nothing at all; it could be completely unconnected to the *Persephone*. But somehow I doubt it. The ocean is still keeping his secrets, just as it always has.

But not for much longer.

# THIRTY-SIX

There's still a crowd of reporters at the end of the driveway and when they notice me in the passenger seat of Grey's car they practically explode with questions. Morales's officers struggle to push them back and it's several moments before we're free.

Grey lets out a long breath as he accelerates down the road and away from it all. "God, I get so tired of them," he mutters, checking the mirrors to make sure we're not being followed.

"I'd have thought you might be used to them, with your father's job and all," I say.

He practically shudders. "No. Dad's a fan of the camera and so is Mom, but not me. I had enough of them after the *Persephone*."

We stop at an intersection and at the press of a button the roof recedes, bathing us in sunlight. I tilt my head back, watching the canopy of old oaks pass by overhead as he continues toward the mainland.

"Was it bad?" I finally ask. "Back then—with the media?" I find that I'm genuinely curious.

"One of them climbed in my window." He glances over his shoulder and then slides into the next lane as we approach the bridge off the island. "I was at home alone, taking a shower at the time," he adds.

"You're kidding me!" In all my research, I'd never heard mention of this.

"Yep, she got pictures of me, naked in all my glory," he says, a smile beginning to ease across his lips.

I groan at how embarrassing that must have been. "What happened?"

"My dad had private security back then—one of them caught her trying to climb back down the tree. He confiscated her equipment and, uh, convinced her that it was in her best interest to forget everything that happened."

I can't help laughing. "Wow, you did have it bad!"

He glances over at me. "How were you able to escape it all?"

My smile turns a bit brittle and he realizes that he already knows the answer. How I'd mentioned all the doctors and shrinks, trying to get my memory back. Trying to recover.

"Sorry, I shouldn't have asked," he says, refocusing on the road. Below us, the marsh falls away under the bridge, receding toward the creek. The day's too beautiful for our moods to be so heavy.

"No, it's okay," I tell him. "Dad thought it would be easier for me if I recovered overseas and then it just seemed like the easiest thing would be for me to stay there for school."

"Were you able to keep up with your old friends at all?" he asks.

I have to choke back laughter. My old friends—the few that I had—thought I was dead. "No. It was just easier to start over. Clean slate."

His smiles wistfully. "I'm envious."

"You still had your family," I point out.

It's a direct hit. Color drains from his face and he swallows. His hands tighten around the wheel. "Look, maybe this isn't really a good idea. We should go back."

I turn in my seat to face him. "*Hey*," I say softly, resting my fingertips lightly on his thigh. "Maybe talking about the *Persephone* is a bad idea. But us, this"—I gesture at us and the car and the bridge stretching out ahead of us—"this is an excellent idea."

He glances at me from the corner of his eye and I watch as he slowly, but visibly relaxes.

"New rule," I say. "No more *Persephone*. Deal?"

He smiles. "Deal."

"So, to very unsubtly change the subject, what kind of books do you like to read? And so help me if you say Greek mythology, I'll turn this car around myself."

It takes him a minute to get my joke, and then he starts laughing and I join in. And there's something about it all—the expanse of the summer sky arcing overhead and my hand still on Grey's warm thigh—that makes me wonder if I could just pause life here and wrap a bubble around this moment, if it would be enough to keep me happy.

Walking with Grey around Charleston, I catch a glimpse of him as though he were just another guy. Not Senator Wells's son or a *Persephone* survivor. Here, in the bustling stalls of the market, he's anonymous. And it's obvious how much he prefers it this way.

His shoulders relax, his smile comes quicker, and the stress lines around his eyes ease. When he laughs, there's something so earnest and carefree about it that I almost wish this could be his life.

Even our life.

Because, somehow, I've become anonymous as well. I relax my grip on the Libby mask I always clutch so fervidly. It's almost too easy, setting aside her desires, her preferences, her habits that so rigidly control my life at every other moment.

When we walk into an art gallery, a brief respite of air-conditioning on the hot, humid day, I allow myself to linger in front of the paintings that *I* like. Not the ones I think Libby would have liked. I stop worrying about making sure my smile tilts sideways, that my laugh is demure, that my passion is checked.

And I remember—more than anything else—I remember just how easy it was to be with Grey. How naturally we fell into stride next to each other, how often we gravitated toward the same things—the same music, the same books, the same foods.

How time could just slip away when we talked—about anything and nothing. There's no awkwardness.

It's almost like falling in love again, and as the day wears into evening and we find a quiet restaurant with white tablecloths and flickering candles, I have to remind myself again and again that Greyson Wells is not for me.

There is a plan. And it involves Grey falling for me so that I can gain access to his life. So that I can get back into his bedroom and find out what's in the envelope hidden behind the picture frame. So that I can turn him against his father and expose the truth.

That's all this is: part of the plan.

But I'm lying to myself. I know this. Because when I look across the table at him all I can do is wonder . . . If the *Persephone* had never sunk. If I were still Frances. Could we have still somehow found ourselves in this place together?

## THIRTY-SEVEN

Grey pulls his car next to mine in his driveway and kills the engine. The Wellses' house hulks like a beast before us—strategically placed outdoor lighting casting sharp shadows. Neither one of us moves.

For a moment today, it felt like I'd actually escaped. I'd gotten a glimpse of what a normal life might have been. And once I step out of the car, reality will drape over me again like a smothering blanket.

He shifts toward me. "Today was . . ." His voice trails off. He doesn't have to finish because it's all there on his face. I know what he looks like when he's starting to fall in love. I've experienced it all before. I recognize it again now.

A ghost of a smile traces my lips. "It was."

With our seat belts still fastened, there's no way for us to move closer, at least not without clearly stating our intentions to do so. And this is all too young and new for that.

The moment breaks when a light on the front stoop flashes on. A shadow moves behind the crystallized glass of the foyer window. Blushing, I reach for the door. "It's late, I should go," I murmur.

There's disappointment in his eyes.

"But, um . . ." I clear my throat, wondering whether there's a way to sneak up to his room and grab that envelope tonight. "Do you think I could use your restroom first? Dinner was a long car ride ago."

He laughs. "Of course." Once inside he leads me down a hallway and points to a powder room. "I'll wait in the kitchen," he says.

I've barely closed the door when I hear voices. Holding my breath, I pull back open the door a crack and listen.

"I told you I didn't want you seeing that girl," Grey's father growls. One side of the hallway is lined with windows and I can just make out his blurry reflection in the glass. He stands in the kitchen, pouring a drink.

"Dad—" Grey protests.

His father spins toward him, finger pointing and expression pulled into a grimace. "She's dangerous for this family, Greyson. And she'd dangerous for you. Get her out of this house and then stay away." He punctuates that last bit by jabbing his finger against Grey's chest.

Grey grabs his father's arm before he can say more. "Shh! She'll hear you."

The Senator whips his head in my direction, and I duck behind the door, heart pounding. I have no idea whether he saw my reflection or not. Carefully I click the door closed as footsteps pound down the hallway. I cringe as they near, waiting for them to stop. But they only slow slightly before continuing past.

Letting out a sigh of relief, I flush the toilet and wash my hands. It's obvious I won't be getting that envelope tonight, which means biding my time—laying the foundation so I have an excuse to come back. Even if it is against his father's wishes.

Smiling as though I've overhead nothing and everything's fine, I open the door and start toward the kitchen. Grey stands with his back to me, hands braced against the island and chin dropped to his chest. His shoulders rise and fall as he struggles to control his breathing.

I pause by the door. "Hey—thanks for today."

He turns, cheeks mottled with anger and my smile freezes in place. "You okay?" I ask, as though I have no idea about the confrontation that just took place.

He clenches his teeth, the muscles along his jaw tensing, before finally he shoves a hand through his hair. "Yeah."

But he's so clearly lying.

"Hey," I say softly, moving closer. "What's going on?"

From somewhere deep in the house there's the muffled *bang* of a door slamming. Grey winces and glances over my shoulder. "Nothing. I'll walk you out." The last bit he says in a defeated voice and I know there's no changing his mind.

I follow him down the hallway to the front door, him lost in thought and me silent. But once outside he pauses and then, just as the door closes behind me, he turns. In two steps he's in front of me, hardly any space separating our bodies.

Instantly my heart begins to pound. But not from fear or

surprise. Grey's proximity sparks everything inside me, memories surging to the surface as I remember his taste, his smell, his touch.

Frances roars to life under my skin.

His khakis brush against my thighs, and when I struggle to take a deep breath, my chest skims against his. A riot of adrenaline courses deep, causing my insides to twist with need. The door at my back seems like the only solid thing in my life at this moment.

He sways, imperceptibly closer, and ever so slightly I arch to meet him. His pupils swallow his eyes with desire and his breath catches, causing my toes to curl.

I lick my lips. Swallow. Wait.

His voice is a rough-edged growl. "Everything in my life has turned upside down since you came back into it." There's an angry undercurrent to what he's saying, but it's tempered by desperation.

"I'm sorr—"

He steps in closer, cutting me off. I make a sound low in my throat, not understanding how there's still space separating us. He looms over me now in a way that causes me to crane my neck just to meet his eyes.

One of his hands reaches out, teases at the fabric of my shirt, finding the hem and slipping to the bare flesh just beneath it. Every touch of his fingertips is a jolt of sensation. Breathing becomes impossible.

"Ever since that first day on the beach, I haven't been able to stop thinking about you."

A burst of warmth breaks free low in my abdomen.

"And then later," he continues, "when you were in the pool, drifting just out of reach." His fingers dance along my hip toward my back, setting me on fire from the outside in.

I press my palms flat against the door behind me, needing to feel something but afraid to reach for him.

His head drops lower and for a moment I think he's about to finally kiss me. But instead he shifts, bringing his lips slowly to my ear. "Do you know how many times I've imagined what would have happened if I'd just gone in after you?"

My nails dig against the wood of the door.

But then his hand drops from my back and air floods between us. I swallow, wanting to protest, until I see his eyes. They burn.

"No one's made me feel this way in years." His whisper is rough, calloused. "I want you, Libby."

For so long, Greyson Wells has been nothing but a target—a means to an end. All of my rage and pain and confusion I've heaped on his shoulders. But in this moment, all of that falls away.

And I realize the mistake I've made. Because I want him as well. Not just the Frances part of me who's always wanted him, but the rest of me. The part of me that laughed with him this afternoon. That was drawn to him in the pool before. That likes the way he looks at me.

*You loved him once*, a voice reminds me.

*This isn't love*, I argue back. *I won't let it be.*

*Then you've got nothing to lose*, the voice says.

And I know I'm just lying to myself, but it's a lie that I want to believe.

I release my hands from the door at my back and I let my fingers finally curl against the waistband of his khakis, my knuckles grazing the warm skin of his hips as I tug him closer. He sucks in a breath at my touch.

"*Then have me*," I whisper.

His lips land on mine, and it's like coming to the surface after drowning. All desperate need that eclipses everything else. He presses me against the door and we're a tangle of heart-hammering desire and panting need.

With one hand I tug the rest of his shirt free of his pants and with the other I grip his neck. Dragging him closer. Needing more of him. His teeth sink possessively into my lower lip and I groan low and long in my throat.

I'm thrown back in time. The feel of his heated breath feathering against my jaw, the taste of him drifting across my tongue. That sharp tang of salt, the sound of the ocean.

Everything is familiar. As though nothing has changed. As though the ship never sank and he never lied and our future is spread out before us.

As if this could become our new truth. Him and me. Together.

I stop fighting and allow myself to believe it all, right then. That such a thing is possible. "Grey," I gasp, my nails digging into his hair, tugging lightly.

He freezes. Every part of him going still at once like a rabbit caught in the floodlights. Bracing his hands on the door next to my head, he pushes back, putting distance between us.

His eyes devour me, confusion and wonder tangling together, and for a split second I think he knows. If he was this familiar to me, wouldn't the same be true for him? The taste of Frances? The sound of Frances? The *feel* of Frances?

I'm instantly aware of just how fast my breathing's become and I realize in that moment how desperately I want to be found out. To hear him murmur my name—my real name—into my ear like he did so many times before.

He lets his head fall against my shoulder and his lips press against the skin there—right where my throat meets my collarbone.

I suck in a shuddering gasp of air. My body is the same as Frances's. My responses the same. He already knows me—how to find the spots that cause my heart to stumble and then roar.

He smiles against me and I'm convinced he's figured it out. Until he murmurs the name *Libby* against my flesh. And it's almost as though he's saying it to remind himself.

I go cold inside. Everything blooming pulled tight once more.

How stupid could I be to allow myself to hope? Why would he think me anyone else?

Who expects to find a dead girl in his arms?

"I wasn't sure I'd ever be able to care about someone again," he confesses. "No one's made me feel this way, not since . . ." He swallows the name but it's still there between us, unspoken. *Frances.*

A surge of possession sinks through me. It should be impossible to be jealous of yourself. Yet, somehow, this is the situation I've found myself in.

Desperate for him to continue loving the girl I used to be.

Desperate for him to forget her so that he can be with the girl I am now.

In the wake of my silence, he raises his head. Lines appear across his forehead. Lifting a finger, he trails his thumb just under my eye, and when I look down I find the dampness of tears.

I realize, then, that this has gone too far.

I've let my emotions interfere. I need to pull myself together and regain control.

I slip a hand between us, pressing against his chest. Trying not to notice the ridges of his muscles flexing under my touch. "I should go." He straightens instantly, worried he's done something wrong.

There's something I should say here, I know this. Some piece to the puzzle of revenge I've so carefully been assembling. But my mind refuses to focus.

Not with the taste of Grey still fresh on my lips. His smell clinging to the air in my lungs. His touch skittering over my skin like goose bumps.

All I can muster is a good night before fleeing down the steps to my car and starting for home. Telling myself the same thing over and over: *He is not yours to have.*

Whether I'm talking to Libby or to Frances, I'm not sure.

## THIRTY-EIGHT

My thoughts are so tangled with Grey that I drive right past the entrance to my driveway. I don't bother turning around, don't even tap the brakes. I just keep going, my headlights illuminating the night ahead only as far as I need to see.

I can still taste Grey on my lips. Still smell him. Still feel the warmth of his fingertips pressing against my back. Even my pulse hasn't returned to normal. I roll down the window, wanting to flush the car of his scent. Needing the fresh air to clear my head.

Of course it doesn't help. The night is thick with humidity and the smells of the marsh: pluff mud; salt water; decaying fish. Even so, Grey fills my head and my senses.

*He's a means to an end*, I remind myself again. But telling myself doesn't make it truth. Somehow that end I've been searching for has grown fuzzier. I've reached the point where my carefully crafted plans are no longer relevant. Too many variables have entered the equation, jumbling things, forcing me to course-correct on the fly—before I have time to stop and think. To play out the consequences in my head before putting them in action.

If I needed any proof of how much my control over the situation has slipped, I need only listen to the stutter of my heart, feel the flexing of desire in my abdomen.

Run my tongue over my lips and taste Grey.

It has to stop. I need to refocus, regain control. And so I head to the one place I know that will remind me of the reason I'm here.

That will reorient me on my quest: the Caldwell Island Marina.

When I turn into the parking lot it's dark and empty, sleek expensive cars lined up like soldiers along the outside rows. I flip open the glove compartment and pull out a set of keys before making my way toward the docks.

Only about half the slips are occupied, most folks taking advantage of the recent good weather to head out for deeper waters. But the boats that remain are impressive, their hulking hulls glimmering under lights strung between towering masts.

It's late enough that everything's quiet, the only sound muffled music playing against the hushing roll of waves. I keep my head down as I walk to the far dock and make my way out to the slip at the end. One of the few reserved for the larger, more impressive yachts.

I approach her slowly and stand for a while, staring at the name stenciled across the hull. LIBBY TOO. Cecil had once told me he named her that because his first yacht—a larger one—

had been named after his wife, and as a kid Libby used to say, "I want one too."

And so he bought her one.

It's the first time I've seen the boat since I was pulled from the ocean four years ago. At the time, the yacht seemed enormous, towering over our tiny life raft. The ship represented every wish come true—the perfect embodiment of heaven to a fourteen-year-old girl who'd embraced the truth that she was going to die.

I step on board, tentative. Unlocking the door to the cabin feels like unsealing a tomb. There's a puff of air as the seal breaks, and when I step inside everything's dim and musty. The blinds have been pulled tight across the windows, everything lashed into place.

Cecil had arranged for someone from the marina to check on her every few weeks, and they've continued to do so after his death. There's no dust on the table, no mildew along the walls. As far as I know, no one's taken her out since my rescue which is perhaps why she carries such a feeling of pervasive emptiness.

As I make my way through the ship, I catch glimpses of my own ghost. A girl straddling the space between living and dead. By all rights I never should have survived.

Arguably I haven't survived.

Eventually I find myself standing in the doorway to the room where they'd put Libby's body. Now it's just a cabin like any other on the ship. But in my mind I still see her on her side, face to the wall and blanket pulled to her shoulders.

Almost as though she'd simply fallen asleep.

I move to the bed and sit, swinging my legs up until I've arranged myself in the same position she'd been in. Ahead of me nothing but a blank wall.

And I think: *What if it had been me instead?*

What sort of life would Libby have lived if she'd been the one pulled from the ocean alive? Could she have returned to her old school, resumed her relationship with Shepherd? Would she have done as her father asked and forgotten about the incident, letting it all fall into the past?

Let me fall into the past as well?

Or, like me, would she have held on. Unable to let go. The screams and images of that night seared so deep that the burn never faded.

But that's not really the kind of person Libby was either. She wouldn't have kept the truth quiet like I have. She'd have spoken out against Grey and his father. Secure in her place in life, she wouldn't have been afraid.

Like I've been.

She wouldn't have let it control her life.

Like I have.

She wouldn't have been content to live a lie.

A tear slips free. Followed by another and another. Lying here in the spot that had been rightfully mine, I realize that my recovery from the *Persephone* has only been an illusion. As superficial as I am.

All I know to do anymore—all I know who to be—is this. And I have no idea what or who that is. For so long I've been a girl who no longer exists, chasing a path no longer visible.

To what end?

It would be so easy to let it go. Walk away. There's no one left to condemn me for such a decision. Except that I don't even know what that means or where I would go. Because for four years my life has been defined by the *Persephone*—by someone else's preferences and desires. Someone else's life.

I slip my phone from my pocket and enter the familiar terms in the image search: "*Persephone* disaster passengers." It pulls up a page of pictures, memorials for those lost when the *Persephone* sank. Formal photos of families, candid pics of friends, casual group shots of coworkers. I've spent so much time researching every one of them that their histories are almost as familiar as my own. The environmentalists by the Amazon; the Dorsey family gathered around a Christmas tree; Jeff and Jane Stier with their latest rescue dog.

And then there's Frances Mace and her horrid school photo. There are other pictures as well, though I have no idea where the media got them—whether someone rooted through our empty house, searching for abandoned photo albums, or whether these were somehow donated by friends.

But they're the only pictures I have left of my family. A Christmas card from six years ago, the photo ironically taken from another cruise we'd been on. We're standing on the gangplank, my mother's wide tortoiseshell sunglasses pushed up on her head, her arm around my father and her other hand draped over my shoulder. Me leaning back against them both, an outline of Darth Vader reading a book on my red shirt, my hair in a frizzing ponytail, and my smiling mouth filled with braces.

That had been my favorite shirt—a birthday gift from my friend Jackie. I used to go over to her house sometimes on the weekend and she'd pull out an old Ouija board and we'd drink root beer and stay up late asking the spirits questions and pretending we weren't the ones pushing the disk around the board, making up stupid answers.

On a whim, I look her up and find a blog filled with photos. Her at graduation, long dark braids twisted into a knot at the nape of her neck, one arm around a tall, lanky redhead and the other clutching her diploma. Her on the beach, her two younger sisters helping her bury that same redhead, his nose an alarming sunburned red. Her slouched with a group of girls, all of them wearing glittering dresses and wrist corsages as they pose in front of a limo.

I try imagine myself with them, on the end with my arm draped over Rebecca's narrow shoulders. But I can't. Because when I picture myself now, it's as Libby. Sleek, sophisticated, always-put-together Elizabeth O'Martin. The kind of girl who knows how to write a thank-you note, who attends boarding school in Switzerland and spends her summer vacations in Provence, who wears couture.

The kind of girl who would never fit in with Jackie and Rebecca. Or rather, they wouldn't have fit in with Libby.

Though who knows how much *they've* changed in the years I've been gone as well.

The only one who never changed at all was Frances. The girl in suspension, stuck in time. Pulled onto the *Libby Too* as one person and stepping off again someone else.

I reach up and slide a finger along the hair covering my cheek, carefully tucking it behind my ear the way I'd wanted to do for Libby years ago when she'd been lying here. And I think about crouching in that cruise ship dumbwaiter, watching through the mirrored porthole window while a man kicked open the door to my family's stateroom.

He'd pointed his gun at my parents and my mother had looked past him to my hiding place. There'd been so much hope in her eyes—that I would somehow survive. That I would *live*—be something more than a victim of these monsters. I know it's the thought that carried her into death: belief in me.

She would be so disappointed to see what I've become. To see how I've wasted everything that came before.

To see how cruel I now am.

A victim of the *Persephone* nonetheless.

She would tell me that it's never too late to change. It's never too late to strike out on a different path.

But she would be wrong.

And it doesn't matter anyway, because she is gone. Something in my chest catches, razor-sharp bands squeezing tight. I clench my teeth against the pain of it. Even now I can't think of my parents without seeing how they were at the end.

Blood-soaked, faces shattered. Gone. Gone. Gone.

## THIRTY-NINE

I snap awake in the darkness, heart screaming in my chest. At first I think it must have been a nightmare, but my body remains rigid, on high alert. I hold my breath, listening.

The *Libby Too* isn't a small boat by any stretch, and yet she still dips under the weight of someone walking on her decks. That, I realize, is what has woken me up. The echo of footsteps, the almost-imperceptible shift in her movement.

Slowly, as silently as possible, I sit up, straining to listen. "Hello?" I call out. Nothing. I stand. "Hello?" I call again.

In response, there's a massive burst of sound and light. I fly through the air. My shoulder slams into the wall and I fall to the floor, knocking my head against the corner of a table. Starbursts explode in my vision as I push to my hands and knees, groggy.

The room's a solid wall of darkness, my own fingers nothing more than deep shadows as I wave them in front of my eyes. There's a loud, horrible groaning noise and the floor begins to tilt under me, sharp enough that I have to brace my feet against the wall to keep from crumpling against it.

Something big and heavy crashes on the other side of the room and I'm barely able to roll out of its path as I hear it skidding toward me. At first I think the rushing in my ears is blood from my racing heart, but as the intensity of it grows and builds, I recognize the sound: water.

The ship tilts again, and cold salt water oozes along the floor, sliding in under the door and sloshing against my legs. The *Libby Too* is sinking.

I pat at my pockets, finding the bulge of my keys but no phone. I'd fallen asleep clutching it. Who knows where it is now? There's no way I'll be able to find it in this wreckage.

"*Damn*," I whisper. It's so impossible to see in the dark that it doesn't matter my eyes blur with tears.

Twice I try to stand, and twice I wobble and fall as the boat pitches beneath me. I half crawl, half throw myself toward the far wall, sliding my hands over it until I find the door.

I flick the knob and push, but it doesn't budge. From overhead I hear a series of crashes, the cabinets in the salon falling open and disgorging their contents. I throw my shoulder against the door over and over, trying to get as much leverage as I can, but there's something on the other side blocking it.

I'm trapped.

"Is anyone out there?!" I scream, slamming my hand against the door. "Help me!"

But there's no one to save me. I'm completely alone.

A series of shudders rocks through the ship—vibrating up my legs and down my arms. Something buckles against the other side of the door, scraping across it. I push again, this time creating a gap large enough to fit an arm through.

There's a muffled blast and somewhere deep in the bowels of the ship something gives way. The floor tilts violently, almost falling out from underneath me. The *Libby Too* is almost completely on her side now, which leaves me hanging, my fingernails digging into the doorjamb as I try to pull myself up. Water pours into the room, pummeling at my face. It's like trying to hold on to the lip of a waterfall and I can't do it anymore.

My hands lose their grip, and I fall. I plunge underwater and come up sputtering. Everything's turned on its side, the wall by the bed now practically the floor, the door out of reach above me.

I can barely stand, my toes just grazing the side of a table. And then even that becomes impossible and I'm treading water. The room's an interior berth and there's no other escape—no porthole or vent.

My only option is to keep my head above the surface and wait until it's deep enough that I can reach the door again. Even to my own ears, my breathing sounds ragged and wheezy. Desperate. All I can do is flail at the water, try to stay calm.

Inch by inch, the water level rises. Once it reaches the door, the hallway will fill quickly, and if I can't find my way out before that happens, I'm dead. A whimper sounds in my throat.

When I'm close enough, I kick as hard as I can, reaching for the edge of the doorway over my head. I grab hold of the jamb, but as I try to pull myself up, my arms wobble and give out. I splash back down again.

I surface screaming. In pain. In rage. In terror. This time, with the water level higher, I'm able to pull myself up, into the hallway. Everything's turned on its side, the water a rushing river creating rapids over the debris scattered in its path. It's a fight to gain traction, to move at all against the current.

The water's at my knees, and then my thighs and hips. I'm only halfway to the stairs when it reaches my waist and suddenly I lose my footing. It's like swimming against a riptide: impossible and deadly.

I dive under, scrabbling for handholds as I pull myself forward. Kicking to the surface to swallow a breath of air before doing it all over again. Inch by inch, I fight my way down the hallway until I push for the surface and it's no longer there.

The hall's completely submerged. Panic's a hot coal burning in my lungs, my brain screaming *breathe, breathe, breathe* as I force my lips to clamp shut. Static hazes around my vision, my thoughts turning fuzzy, and then my hand brushes against the edge of the staircase railing.

I'm clawing at it, wrenching myself forward hand over hand. My mouth is already open, my lungs already sucking in when my fingers break into air and I come up sputtering and coughing. Retching, doubled over, as I shudder and gasp.

All around, an orange haze echoes off the surface of the water, the air thick and sticky, burning my eyes. Fire eats at the stern of the ship, loud and frenzied. I push myself in the other direction, toward the bow. The salon is a chaos of broken furniture and floating debris. And though the water continues to rise, it's not rushing as furiously.

The double doors leading out to the front deck are broken open, the glass shattered and jagged. As careful as I try to be easing through it, the sharp tip of one of the shards catches at my arm, tearing open the skin. Blood glistens black, like oil, under the glow of the fire.

Outside I'm surprised to find the ship unmoored. It's drifted into the middle of the bay—the marina a collection of lights in the distance.

Underneath me the boat groans and shudders again and I feel the vibrations of her tearing apart. The entire deck of the bow is tilted, a smooth wall of varnished teak. With nothing to hold on to, I slip down it like a child on a slide at an amusement park. When I crash into the water, the world goes muffled and dark.

I kick away from the sinking ship, swimming as hard as I can to put distance between us. I reach the surface and gasp, fighting against the churning water, bubbling and frothing as the *Libby Too* lets out her last protests and breaks apart.

The night's lit by her flames and little else. Behind me, the marina's several football fields away, the crowds beginning to gather, appearing little more than flickers of fireflies with their flashlights aimed toward the sinking ship.

I swim into the darkness, cutting through the water as smoothly as I can, trying not to draw attention. There's enough debris and chaos surrounding the dying ship that I can easily go unnoticed, just another shadow against the midnight water.

The far side of the marina is practically empty, everyone else crowded at the other end, eyes glued on the spectacular wreckage. I'm able to haul myself onto one of the docks and slip back toward the parking lot, leaving a trail of water in my path.

I reach my car just as two fire trucks and a cop car come screaming through the entrance, barreling their way toward the docks. The air becomes a riot of color and sound, activity and screaming orders. Thankfully the keys are still in my pocket and I slip behind the wheel, slumping gratefully into the cradle of the leather seat.

*Safe*, I tell myself. And the thought causes my breath to strain, my body quivering and teeth chattering, as the reality of it all crashes through me. I let out a gasping sob.

How safe can I really be? There'd been someone on board. Someone had unmoored the ship. Someone had set her adrift, rigged her to blow, intending for her to sink. And someone had barricaded the door to my room.

Goose bumps flare down the back of my neck and along my arms. They'd known I was there. They'd known exactly where I was on board.

And I'd been completely unaware.

*They could still be here now. Watching.*

I fumble for the door lock button and then push it again twice more just to make sure before staring the car. As I pull out of the parking lot, I keep my eyes on the rearview mirror, watching to see whether anyone follows.

But all I see is the final belch of flames and frothing water as the *Libby Too* sinks beneath the surface. The ship that rescued me had almost taken me down with her.

# FORTY

I've barely made it home and up to my room when the doorbell rings. Carefully I tiptoe across the hall, pushing aside the curtain to look outside. There's a cop car in the driveway. I curse under my breath and dash into my bathroom where I peel off my wet clothes, running a brush through my hair before pulling on a robe.

Shepherd's already at the door when I reach the stairs. "Detective Morales," I hear him say. She says something in return that causes him to chuckle as he steps aside to let her in.

My pulse jumps. I can only assume she's here because of the *Libby Too*. But what I don't know is whether someone saw me. I have no idea how much Morales knows and she's not likely to give any hints. She's too good to make that mistake.

I retreat around the corner and close my eyes. Taking a second to put myself in character before calling, "Sorry! I was in the shower." I start down the steps but pull up short when I see Morales in the foyer. "Oh! Detective Morales," I exclaim. I tilt my head to the side, concerned. "Everything okay?"

She isn't wearing a uniform and her hair's scraped back haphazardly, as though she'd been called out of bed. Even though it's muggy outside, she's wearing a sweatshirt with a faded and worn logo from Carolina. Her eyes sweep the foyer, and when they land on me, her expression slides toward formality, any humor left over from her quip with Shepherd erased.

She nods rather than saying hello and then dives right in. "There's been an accident down at the marina and I wanted to make sure you were okay."

I frown, feigning confusion. "I'm fine—why would you be worried?"

She keeps her eyes trained on me, waiting to gauge my response as she says, "Your father's yacht, the *Libby Too*, pulled free from her slip, caught fire, and sank."

I let my jaw drop, as though trying to find words through the shock of such news. "I . . . Oh my goodness." I look toward Shepherd, who says nothing, just watches me. "Was anyone hurt?"

Morales shakes her head. "There haven't been any reports of casualties."

"Well, that's good." I sigh in relief. "Here," I say, moving down the rest of the stairs. "Can I get you something to drink? Coffee? Tea?"

I don't expect her to take me up on the offer and am surprised when she nods. "Some tea would be great—thanks."

I lead her through the house to the kitchen, Shepherd trailing in our wake. "So what happened?" I gesture for her to take a seat at the island and busy myself with the kettle.

"We don't have a full report yet," she says. "One witness

says they thought they saw a young woman headed toward the yacht late this evening—that's why I wanted to stop by tonight and make sure you're okay."

The unasked question hangs in the air for a moment, the only sound the clicking of the pilot light on the stove before the soft *whump* of the gas catching. "Of course, I'm glad you did," I finally say, straightening. I pull down a selection of teas for her to choose from.

She waits until I've turned to face her before saying, "I'm sorry I have to ask this, but where were you tonight, Libby?"

My eyes flick to meet Shepherd's. He leans against the doorjamb, silent. His expression is an impassive mask, but his gaze burns holes through me as he too waits for the answer. I clear my throat. "I . . . uh . . . I was with Grey Wells." I pretend to be uncomfortable with the admission, as though I've done something wrong. "We were . . . out."

She doesn't immediately say anything, letting the silence stretch. Hoping I'll fill it. But I know better than that. I've trained myself to be comfortable with the silences. "Other witnesses at the marina say they saw a man walking around the *Libby Too*'s slip," Morales adds. "Middle-aged, skinny. Anyone you know?"

I look to Shepherd. "Could it have been the caretaker?"

He shakes his head. "He's captaining another yacht down to the Caymans this week."

"That's good," I say. "I mean, that he's okay."

Morales considers me a long moment. Her demeanor is more reserved than last time we spoke and I can't decide whether it's the late hour or something more. She seems somehow suspicious of me but I can't figure out why. It makes me uneasy. Without taking her eyes off me, she says, "Shepherd, do you mind giving us a moment?"

He lifts his eyebrows, clearly not pleased at the request. But then he shrugs, pretending otherwise. "Sure," and takes his time retreating down the hallway.

It can't be a good sign that she wants to talk to me alone and I busy myself with the teakettle, pulling it from the stove and pouring a mug of hot water for her. I set it in front of her along with a few tins of tea, but she ignores it.

Instead, she pulls a small plastic Baggie from her pocket. The word EVIDENCE is emblazoned in red across the top. She places it on the counter. "Do you recognize this?"

Inside is a gold ring, the face of it scratched and crusted with dirt. The edge of the O'Martin family crest is just visible. Immediately I reach for my ring finger, finding only empty skin instead of the familiar hard metal band. Something slithery and cold starts deep in my gut, pressing outward.

I nod, mind whirling. "Yes. It's mine, but . . ." I frown, trying to remember when I'd last taken it off. It had been the night I'd told Shepherd the truth. I'd held it up to the mirror and then set it down on the bathroom counter. I don't recall ever putting it back on.

Which means someone must have taken it.

My pulse thunders in my ears. "Where did you find it?"

"Do you remember when you were last wearing it?" she asks instead of answering. I clench my teeth—it's an old trick, avoid divulging information by responding to a question with more questions.

I shove a hand into my hair, dislodging droplets of water that fall against the counter. "A few days ago?" Morales watches me closely and I struggle to figure out the best approach here. How much to admit. If I let her think someone broke in, she might push for me to file a report, which will only mean more questions. Maybe even an investigation and dusting for fingerprints.

That's the last thing I need.

"I noticed it was loose when I rescued Mrs. Wells. I kept meaning to take it in to be resized . . ." I let the thought trail off, leaving it as vague as possible. "How did you end up with it?"

This time Morales relents and answers. "One of the officers found it down at the marina. By *Libby Too*'s slip. It was caught on a cleat for one of the mooring lines."

She pauses and it takes all my concentration to keep from recoiling at the information. My lungs constrict, making breathing difficult. Someone had not only taken my ring, but planted it at the marina. Probably when they untied the *Libby Too* and set her adrift to catch fire and sink.

I clutch at the edge of the counter. If I'd died, this ring would have been evidence that I'd been there. Maybe even been the one to unmoor the ship. They'd probably intended for it to look like some sort of elaborate suicide attempt.

"I must have lost it when I went to check on the *Libby Too* the other day. You know, with the caretaker gone and all," I force myself to say. "Like I said, it was loose. Please thank the officer for finding it," I tell her. "My father gave it to me on my thirteenth birthday. It means a lot to have it back." I shift toward the foyer, hoping she'll get the hint.

She frowns, as though still not satisfied by my answer, and for a moment I think she'll press the issue. But finally she nods and I lead her back through the house. "The insurance company will want the police report," she says once we reach the front door. "I'll have someone drop it by when it's ready."

"Thank you." My cheeks strain with the effort of smiling as I pull open the door.

"Let me know if you think of anything else." She says it more as a standard formality, but then her eyes sweep over me again and she pauses on the threshold. "Libby, if you're in trouble, you know you can call me at any time, right? You have my cell number."

I'm so surprised by the sudden earnestness of the statement that I don't know how to respond.

"Don't forget to lock up," she adds. She glances over my shoulder, nodding good-bye, and that's when I realize Shepherd's in the foyer behind me.

"Good night, Detective," he says, coming to stand beside me. "We appreciate you stopping by."

She grins. "Night, Mr. Sheep."

The minute the door closes, Shepherd grabs my arm. "What the hell are you doing?"

I hiss in pain as his fingers dig into the fresh cut from the broken glass on the *Libby Too*.

His eyes widen and his grip immediately eases. But when I try to pull away, he keeps hold of my wrist, yanking the sleeve of my robe up before I can stop him. A bright smear of blood runs toward my fingertips.

He lets out a long breath. "Frances—"

"You shouldn't call me that," I bite at him. I jerk my hand away, yanking down my sleeve.

"I'm not calling you Libby," he snaps back. After a beat of silence during which we glare at each other, he eases back, letting out a long breath. "We should get that cleaned up. Who knows what kind of bacteria's in the water at the marina."

I freeze, eyes meeting his. "I don't know what you mean—"

He snorts, cutting off my protest. "You smell like salt water, not shampoo. Don't think Morales didn't figure it out either." He starts toward the kitchen and I chase after him, panic setting my heart racing.

"Wait—what do you think Morales figured out?"

He pulls out a small first-aid kit, placing it on the counter. He leads me toward the sink, turning on the water and holding my arm underneath. Hissing at the pain, I swallow a few more times before again asking, "What did Morales figure out?"

"Not all of it," he says, focused on cleaning the cut. "Not the big stuff. But she's smart and she pays attention. And she clearly thinks there's something wrong—she has a soft spot for orphans who could use some help."

The statement catches me off guard and I let it sink in a moment. "Is that how you know her so well?"

He lets go of me, busying himself with pulling out strips of gauze and alcohol from the first-aid kit. "After the *Persephone* I got in trouble around town." He swabs at the cut, his touch featherlight.

"Doesn't take much for most of our neighbors to call the cops on a kid who looks like he's not from around here." It comes out both bitter and resigned. He lifts a shoulder, gaze meeting mine again. "Morales took a special interest. Started looking out for me."

He considers me for a moment. "She's someone you can trust."

I'm already shaking my head. "Out of the question."

"What happened on the *Libby Too*?"

"Nothing." I pull my arm away. "It doesn't matter," I add.

He barks out a laugh. "Sounds to me like you were almost killed."

"I'm fine," I grit out between clenched teeth.

"This is getting too dangerous." He runs a hand over the top of his head. "The *Libby Too* catching fire and sinking with you on board—that sounds an awful lot like someone trying to hurt you."

I lift an eyebrow. "Then I guess the sooner we figure out and expose the truth, the better." He's about to protest but I cut him off, steering the discussion in a new direction.

"And about that, I found something at Grey's I think will help. There's an envelope taped to the back of a picture frame in his room and I'm pretty sure it has something to do with the *Persephone*. I found it when I was over there earlier but didn't have the chance to grab it."

I step forward so that I'm having to look up at him, and bite my lip. "Just a little more time—one more day," I ask, as though begging permission. Knowing this will all be much easier if he believes he has a say in the matter. "Let me get that envelope and see what's inside. Then we can figure out what to do with Morales."

He presses his lips together, eyes searching mine.

"I'll be safe," I tell him. "I promise. I know what I'm doing."

Finally, his shoulders drop and he nods. I smile, wondering why he thinks he can trust me. Haven't I already proven that everything about me is a lie?

## FORTY-ONE

The next morning I dig up the clone to my cell phone I lost the night before and charge it up before making a few calls. Thanks to chatty Mindy Gervistan in Senator Wells's office, I learn that the Senator and his wife will be at the dedication of a new war monument up in Charleston that afternoon. It's the kind of event at which there will be boundless media opportunities, which means Grey will be expected to attend as well.

Once I'm sure they've all left, I make my way up the beach and knock gently on the kitchen door. As I'd expected, the housekeeper greets me with a broad smile and a hug. "Get out of that heat," she says with a laugh, hauling me inside.

"Thanks." The air-conditioning hits like a frigid wall and I put on my best-mannered girl-next-door face. "Is Grey here?" I ask, grinning shyly.

Her forehead furrows with concern. "I'm afraid not, sugar. He's up in the city with his parents all afternoon." I bite my lip and she adds, "Everything okay?"

"Yeah," I say quickly. "It's just that I think I left my phone up in his room yesterday." I sigh. "I guess I'll just come back later and . . ."

"Nonsense!" She waves a hand, both cutting me off and gesturing toward the stairs. "Go on up and look."

"You don't mind?" I ask

She shakes her head and chuckles as if the very notion were ridiculous. I smile as I make my way through the house. It's amazing the doors that open when you save someone's life.

Once in Grey's room I act quickly, jumping onto his bed and snatching the frame from the wall. I rip the envelope free, surprised to find that it's bulky and heavy. I stare at it a moment before shoving it into my purse. After another quick circuit of his room, I make sure the picture is straight on the wall and that his sheets are smooth.

Then I pull out my phone and jog back down the stairs. "Found it," I tell her, holding it up as I enter the kitchen.

"Oh, good. How about some tea before you head home?" she offers.

"No thanks, I don't want to get in your way." I start for the door and then hesitate. "And um . . . do you mind not mentioning to Grey that I stopped by?" I bite my lip, letting my cheeks pinken with a blush. "It's the second time I've left my phone here by accident and don't want him thinking I'm an airhead." I fight to smother a smile—the kind that makes it clear how enamored I am with Grey and want him to think the best of me.

As I'd hoped, this delights the housekeeper. Everyone loves to root for romance. "Your secret's safe with me."

If only she had any idea just how dark my secrets really are.

To avoid the reporters, I jog back to the O'Martin estate along the beach, feeling the weight of the envelope in my purse with every step.

I'm not surprised to find Shepherd waiting for me in the kitchen. "You get it?"

I nod, out of breath, and pull the envelope from my purse. Without hesitation, I rip the end open and tip the contents out onto the counter. It's an old cell phone, wrapped in a waterproof case. My heart begins to hammer as I pick it up, turning it over in my hands.

It's an older model, clunky and heavy. But I still remember how new and advanced it seemed when Grey first showed it to me four years ago.

*Grey treads water less than a foot in front of me, and with every swish of his arms and legs, I feel the sweep of currents from his movements buffeting against my body. It's a perfect day in the Virgin Islands: impossibly blue sky, perfectly pristine beach, water clear as glass. In the distance, the cruise ship sits at anchor, waiting for all the passengers to return so it can start the long ocean journey back up to Bermuda.*

*"I want to try something," Grey says, holding up his cell phone in its waterproof case. Droplets of water glisten from his eyelashes, and when he blinks they sprinkle to the surface.*

*"We should probably get back," I say, anxious. There are only a handful of stragglers behind us and we still have a decent swim back to the launches.*

*When he grins, it does something to my insides. The tips of his fingers brush against my bare side, tiny pinpoints of heat* searing through me. "It'll be worth it, I promise."

One of his legs tangles mine, the inside of his knee pressing against the inside of my thigh and I nod. The last thing I hear him say is, "Trust me," before he pulls me below the surface.

I'm caught off guard and don't even have a chance to take a deep breath. I'm about to push against Grey and kick toward the surface when his palm cups the back of my head, gently pulling my face toward his.

His lips meet mine and then I feel the pressure of air. Surprised, I open my mouth and then I'm breathing. I inhale slowly, the heat of air from his lungs heady and intimate. The only sound is the thumping of my heart, the rush of air as it passes from one of us to the other.

The salt water doesn't even sting my eyes as I open them and find Grey watching me. Our bodies are almost fully intertwined now, arms and legs twisting around waists and hips to keep us pressed together. All except for the one hand that he holds outstretched, his camera phone tilted toward us to record the moment.

His lips move against mine and at first I think it's a kiss until I feel the vibrations of noise. I love you. He says it again until he's sure I understand. I love you. I swallow his words, breathing them in so that they will sing through my veins always.

And then, because my body can no longer contain the euphoria of emotion, I grin, throwing my head back, and a trailing bubble of laughs breaks between us. I love you too! I shout through the water, imagining that, like the call of a whale, these words will echo throughout the ocean.

He kisses me then. On the mouth, the chin. The hollow at the *base of my throat and along my collarbones. As he pushes me to the surface, his mouth carves memories across my flesh.*

My finger trembles as I press at the power button, not knowing what to hope for. Would I want to see those pictures of us again? After everything else, would he have even kept them?

*And why hide them away?*

"Battery's dead," Shepherd points out needlessly when the screen remains blank. I bite back a sarcastic retort and examine the plug. Of course it's several generations old, which means having to find the right charging cord.

With a sigh of frustration, I begin searching through the kitchen drawers. Growing up we always had a junk drawer in the kitchen where we stuffed odds and ends like batteries, random tools, old power cords, loose change, and other detritis that accumulated on the counter. Once a year my father would tip it out and let me keep the money in exchange for sorting through it all.

My lips twitch at the memory. How my father would make a big production of carting the drawer over to the kitchen table. How he'd sit next to me, pretending to be a pirate in search of treasure as he helped me paw through the debris. How he was able to turn something that should have been a chore into an adventure.

"What are you thinking about?" Shepherd's question breaks me from the memory.

"Nothing really," I mumble, still intent on my search. "Why?"

"You looked . . ." He frowns, searching for the right word.

"Happy." This makes me pause and I glance up at him, meeting his eyes. "It's a good look on you," he adds. "You should be happy more often."

The comment takes me aback. "I didn't realize I wasn't."

He shrugs. "I think I have a charger that'll work up in my room," he says, changing the subject. He starts out of the kitchen, motioning for me to follow.

# FORTY-TWO

Shepherd's bedroom is above the garage, and the only way up to it is a set of narrow stairs tucked away in the back of the house. I'm surprised when we reach the top to find a sprawling open space with slanted ceilings and dozens of dormer windows. The space is bright and airy with long countertops running down one side and a narrow bed pushed into the corner.

Maps of Caldwell and the surrounding counties line the available wall space, plots of land outlined in heavy black Sharpie and color coded by status and ownership. A vibrant green marks the conservation easement, an angry red indicating formerly protected land slated for development.

Shepherd pulls a basket onto the counter and riffles through a tangle of cords, comparing the ends against the phone until grunting, "Aha!" He plugs in the phone and I stare at it a moment, willing the screen to flash to life. "If the battery's all the way drained, it's probably going to take a few minutes before it's charged enough to turn on."

I bite the inside of my cheek and pace the length of his room impatiently. The far wall is dominated by built-in bookcases, each shelf piled with paperbacks. Most of them have broken spines stamped with the names of various libraries and I trail my fingers across them. *Richland County Library, Greenville County Library, Aiken County Library.*

"Why was Morales asking about your ring?" Shepherd's question breaks the silence.

I shrug, pretending that my attention is still focused on the books. *Calhoun, Charleston, Georgetown.* "How many late fees do you owe for having all of these books?"

"I bought them all at library sales. You going to tell me about the ring?"

"Why not just buy new ones? Cecil would have given you the money for it."

"Money from the sales goes to support the library."

*Lancaster, Marion, Florence.* "You could have just made a donation."

"Libby—" he starts and then all the air leaves his lungs and even his shoulders cave as though he'd been punched.

*Libby.* The name echoes in the silent bedroom.

"God, you look like her," he mumbles. "I can't believe she's . . ." He shakes his head. We stare at each other, for that one horrified moment as it hits him all over again, the truth of this situation. That I'm not her. That's she's gone. Dead.

It's one thing to know something in your head, but it's another thing entirely to convince your heart of it. I can see it in his eyes, the realization that the name *Libby* means nothing anymore.

It's dead, just like the girl it had belonged to.

He presses a curled fist against his forehead as he struggles to regain control, his breath coming in tight gasps.

And I realize, he hasn't had time to mourn. Even though he hadn't talked to Libby in four years, he still loved her. She still mattered to him. He still got to think about her being out in the world, living her life.

He still had hope that one day she might return. She might again love him back.

Now all of that is gone.

Has been gone for years and he just didn't know.

I move across the room and perch on the edge of the bed. "Maybe I should have told you the truth four years ago." I stare at my hands. "Libby trusted you. Maybe I should have too."

He doesn't respond, just continues to stand there, his eyes squeezed shut and jaw clenching, everything about him wound tight. I wish I knew what to tell him to make it all better.

But maybe that's the problem. Maybe there is no such thing as better. Maybe there's only grief and loss.

Maybe, for some people, that's all their life will ever be.

"She talked about you more than anyone else at the end," I tell him. He tenses, listening. "I think what upset her most about dying was leaving you behind." Shepherd draws a sharp breath at this, his fist digging harder into his forehead.

There's no way for me to retreat from the intensity of his emotions. No way to avoid them leaking past my defenses. Making me care. Making me *feel*. How did I not realize that this was always going to be the problem with coming here? I'd spent so many years freezing my heart. But then Grey set fire to it all over again. Now that it beats, I don't know how to stop it.

Being here wasn't supposed to change me.

I wasn't supposed to second-guess myself.

Past Me didn't prepare for this and now Present Me is floundering.

I swallow. Knowing that I've been a horrible person for keeping Libby from Shepherd. *He deserves better*, I think to myself.

"What did she say?" he asks. His voice is calm, though all the sharp edges to it are honed and deadly.

"That you were the best thing that ever happened to her. That you opened her eyes in a way no one else ever had and she was grateful for it."

He walks to the window, stares at the ocean. "*I'm sorry*," I whisper. "I shouldn't have kept that from you." He doesn't respond.

A small *chirp* sounds from his desk where the face of Grey's phone now glows. Quietly, I push to my feet and make my way over to it.

"Why are you doing this?" Shepherd asks just as I've picked up the phone. I stare down at the face of it. The home screen is a picture of Frances and Grey underwater, his lips pressed against hers. I suck in a breath, trying to focus on Shepherd's question.

"Because you deserved to know," I tell him.

He turns, facing me. "I don't mean this." He gestures between us. "I mean that," He points to the phone. "Grey, the Wellses, all of it. What are you expecting is going to happen? What do you *want?*"

It should be such an easy question. All the usual answers are there at the tip of my tongue. I want the truth. I want revenge. I want relief. But none of them feel right anymore.

"I want it to be over," I finally say, my voice betraying my exhaustion. Who knew guilt and rage could weigh so much?

"Then let it be. You're so full of anger—you let it fill you up so that there's no room for anything else. You never talk about your parents or what your life was like before the *Persephone*. Or what you want your life to be like now. Everything you do is so focused on getting back at the Wellses. If you want it to be over, then it's over."

I shake my head, wishing I could explain that it's not that easy. My finger hovers over Grey's phone, ready to swipe it open. "Do you think if it had been different, if it had been Libby who'd survived and me that died, she'd be the one here doing this?"

Shepherd doesn't answer immediately. "I doubt it."

I nod. It's what I'd expected to hear, but it still stings. "You're right, she'd have been able to put the past behind her and move on."

He crosses the room, places his hand over mine so that it blocks the phone's screen. Forcing me to look up at him. "No," he says, meeting my eyes. "She wouldn't be here because she wasn't strong enough to survive in the first place. And you were."

I let out a laugh and shake my head. "Surviving had nothing to do with strength and everything to do with luck."

A frown furrows between Shepherd's eyebrows as his eyes

search my face. Then he makes a noise in the back of his throat as though he's just figured something out. "So that's why you pretend to be someone else."

"Because I had no other choice," I point out.

He shakes his head. "There are always other choices."

I let out a snort, rolling my eyes. "Then why?"

"Because you don't have enough faith in yourself."

It's as though he's poured frigid water into my veins. I stiffen, the heat around my heart rapidly cooling past the point of freezing.

He must notice the shift in my demeanor because he steps back, giving me space. But he keeps one eyebrow raised and I hate that he might think my reaction has proven his point.

"No, I pretend to be Libby so that I can get things like this." I hold up the phone. "Now let's see why Grey felt like this was something worth hiding."

# FORTY-THREE

I lean my hip against the counter, Grey's phone still tethered to the wall in order to keep charging. Shepherd stands facing me, his head only inches away so that he can see the screen as well.

For a moment I want to push him away. This phone feels somehow private, a piece of my past with Grey, and I hate the idea of sharing it. But Shepherd's a part of this now too; it's only fair he be here.

"Maybe put it in airplane mode first," Shepherd suggests. "So no one can trace it."

"Right," I say, making my way through the settings. I realize I'd have probably forgotten to do that and am grateful he's here to remind me.

Then, blowing out a long breath, I brace myself and open the photo app. The screen fills with familiar thumbnail-sized images. I click on one at random and it's a candid shot I don't even remember him taking. I'm sitting on a lounge chair out on deck, my face scrunched in concentration as I lean over a book reading. In the next picture I'm glaring at him. Then I'm laughing. Then I'm reaching for him. Then it's a selfie of the two of us, his lips pressed against my cheek.

I flick through them maddeningly fast, knowing that if I pause at all it will break me. Already I remember too much. The feel of him and the smell and the way his breath tickled the edge of my ear as he hovered, hovered, hovered, until finally flicking his teeth against the lobe, causing me to gasp and shudder.

But then Shepherd mutters, "Stop." He gently nudges my finger from the screen and flips back to an earlier picture. It's me and Libby. We're in our bathing suits by the pool, hair wet and slicked from our faces. I'm making a funny face and she has her head thrown back laughing.

She's so stunningly vibrant and full of life that it makes me ache just to remember it. I'm hit again with how unfair it is that she died and I didn't. She was the brighter person, how could her light ever go out before mine?

After a moment Shepherd grunts, "Go on," he says, and I do.

Five photographs later, I understand why Grey kept this phone hidden for long. At first I think he just mistakenly photographed the inside of his pocket or something. The image is so dark it's almost impossible to make out any shapes. Then Shepherd reaches forward to tap the screen and I realize it's a video.

At first all I hear is shuffling, the sound of something like fabric pulling across the microphone. The image remains dark, no objects distinct enough to stand out. There's a blur of light and the sound of someone breathing in heavy, terrified gasps.

And then the screaming. It's in the background, far enough away that I have to strain at first to figure out what it is. A woman's high-pitched shriek. A series of *pops* like fireworks and she falls quiet.

I collapse against the counter. Letting the phone drop from my hands, I slide until I'm on the floor. Knees clutched to my chest, fingers shoved into my hair and pulling as the memories assault me.

The video continues. "Ohgodohgodohgodohgod." The same words playing through my head, but it's Grey's voice coming from the phone. Laced with panic.

I struggle to breathe, choking on the terror of that night clawing its way free again. Shepherd fumbles to stop the video but I shake my head. "No. I want to hear."

He hesitates. "Do it!" I yell. Reluctantly he crouches next to me, one hand on my back, the other holding the phone. Thumb poised to press stop at any moment.

There's not much more to the video anyway. Just more dark. More screaming. At one point Grey mumbles something that I think might have been *Frances*, but it's too hard to make out in the midst of the chaos.

It ends abruptly. Leaving us in silence. Shepherd lets out a long breath while I continue to curl as tightly into myself as possible. I feel him slip his arm around me and pull me against his chest. "It's okay," he says, holding me.

Only then do I realize I'm sobbing.

"I'm sorry." It's probably the tenth time Shepherd's said this in the past half hour. At first I appreciated his concern, but now I just wish he'd stop. I don't like being coddled.

I don't like someone else feeling like they have a right to comfort me. Or that I'm weak enough to need it.

It's obvious that any doubt he may have had about my version of events has been erased by the video on Grey's phone. Now he's all in. "We should call Morales," he suggests. We're sitting on the floor in his room, both of us cross-legged with the phone between us. The screen is dark. Once or twice Shepherd has reached for it, but he always hesitates and leaves it be.

I've been chewing on my lower lip, thinking. Now I shake my head. "It's not enough."

He looks up at me with wide eyes. "Not enough for what?" he asks, incredulous.

"You can't really see anything—there's no proof. Grey could have taken the video days or weeks later."

"Why would he?" he sputters. "Won't the file have the date and time the thing was taken?"

"You have to think of this the way *they* would—the outside world. As far as they know, they already have the real story. It takes a lot to change someone's mind once they've made it up. The burden is heavier on us."

He pushes to his feet and begins to pace, clearly agitated. "You can trust Morales."

"But she can't trust me!" I counter. "Look, unless we have absolute proof, it won't matter. Even if she did believe us, what can she do about it? Maybe, if we're lucky, we'll convince some crackpot conspiracy theorists. But no one else."

"How can that *not* convince them?" He throws his hand at the phone. "You hear a woman screaming! You hear the shots!"

"Maybe Grey was watching a horror movie in the background," I offer. He scoffs. "Or the video is from when the rogue wave struck and the woman's screaming because of that and the sound you think is gunshots is really support wires on the ship snapping."

He opens his mouth to argue and then closes it.

"I'm not saying this isn't useful," I tell him. "I'm just saying that on its own it's not enough. We need more."

He runs a hand down his face. "Someone tried to kill you last night, Frances. This isn't a joke anymore."

"This has *never* been a joke to me," I remind him. "They sank the *Libby Too* because they're scared we're too close to the truth. They're worried, which means they're likely to make a mistake." I step toward him, allowing a desperate note into my voice. "We're close, Shepherd."

He considers this for a long moment and then lets out a sigh. "So what now?"

The plan has always been to shake the tree and see what falls. Now I just have to shake a bit harder. "It's time for Libby to start remembering a few things from that night. Put a little more pressure on Grey."

## FORTY-FOUR

I wait until that night to text him.

*I think I'm starting to remember.*

The words glow on the phone's screen and I drum my fingers on the kitchen counter, waiting for Grey to respond. A bubble pops up beneath my text signaling that he's typing. He takes his time, pausing and then starting again, as if he can't decide what to say.

Finally he comes back with: *Can we meet?*

I smile, pleased he's fallen for it. *Tomorrow maybe? Lunch?*

But of course I know he won't want to wait that long. *Any chance you can come now? Start walking up the beach and I'll meet you halfway?*

I don't answer immediately, letting his tension mount. Making him more desperate. *Sure,* I eventually type. *See you in a min.*

"Got him," I tell Shepherd, even though he'd been reading the screen over my shoulder. I start toward the door. "I'll be back later."

He grabs my wrist. "I'm going with you."

My back bristles. "No way will he talk if you're there."

"I'll stay out of sight," he counters.

"And if he sees you, it's all over," I point out. "Everything I've done to win his trust, to wind him up so he'll have no choice but to find someone to confide in—the entire plan—all of it will have been for nothing."

"It's too dangerous, Frances."

I throw my hands in the air, exasperated. "Haven't I already proven that I know what I'm doing?" I tell him. "Besides, I don't need you to be my keeper—I can take care of myself just fine, thank you."

He tenses, standing straighter, and the expression on his face hardens. "If I don't hear anything from you in thirty minutes I'm going after you. And if you're not on the beach, I'm calling Morales and telling her everything."

I know he doesn't mean it as a threat, but his words rankle me all the same. "Fine, do what you want," I tell him on my way out the door.

"Frances," he calls after me, voice stern.

I turn, forcing my mouth to smile and my expression to soften as though I'm relenting. "I promise I'll be careful." I say it sweetly, earnestly. Convincingly. He nods and the moment my back is turned, I let my face fall back into a scowl.

Outside, it's a mostly clear night. Though a storm threatens from the mainland, a half-full moon shines over the ocean, dusting pearlescent glances along the wave crests. I walk briskly, so by the time I see Grey in the distance, we're far closer to his house than to mine.

As soon as he sees me, he begins to jog and as he draws near my glance falls to his lips, remembering how just last night they'd been pressed against my own. And my jaw. And my neck and the crest of my shoulder.

I clench my hands into fists, forcing the memories from my mind. Forcing myself to focus.

"You okay?" he asks, reaching for me. His face is cast in enough shadow that it's difficult to read his expression. But his voice betrays his anxiety. I nod.

There's a brief pause while he swallows. And then he asks, "What do you remember?"

I bite at my lip, crossing my arms and holding myself tightly. Knowing that it makes me appear more vulnerable. "Men," I tell him. "With guns," I add, trembling.

His eyes flutter shut, chin falling to his chest.

"How can that be right?" I ask him.

He lets out a resigned breath, everything about him deflating. He drops his hands from my shoulders and steps toward the ocean, stopping just beyond the highest reach of the tide. He doesn't respond and my heart pounds harder. Even knowing the truth, I find myself trembling.

"Wait, how can that be right?" I ask coming up beside him. "It can't be. Right?" I sound like I'm on the edge of panic. "Tell me I'm wrong!"

He shakes his head. "You're not wrong."

I gasp. I don't have to feign surprise because a part of me still expected him to deny it. Can't believe he's actually giving in. "What are you saying?" I press my fingers against my lips, my breathing strained. "I don't understand."

He glances back toward his house, and then at me. "The *Persephone* didn't sink because of a rogue wave. It was attacked." His voice barely exists over the whisper of the tide crawling its way toward us.

And for a moment, I truly am stunned. To hear him say the words. To have confirmation.

To finally have the truth.

I need to hear it again. "*What?*"

He glances again toward his house and then turns, hands reaching for me, but I shrug out of his grasp. "Listen, Libby, you can't let anyone know about this. If my father figures out you remember, he'd . . ." He swallows, realizing he's already said too much.

"He'd *what?*" I press.

He shakes his head.

"What would your father do if he knew I remember the truth about the *Persephone?*"

"God, Libby." He fists his hands through his hair, anguished and frustrated. "I can't talk about it." His eyes silently beg me to believe him.

I refuse. And I ask the question that's been banging against my heart for four years. "Why did you lie about what happened?"

His face is ashen, paler than the moonlight. "Because I was scared," he says in a small voice. "I didn't know what else to do."

"You could have told the truth," I snap. "They would have kept looking for us."

He shakes his head. "They wouldn't have found you." I

open my mouth to protest but he cuts me off. "Where they found us? Where they think the ship went down? It was all a lie."

The blood drains from my limbs and my lips go numb. This is new information. I'm having a hard time standing and so I crouch, my fingers digging into the damp sand. "How?" I wheeze.

"Before they attacked, they hacked the *Persephone*'s frequencies—broadcasting the wrong coordinates," he explains. "The coast guard was always looking in the wrong place. That way they wouldn't be able to find any wreckage or debris and figure out what happened."

"Then how did they find you?"

"The men took us with them. Left us at the other coordinates for the rescue crews to find."

It's difficult to breathe. All this time I'd assumed that if the coast guard had just kept looking they'd have found us. And they never would have. They were searching in the wrong place.

Grey crouches in front of me, not caring about the waves curling up and around his feet, drenching the hem of his pants. "You have to believe me! I didn't know anyone else had survived the attack," he pleads. "They told me everyone else was dead. If I'd thought for a second . . ." He clenches his teeth, eyes glistening.

"Did you know?"

He frowns, puzzled.

"Did you know about the attack beforehand?" I clarify. "Did you know it was going to happen?"

## FORTY-FIVE

Grey's eyes widen, horrified at the idea that he might have known about the attack ahead of time. "God, no! I had no idea—*none*! You have to believe me. Neither did my father."

I laugh at that, the sound sharp. "Believe you?" I shake my head like it's the most ridiculous suggestion in the world.

He winces at the bitterness in my voice. "Libby, please, I'm sorr—"

Hearing that name on his lips is too much, like a slap to the face. I can't bear for him to say it again. "Why did they attack the ship?"

His shoulders drop, resigned. "I don't really know for sure. But from what I've overheard . . . Money. Power. I think there were some people on the ship who were in the way of something." He runs a finger through the sand, watching the divot refill with water. "And they needed someone in the government to protect their interests—they completely control my father now."

"So, what, they took out an entire ship of people so they

could blackmail one Senator?" I scoff. "That seems like a lot of effort—they could have just paid him off."

"But that's the problem, isn't it? If they could buy him off, then someone else could too," he points out. "This way they never have to worry about my father's loyalty."

I press the back of my wrist against my forehead, trying to wrap my head around this. Grey's voice is so calm and even. Whatever rage or fight he may have felt in the past has been tamed, any indignation curbed. "That's not a reason to take out an entire ship full of innocent people," I shout.

"How many wars have been fought—how many people have died—because someone wanted more money or power?" he asks. "Hitler? Pol Pot? Stalin? Alexander the Great? Emperor Hirohito? Napoleon?"

"I know," I cut him off. "It's just . . ." I realize that, more than anything else, I'm disappointed. "I guess I thought there'd be a better reason. Something important."

"People do shitty things for shitty reasons."

The statement hangs in the air for a while before I ask, "Who was behind the attack?"

"I don't know," he mumbles. But his hand reaches up to rub that spot behind his ear. And this is what enrages me. That he would continue to lie. I smack his arm, pushing him backward so that he splashes onto his back in the shallow tide.

"Stop lying!" I scream, kneeling over him. "I deserve the truth!"

He reaches for my wrists but something over my shoulder catches his attention and his eyes go wide. The last time I saw such naked terror on anyone's face was on the *Persephone*. I stiffen, about to turn and look, when Grey flips me over so that I'm beneath him.

His chest crushes mine. I'm so surprised by the move that it takes me a moment before I can even struggle. But Grey's stronger than I am and he has me pinned. I've just drawn a breath to scream when I feel his lips against my ear.

"Please," he begs, "if you've ever trusted me in the past, please just trust me again now." The breath catches in my throat. Frances holding back the scream, giving Grey a chance.

"There's someone watching us from the boardwalk to my house and if he suspects you have your memory back, he'll kill you." My body goes rigid with fear and he runs a hand down my arm, trying to calm me.

Bringing my wrist to his lips, he kisses his way toward my shoulder, making this moment appear romantic to anyone watching. "You have to understand," he continues to explain. "The men behind the *Persephone* are powerful and they'll do anything to stay that way. *Anything*. Why do you think I've stayed silent about this for so long?

"I know you hate me right now, and you should. But just this once, please pretend you don't." He pulls back so that he can meet my eyes. His fingertips whisper against my temple. Our mouths are centimeters apart, his breath spilling and tangling with my own. "Please, I can't bear to lose you."

He doesn't add the word *again*, but it's there in his eyes. Frances reaches for it, consuming every part of me in her effort to break free. And I let her. Because for Frances, Grey will forever be as he was that last night on the cruise ship, unerringly in love with her.

She's never had to confront his lies. Never had to feel the slice of his betrayal. She will never have to sort through the things he's confessed tonight.

Frances is still there on the deck of the *Persephone*, still kissing him as the rain pours down around her. Blissfully unaware that in moments everything she knows about her life will come crashing around her.

Feeling the surge of her passion, I tangle my hands in Grey's hair and drag his lips to my own. I kiss him hungrily, my heel hooking around his calf, pulling him tighter. Tendrils of waves lick up around us, the night a roar of the ocean and the flavor of salt.

And then a man loudly clears his throat nearby. We jerk apart. Grey twists, looking up. That's when I catch a glimpse of the man who's been watching us and the world narrows to one brilliant point of light, focused entirely on him.

There's nothing really all that exceptional about his appearance. He's middle-aged with salt-and-pepper hair and narrow shoulders. The kind of guy you might find behind the window at a bank and then easily forget. Innocuous.

But all I can think is *How is he here?* while in my head it all explodes at once: the sound of screams; the smell of blood; the terror. This man, gun in hand, walking down the hallway of the *Persephone* toward me. Pointing it at Mrs. O'Martin's writhing body and pulling the trigger without hesitation.

*He kicks open the door to our stateroom. My parents huddle on the floor. Nowhere to hide. Their arms around each other. He raises the gun.*

I take a sharp breath, forcing the images away. Forcing my heart to calm and breathing to steady and hands to stop trembling. Forcing myself to remember that I'm not supposed to know this man. Not supposed to recognize him.

I'm not supposed to remember.

*He's a stranger*, I tell myself. *A stranger*.

"Your father's looking for you, Grey," the man says.

Grey's head drops as he curses under his breath. But his eyes are on mine as he rolls off me, searching to see if I have the strength to pull off this charade. An insane part of me wants to laugh at his concern.

If there's anything in life at which I excel, it's playing the role I'm given.

Grey stands, offering a hand to help me up. "This is Thom— head of my dad's security," he explains. His gaze holds mine, begging me to play along with the lie. "With all the media around after Mom's accident, Dad called him in to keep an eye on things."

What goes unspoken is that the "thing" Thom's been charged with keeping tabs on is likely me.

Thom's focus crawls over me, sharp like razor blades slicing up my spine. "And you are?" His voice is more curt than before, keenly honed.

Beside me, Grey tenses, but he needn't be worried. "Hi," I chirp, my own voice grating against the walls of my skull. "I'm Libby. I'm the one who rescued Mrs. Wells."

I hold out a hand and as Thom's fingers slide against mine I bite my cheek hard enough to draw blood. "Thom Ridger," he says. "I'm in charge of the Wellses' personal security and I'm afraid I'm going to have to ask you to go, Libby." His eyes bore into mine, probing to see if I remember.

Bile rises in my throat. Going into this I'd been prepared to see Grey again. To see his entire family and throw myself into their world. But I'd never even considered I'd encounter any of the gunmen from the ship that night. In all my research, I'd never come across a hint of Thom. Never a photo or reference.

I'd assumed the Senator would keep the men involved in the attack at a distance. Unless he wasn't the one pulling the strings. Unless the men behind the *Persephone* were here to make sure the Senator and his family stayed in line.

To make sure I stayed in line as well. I think of Libby's ring, the face scratched. Of the *Libby Too*, now at the bottom of the harbor.

A shiver presses through me. "Sure, I should go," I murmur. I turn to Grey and push up on my toes. "Good night," I whisper against his lips before brushing a kiss across them. Then I'm on the beach, running. Tears blurring my eyes and my heart screaming against my chest as storm winds crest over the dunes.

## FORTY-SIX

The moment Shepherd sees me, his eyes go wide. "Frances!" He races toward me as I stumble through the kitchen door. I'm struggling to breathe, and not just from my sprint down the beach. Every time I close my eyes Thom is there. Standing in front of me. Shaking my hand.

*Kicking down the door to my family's stateroom.*

Shepherd grips my shoulders tight, trying to get me to focus on him.

*Lifting the gun.*

"Frances!"

*My mom staring past him. At me.*

He shakes my shoulders.

*My dad's head snapping back surrounded by a halo of red.*

"Shh, hey." Shepherd's hands shift to my cheeks, pulling my face close to his. So that his eyes meet mine only inches apart. "*Frances*," he whispers. And I blink, struggling to focus.

"It's okay." He tucks my hair behind my ears. I can't stop my teeth from chattering.

"Grey confessed." I choke on the words. "All of it."

Shepherd lets out a long breath in a hiss and eases back. I struggle to bring myself under control. Hating how my body shakes, how my voice trembles. How tears still leak from my eyes. I shrug out of his grip and turn, pressing my hands against my face and inhaling deep.

"Frances . . ." His voice is soft, filled with concern. I shake my head and he says nothing more.

With effort I force my blood into a hum, my heart into a duller rumble. Adrenaline still spills through me, making my stomach roil, and I twist it into cold anger rather than fear. "Grey told me everything."

When I turn to face Shepherd, he leans against the kitchen island, hands braced on the counter by his hips, giving me space. Outside lights flicker in the distance, the storm huddled on the horizon, kicking up lightning. It takes several moments for the thunder to find its way to us, a muffled *thump* and shudder.

I move to the windows, watching the shadows thrown by the patio floodlights—sea oats tangling and dipping in the wind of the approaching storm. Pressing my hand against the glass, I think of the waves, whipping and rising under the pressure of the roiling clouds. Turning from smooth glass to jagged shards.

In a steady voice, I recount everything Grey told me about the *Persephone*. Shepherd pulls out a chair, sitting with his elbows braced against the kitchen table and his head cradled in his hands. He says nothing, just listens, and when I'm finished there's only the sound of the wind and rain.

"But he doesn't know the men behind the actual attack? Why they did it?" he asks.

I turn and lean against the wall, shaking my head. "Only that there was someone on the ship in their way and they needed to get rid of them and secure the Senator's loyalty."

I blow out a frustrated breath, trying to put all the pieces together and failing. "But I've already researched the other passengers. I checked them all and there was nothing."

"Maybe Grey was lying," Shepherd offers.

There'd definitely been something he was holding back, but I don't think it was this. "No, I'm missing something—some connection." I shove my hands through my hair, tugging.

"Then let's go through it again," he says.

Sighing, I pull my cell from my pocket, call up the familiar webpage with photos of the *Persephone* passengers, and toss it toward Shepherd. "Ship's manifest," I explain.

His forehead furrows as he scans down the page. But I don't hold my breath. I've spent so many hours scouring every last detail of the *Persephone* that I practically have it all memorized. I let my head fall back against the wall, remembering.

"Three hundred twenty-seven souls on the ship," I recite. "One hundred seventy-nine male, one hundred forty-eight female. Forty-seven of them kids. Mostly all of them families on vacation. A few girl trips. A couple of corporate retreats. Five couples were celebrating anniversaries and—"

"*Holy shit*," Shepherd breathes, cutting me off.

I swallow what I'm about to say next. I don't even have to ask, Shepherd just turns the screen for me to see. The photo is familiar—the environmental group by the Amazon River, their arms around one another.

I don't understand the significance. "That's the Gaia Agape group," I tell him. "There were fourteen of them on the *Persephone* for their annual meeting. I checked them all out—nothing stood out about any of them."

He stands, running a hand over his head, agitated. "You wouldn't have noticed." He lets out a bitter and incredulous laugh. "That's the thing, *no one* would make the connection unless they were really looking."

"I looked," I interject.

"But you didn't have the right perspective," he explains.

I cross my arms over my chest, hating the implication that in all my years searching I'd missed something. "Which is?"

"I'll show you," he says as he turns and starts from the room. He keeps talking as I chase after him. "The Senator likes to talk about conservation and all of that—gives lip service to the stuff I've been working on down here. It looks good and all, but there's no action behind it. It ticked me off, which is the reason I started looking into his position on other environmental issues—to see how big of a hypocrite he was."

He weaves his way through the house to a tall dark door at the end of a marble hallway. Without the slightest hesitation, he throws it open and steps inside, but I pause on the threshold.

It's Cecil's office. I'd come in here my first day here to grab the bottle of bourbon so I could poison it before handing it over to Cynthia the party planner. But I hadn't lingered. Hadn't wanted to spend any more time than necessary surrounded by things that were so very much *him*.

As Shepherd boots up the computer, I take my time circling the room. Two of the walls are dominated by bookcases, most of the shelves filled with what you'd expect from a man of Cecil's stature and wealth: a collection of leather-bound first editions, framed photos of him with important individuals, antique tchotchkes brought back from faraway lands. I run my finger across them all, wondering about the man who in one breath lost his daughter and wife and in the next gave refuge to a total stranger.

It's hard to find fault with the kind of man who takes in strays like Shepherd and me. Because of Cecil, there was no door closed to me. Except the one to my past. That is why I both love him and hate him.

He saved me, in so many ways: from the ocean; from the tides of whatever system I'd have been thrown into back in Ohio. But the one lifeline he'd cut from me was to that of my own identity.

At the time it had seemed so simple and clear, his reasoning so solid and understandable. Of course it would be easier for me to take his daughter's place, to assume her life. And it's not like the thought of becoming Libby didn't hold its own appeal.

Frances's future was nothing but a gaping black hole. Not Libby's. She still had a brightness to her. Alive I'd envied her. Dead I could become her.

Sometimes I think I had no idea what I'd been giving up when I accepted Cecil's offer. But that's not the truth. I'd known exactly what I was jettisoning—a solitary life of uncertainty, trauma, and pain. It had never occurred to me that the *Persephone* was something Frances could recover from. It had destroyed her more thoroughly than a bullet.

Except that she is still there inside me, growing restless. Perhaps I should have had more faith in her. Perhaps I should have given her a chance.

Perhaps she is stronger than I realized.

"So here's the thing," Shepherd says, interrupting my thoughts. He calls up a webpage and starts typing. "I noticed that the Senator's played a pretty big role in the United States' acquisition of oil from Ecuador. Which is, of course, pretty shitty for the environment. But there's one area in particular that's been at issue."

He clicks on a map, zooming in on an area in South America. I move around the desk to peer over his shoulder. "The Bundios National Park," he says, pointing. "Thousands of square miles of pristine rain forest with a couple of isolated indigenous tribes. And, of course, it's sitting on massive oil reserves." He turns and looks up at me, his eyes bright with conviction.

"Close to a decade ago, Ecuador entered into a deal with the Bundios Preservation Fund that, if they could raise the money, Ecuador would put the entire area under protection and prohibit drilling."

"Okay," I say, wondering where this is going.

"Well, the Bundios Preservation Fund was really just a coalition of various environmental groups, the most prominent being Gaia Agape. For a while it actually looked like they were going to pull it off and then . . ." He lifts a shoulder. "The whole deal just sort of collapsed. But not all at once. A few celebrities stepped in, trying to raise awareness but they were never able to raise the money they needed. It was never all that clear what caused it to fail, but it seems like the trouble started about four years ago."

He pauses, waiting for me to make the connection. When I do, I frown. "Which is when the *Persephone* sank," I point out.

He nods. "Exactly. The *Persephone* went down, wiping out most of the Gaia Agape leadership. The same people who were the key players in the Bundios Preservation Fund."

My heart races at the possibility that we've uncovered something important, but I hold myself back, not wanting to set myself up for disappointment. "You think that's who Grey was talking about?"

He sits forward, face flushed with excitement of this discovery. "Here's the connection: Once it was pretty clear the whole endeavor was going to fail, a small private company stepped in and offered Ecuador a substantial amount of money for drilling rights in the area. And Ecuador didn't have much of a choice in accepting it because the US had just significantly cut the amount of aid we sent to them."

He waits for me to put the pieces together, and when I do a flood of anger pours into my system. "Let me guess," I bite out. "As a ranking member of the Senate Foreign Relations Committee, Senator Wells was influential in determining how much aid the US sent to Ecuador. Which means he could push the US to cut that aid in order to force Ecuador's hand with the Bundios National Park."

He nods. "Plus he was instrumental in negotiating a deal so that the US became one of the largest purchasers of Ecuadorian oil."

I pace across the room to the wall of windows. Outside, rain pummels the ground, sending steam from the sunbaked concrete hissing into the night air. But as I think it all through I realize just how absurd it all sounds. "So, what, take out an entire cruise ship just to kill fourteen people?" I ask, turning toward the desk.

He lifts a shoulder. "It worked, didn't it?" He says it so matter-of-factly that my rage only grows.

"It shouldn't have!" I spit back.

"Think about it—there's no easy way they could have killed that many people without arousing suspicion," he offers. "They had to make it look like an accident so no one would ask questions."

I yank on the ends of my hair in frustration. "There are so many other ways to pull it off," I shout. "Think about the amount of effort that attack took! All the ways it could have failed."

"But it didn't," he points out again. "Everything worked out. They got rid of the core Gaia Agape leadership and put Senator Wells in their pocket. The Bundios Preservation Fund failed and the Senator fixed it so that Ecuador had no choice but to sell off the oil rights."

My head aches and I rub at my temples. Exhausted. Heartsick. "To what end?"

"Money?" he offers. "Power? The company that bought those drilling rights—DMTR—took in several billion dollars in sales last year alone. Almost all of it from the US."

Something jolts in my memory. That name—DMTR. I think back to when I'd hastily searched the Senator's office after rescuing Mrs. Wells. There'd been a stack of folders filled with financial documents—all of them with DMTR stamped across the top. There's no way it can be a coincidence.

"*Holy shit*," I whisper, dropping into a chair as it all falls into place. "The Senator's been getting money from DMTR," I explain. "He's had a stake in this entire scheme."

# FORTY-SEVEN

S hepherd and I sit in silence, minds spinning through the revelations. Now that I know the truth I feel numb.

*And I wouldn't have figured it out if it hadn't been for Shepherd.*

He'd held the piece of information I'd been missing. "Why didn't you mention Gaia Agape and the connection with the Senator before?"

He lets out an incredulous laugh. "Why would I? Until this week I didn't know there was any reason to question what happened on the *Persephone*. I didn't even realize that's what caused Gaia Agape to fold—I had no idea they were on that ship. I just knew they couldn't raise the money and the whole deal collapsed."

I run a hand over my face, reading between the lines of his answer. If I'd only talked to him earlier . . . if I hadn't kept him at a distance all this time . . . if I'd trusted him . . . the truth would have come out years ago.

The what-ifs unravel endlessly.

Except there's still a piece missing. "You ever heard of a guy named Thom Ridger?"

Shepherd thinks for a moment before shaking his head. "Why?"

I consider telling him that Thom's the man who killed my parents and who shook my hand earlier tonight. A shiver presses through me at the memory and I pull my feet up onto the chair, wrapping my arms around my legs.

He stands, coming around the desk. "Why?" he presses.

If I tell him that one of the men involved in the attack is in town he'll want to call Morales. He'll say it's too dangerous. If he was worried about me meeting Grey on my own earlier tonight, there's no way he won't pull the plug once he learns about Thom.

And he's right. Thom is deadly. He's a murderer and probably the one who sank the *Libby Too*. But once we call Morales, this is all over. I lose control.

The cops have to follow rules. I don't.

If there's one thing I know for sure, it's that no one else will ever be able to make the Senator pay. Even if there was an investigation, the worst that would happen is there'd be a few hearings. Maybe his Senate seat would be at risk; though, given South Carolina's history of reelecting disgraced politicians, even that is unlikely.

No, I want Senator Wells to pay. And I want to be the one who makes it happen. That's why I'm here. There's nothing else left for me. No future to return to.

There is only this. And I don't intend to let anyone stop me.

Shepherd looks at me expectantly, waiting. I lift a shoulder. "He's no one."

He frowns, eyes searching mine, waiting for more. But he should know by now that I can outlast almost any silence. Finally, he lets out a long sigh and sits back against the edge of the desk. "Have you ever talked to anyone about what happened on the *Persephone*?"

I lift a shoulder. "Dozens of people. Shrinks, therapists, hypnotists, doctors. You name it, I've talked to it."

"But did you tell them the truth?" he counters.

The corners of my lips twitch, but not in any way that resembles a smile. "Who cares about the truth?"

"Look, I'm your friend here, okay? This is what friends do—they talk. They help each other out." When I don't respond, Shepherd tilts his head to the side. "Do you even have any other friends?"

I'm about to shoot back a smart-ass response but the way Shepherd's looking at me I realize he deserves better. I actually consider the question. There were girls at school I was friendly with, but none I felt comfortable getting close to. We always hit a wall, a limit to how much I was willing to share about myself. I was afraid of messing up—mixing Frances's memories in with Libby's.

Plus, a part of me had grown to resent the other girls in my class. Girls who complained about inconsequential things like allowances, homework, and vacation destinations. There were times my palms bore bloodied indentions from my nails, me squeezing my fists to keep from erupting.

*Your problems are petty!* I wanted to scream at them. *Watch your parents get murdered and then spend a week lost at sea as the only person you have left in the world dies! Then see what really matters in life!*

It was safer for everyone for me to keep to myself. That way I wouldn't have to care when I was the only one left in the dorm during a school dance. I wouldn't have to care when none of the other girls invited me home over long weekends.

And I wouldn't have to care when school ended and we all went separate ways.

"Anyone?" Shepherd prods.

I shake my head.

"Has it been this way since the *Persephone*?" There's concern in his voice—but there's more than that. Anger, almost. I can't stand the thought of his pity. The thought of his caring at all. I don't want anyone caring about me anymore. The reason I don't have friends is because I don't need them. I don't need anyone.

"I'm going to bed," I tell him, standing.

But his hand shoots out, grabbing my elbow. "You can't keep pushing people away."

"Watch me," I fire back, trying to twist out of his grasp. The girl trapped inside me—the girl still drowning and desperately in need of help—howls to give in. To fall against him and let him put his arms around me and tell me it will be okay.

Just please, for one minute, let someone else carry the burden of all this pain. I fight against her, wrestling her into submission.

I'd given in to her once tonight and look where it got me.

"Frances." He says it like a warning but it strikes more like a slap. A bitter reminder of who I'm supposed to be and why I'm here.

*I am Elizabeth O'Martin*, I remind myself. *I am cold destruction, calculated retribution.* I try to pull ice around my heart, but Shepherd's touch on my arm is too warm, melting through it.

"So if you don't get close, you can't lose them? You can't get hurt?" he asks.

"It's worked for the past four years." I glare at him, daring him to contradict me. "I was doing just fine before."

"No, you weren't." His grip softens along with his voice. "That's a lonely way to look at life. Trust me," he says, trying to meet my eyes. "You have to let someone in, Frances."

I think about Grey. About his lips against my collarbone, his hands dancing along my hips. I think about how easy it is to see that he's broken when you know where to look.

And how I'm broken in all the same ways.

*But I wouldn't be broken if it weren't for the* Persephone, I remind myself.

If it weren't for Grey and his lies.

For the Senator and his greed.

The familiar warmth of rage fills my heart. Who needs anyone else when I have this? "No, I don't." I turn on my heel and stride from the room.

"You don't know how to let people care about you, do you?" he calls after me.

I freeze, my back bristling.

"You should try it sometime. You might actually find you like it."

As much as I'd love to turn and face him, I don't. Because I don't want him to see the truth: that I know he's right. And it still doesn't matter. "I did once," I tell him. "And then they all died."

He comes up behind me. Not close enough to touch. Just enough to lower his voice. "Everyone dies, Frances."

I shake my head. "Not like that, they don't. Not ripped away."

"You blame them for taking your life away back then, and maybe they did. But you're the one keeping life at bay now."

I inhale sharply, ready to argue, but he doesn't let me. "You've got to let someone in, Frances," he says, slipping past me into the hallway. "Even if it's not me. Yes, it's a risk and, yes, it's scary. But that's what life is." He shrugs and starts for his room, leaving me standing alone. "You should try it sometime."

## FORTY-EIGHT

After everything that's happened, it should be easy to sleep, but I lie in bed awake, Shepherd's words churning through my thoughts. No matter how many times I tell myself he's wrong, I know he's right. I can't go on like this forever—so alone and removed. Isn't that why I came here after all? Because living as Libby had become untenable?

Something had to change and if I wasn't willing for it to be me, then the only other option was to change the situation.

And yet now that I know the truth, now that all the pieces are falling into place, there's still something missing. Shepherd was right: I've been afraid. And I'm tired of being afraid.

Cursing under my breath I slide out of bed and make my way down to the kitchen. My cell phone is still on the table from earlier tonight, and I reach for it. After a moment of thought, I text Grey.

*Your father's been getting payouts from the men involved in the* Persephone *attack.*

I've just pressed send when my phone rings. Unsurprisingly, it's him.

"Jesus, Libby, you can't just say something like that!" His voice is barely more than a breath. "What if my father or Thom had seen it?"

"Aren't you tired of being afraid of them?" I ask.

There's silence. And then this, "I have to go." The line goes dead.

I stare at the phone, waiting for something more. But it doesn't come. And eventually I give up. *It was a stupid thought anyway*, I tell myself as I push back from the table.

Outside lightning dances over the ocean, thunder rolling through the waves to reach shore. I watch the storm roll in for a while, tapping my fingertips against the kitchen window as my mind continues to spin.

I'm just turning to make my way back to bed when a sharp noise sounds outside. Through the darkness a figure reaches for the door. I open my mouth to scream when he looks up.

It's Grey. My pulse hitches and then roars. I throw the latch, pulling it open. But he doesn't come inside. Instead he wraps a hand around my wrist, pulling me into the rain.

I suck in a breath against the sudden deluge, water instantly drenching me. "What—?"

But he doesn't let me speak. "You're the one I'm afraid of," he says, voice rough and insistent. "Don't you understand? For four years I've tried to forget. About the *Persephone*. About Frances. About all of it. And you show up, bringing it all back to the surface."

"Grey—"

He backs me against the wall, crowding close. His wet fingers slide up my cheeks to bury in my hair. "I'm drowning," he whispers, his forehead touching against my own.

And then I don't care about the rain. I don't even feel it. I only know the rise and fall of his chest. The pulse in his fingertips.

I tell him a truth I didn't even know existed until this moment. "So am I."

His eyes search mine for a long moment. "Run away with me."

I laugh, but it's rueful.

"I'm serious," he insists. "Let's go somewhere where none of them can find us. Leave it all behind and start over."

The heel of his palm is warm against my temple and I lean into it, turning my head to press my lips lightly against his wrist. "I can't."

He drops his hands, turning away in frustration. He paces across the patio, gripping the back of a chair, shoulders straining against the tension. Rain falls around him, against him. His shirt clings to his wet skin, water dropping from the hem of his shorts.

"Don't you want to know the truth about it all? Don't you want it to all come out?" I ask, stepping toward him.

He turns to look at me. "Is that what matters most to you?"

I open my mouth to answer, but no words come.

"I'm falling in love with you, Libby." He says it desperately.

The words strike like a blow to the chest. There's no way he can know just how cruel it is. How that name renders meaningless any statement attached to it. For a moment I allow myself to believe he could be telling the truth. That it could be real.

And then I touch a hand to his shoulder, gripping it like it's the only thing keeping me from falling up into the water-filled sky. "You can't be," I tell him softly. "You barely know me."

His head drops and he says nothing. And then this: "You do handstands in the pool when you think no one's looking. When you pick up a book in a store, you stand on one foot and tuck the other against your knee while you read the first page. You close your eyes when you take the last bite of anything chocolate."

My breath catches and he looks over at me. "You can be bitter and angry, but when you laugh . . ." He smiles. "When you laugh you completely let go." He reaches out, grabs a tendril of my wet hair, and lets it slip through his fingers. "When you're scared you wrap your hair around your finger."

His eyes meet mine. "Frances did the same thing."

And I'm sure that he must know. That, like Shepherd, there are too many tiny things that make up the uniqueness of a person and there's no way I've captured all of Libby's.

No way I've eradicated all of Frances's.

Except that Grey keeps going. "But the difference between you and Frances is that you're scared—all the time." The statement hits so true that my gut clenches. He's close enough that I have to tilt my head back. "And I know this because I'm scared all the time too. I just didn't realize it until I saw the exact same thing in you."

His lips hover, just over mine. "So when you ask me if I'm tired of being scared, my answer is yes. I'm tired of being scared of the way you make me feel. I'm tired of being scared of letting myself be in love with you. I'm tired of being scared of life."

Then his mouth is on mine in a kiss, raw edged and hungry. There's anger in the way his lips press against mine, the way his fingers dig against my spine, pulling me closer. My own anger responds to the call, surging within me and setting every nerve ending on fire.

His hand wraps around the back of my neck, holding me steady as he pulls away slightly. Our breath tangles a fast rhythm between us. His pupils are dangerously dark, eclipsing the deepwater blue of his eyes, as his gaze bores into me.

"Don't you think we deserve to move on from the past?"

Somewhere inside me, Frances crashes through all the walls I've used to hold her back. She bursts under my skin, howling. For having her future taken from her. From being denied all these years. Until now I'd been willing to burn down my own life in order to out the truth, but now I'm not so sure.

Because I remember the moment on the *Libby Too* four years ago, right after I'd been rescued, when I learned that Grey was still alive. I remember how it made me feel, that perhaps in this darkness there was someone else out there, someone who understood, and maybe together we could find a spark of light.

Looking at Grey now, tasting him and breathing him in, I realize that's what he's been. A beacon for Frances, a way for her to reach forward—to want again.

And what she wants so desperately is to move on from the past. She wants exactly what Grey is offering. But there is only one path to that place and it involves the truth.

Not the truth about the *Persephone*. The truth about me.

I say the words fast, before I can stop myself. "I'm Frances."

Silence. Even the rain stutters for a moment before resuming with a roar that matches the rush of my pulse. Grey blinks slowly, water dropping from his lashes. Then he steps back. His eyes scour me, top to bottom.

"What?" he asks, though it's clear he heard me. He just doesn't understand yet.

I swallow. "I'm not Libby. She died out on the life raft. When we were rescued I took her identity." I chew my lip for a moment, waiting for him to say something.

He shoves his hands through his hair. "I don't . . ." He turns to face the ocean and then back to me. "Frances?"

I nod, the thrill of that name on those lips. There's such an unbearable freedom in having told him the truth. Having unleashed this last secret. I reach for him but he jerks away as though my touch were molten.

He can't seem to find the right question, just shaking his head as he says, "What? I don't . . . How?"

"I was an orphan and Cecil was afraid the men who attacked the *Persephone* would come after me," I rush to explain. "He did it to keep me safe." I step closer, not quite touching him. "It's me. I'm Frances."

There's a flash of hunger in his eyes and that seems to pull him from his trance. He staggers back, putting distance between us. "*You lied*," he whispers.

"Only because I had to," I argue.

"The real Frances would have trusted me." Had his words been daggers they could not have landed more sharply in my heart.

"I *am* the real Frances."

But he just shakes his head. "Maybe you were Frances in the past." His eyes sweep over me one last time. "But you're certainly not anymore."

He starts across the patio to the beach, his steps ragged. "Grey!" I start after him, but he holds up a hand.

"Whatever there was between us—it's done."

Everything inside me is sliding out of place. "Wait," I cry, my eyes blurred with tears and rain. "Give me a chance to explain!"

He stops at the base of the boardwalk. The way he looks at me is how I know that we're done. Fundamentally and irrevocably. "No," he says simply. And then he's lost to the night and the rain. And so am I.

# FORTY-NINE

Shepherd's the one to find me outside on the patio, curled over myself as the rain continues to crash down around me. Lightning splits the sky overhead, sending thunder shuddering through my bones. Right now I would love nothing more than to be struck by it, laid low in one fell swoop.

"What the hell are you doing out here?" Shepherd shouts, grabbing my elbow and hauling me to my feet.

I'm so numb emotionally that I'm not even sure how to answer. "It's over," I tell him.

With an arm around my shoulders, he guides me inside. "What's over?" he asks once we're out of the rain.

I shake my head. "All of it. I told Grey the truth. I told him who I really am."

Shepherd sucks in a breath. "And?"

I slip out from under his touch, turning to face him. Drops of rain glisten in his hair and across his cheeks. I consider him for a moment. "Could you have ever loved me?"

He's so taken aback by the question that he actually,

physically recoils. Which should be all the answer necessary. But still, I need to hear it.

"You as Libby or you as Frances?" he asks.

"Me as me."

To give him credit, he actually thinks about it. But after a long while, he eventually shakes his head.

It's what I'd expected, but still it hurts. "Why not?" He squirms and I press him again. "Why not?"

"Because I could never trust you," he eventually confesses. He braces for my response.

We stand that way for a moment until finally I nod. "That's because you're smart." And the irony is that this is perhaps the most honest either of us has been with each other. I turn and start for bed.

"You never could have loved me in the first place," he counters. "Not like that."

I glance over my shoulder at him. "Why, because I'm incapable of love?"

He shakes his head. "Because your heart has always belonged to someone else. Just like mine."

A bitter laugh rises up my throat like acid. "Then I guess we're both screwed, aren't we?"

"You can fix it, you know," he calls after me.

I hesitate only a second, considering the possibility. But he didn't see the way Grey looked at me. Grey's done with me. "No," I tell him. "I can't. Not this time."

When I wake, it's close to dawn and I frown. Sitting up, I clutch the sheet as I hear the pounding from downstairs, followed by the bright peal of the doorbell. And I realize that this is what has woken me up. Something about the moment feels off, out of step—the banging on the door too urgent for the sun not to have risen yet.

Cold dread begins uncurling in my gut and I race down the stairs. When I throw open the door to find Morales standing on the porch, I'm somehow not surprised.

As though this moment were inevitable—already written and simply being played out.

"Libby," she says with a tight nod. The whites of her eyes are red, the rims raw. "There's been an accident." She's so formal the way she's standing on the porch, rain still dusting her shoulders from her dash from the car.

A sharp wind blows across the yard, sending a wash of wet mist to surround us. Behind me, the house yawns empty and I know. Shepherd's not here. In that way that the air shifts when it has to accommodate another body in the same space.

He's gone.

I shake my head.

My hand clutches the edge of the door.

"May I come in?" Morales asks gently. Her eyes are broken, though, and I wonder how many times she's had to do this. How many people she's pulled out of bed to shatter their life.

A part of me wonders if I tell her no, will it undo any news she's come to tell me. But if it were possible to do such a thing, I'd have figured it out long ago. If there's one thing the *Persephone* taught me, it's that the saying is true: Not being known doesn't stop the truth from being true.

I step aside and Morales follows me into the living room. I

gesture toward the couch but I'm too restless to sit and so I stand behind a chair, fingers gripping the back of it.

There's no preamble. She's not that kind of person. "I'm sorry to be the one to tell you this," she says. "But Shepherd was in a serious car accident earlier this morning. He's been airlifted to MUSC up in Charleston for surgery. He's suffered a severe head injury, and though the doctors are optimistic, they won't know for a day or two the extent of the damage."

With every word, the world begins to constrict around me. It becomes difficult to breathe. There has to be something I'm supposed to do here. Something I'm supposed to say. "I need to see him," I tell her. But I take only one step toward the door before I stop.

I don't even know if he'd want me there.

But it doesn't matter anyway. "He can't have visitors yet," Morales informs me. "I've already asked. I've given them your number and told them you're family. They'll call when they have updates."

It was a mistake not to sit, I recognize this now. I sink into the chair. "What happened?" I'm the one asking the question, but it feels as though the words come from someone else's body.

"It looks like his car crashed through the guardrails on the connector to the mainland and fell into the marsh. There's still no word on the cause, but we're investigating." She leans forward. Exhaustion pulls at the skin beneath her eyes. "Do you know where he might have been going?"

I think through the night before, but nothing stands out. "No, he didn't mention anything. He was here when I went to bed."

I pull at my hair. It's still wet. And I have to bite my lip to keep it from trembling as I remember him finding me in the rain, bringing me inside.

Telling me that I could fix what was broken.

She nods, staying silent. Waiting for me to add more. But there's nothing else to say. Her eyes wander across the pictures scattered across on top of the coffee table. She reaches for one and my back stiffens. In it Shepherd and Libby hang upside down from the monkey bars of a swing set.

"He's a good kid," she says. I nod. There's a long stretch where we both stare at the photo. And I realize that there's no one left to remember that moment with him.

I press my fingers against my temples, trying to keep my emotions from cracking through to the surface. Trying to hold it together.

Finally Morales sets the frame down and moves toward the door. "If you think of anything else, will you let me know? You still have my cell number?"

I nod again. She starts to let herself out but then pauses. "Shepherd's tough—he'll make it through this," she reassures me. "I'll be keeping him in my prayers." Before she closes the door she adds, "Make sure to lock up."

Once she's gone, I sit silent for a moment. I've been so alone for so long you'd think I'd be used to it. Yet somehow the house feels too empty. Too wrong and cold.

My first instinct is to reach out—call someone to share the burden of this pain. But there's no one. It hits home what Shepherd told me earlier tonight: that by keeping everyone at bay, I've made it so that there's no one there when I need them.

Restless, I wander into the kitchen. My cell phone still sits on the table and I grab for it, intending to call MUSC and check on Shepherd. But when I swipe it open, a series of texts fills the screen.

The first is from Grey: *About earlier. Can we talk? In person?*

And then one from me: *Yes.*

Except that I never sent that. My blood runs cold.

From Grey: *My dad has the place on lockdown so it can't be nearby. There's an all-night diner where the connector hits 17—meet there?*

Me: *Leaving now.*

The last message is from Grey: *Thank you, Libby. You don't know how much this means.*

I close my eyes, chest tight and breathing difficult. Imagining Shepherd standing in the kitchen after I've gone to bed, my phone on the counter vibrating with an incoming text. Shepherd glancing at it. Deciding to answer.

Deciding it was time he faced Grey himself.

Morales's question from earlier echoes through my head: *Do you know where he might have been going?*

Apparently he was going to meet Grey.

And then a horrible realization tears its way through me: No, *I* was the one going to meet Grey. I run to the garage, throw open the door. The car I've been using is missing.

Feeling weak, I brace myself against the wall, sinking until I'm sitting. In the dark of night and with all the rain, it would have been impossible to tell who was driving. And why would anyone expect someone other than me?

I'm the one they've been after. I'm the witness from the *Persephone*. I'm the one they tried to kill on the *Libby Too*. I'm the one who's been making waves, stirring things up.

I curl over myself, pressing my forehead against my knees. I'm the one who was supposed to be run off the road tonight. Not Shepherd. It's my fault Shepherd's in the hospital. My fault he was brought into this at all.

Every life I've touched since jumping from the *Persephone*, I've ruined. I begin to sob, finding it difficult to breathe. The pain is too great, an undertow dragging me too deep. Already I feel Frances beginning to drown inside me. She'd broken through the surface for one last choking gasp but it wasn't enough.

She was never strong enough for this. From the beginning it has always *my* job to survive. It's what I do best. What I was made for.

A familiar heat starts at my toes, roaring up my body. Like stepping into a scalding sea it sears through me, this familiar haze of red, burning through my grief. Rage tastes like bitter fresh blood and cut grass, and it is as comforting to me as a summer afternoon.

Swiping the tears from my eyes, I reach for my phone and pull up the map. I type in a destination: Winter Hills Cemetery, Ohio. It will be long drive, but the anger coursing through me will keep me awake.

It is time for this to end. For everyone to finally pay. But it will be on my terms and no one else's.

# FIFTY

Once, only a few weeks after I'd been pulled from the ocean, I begged Cecil to take me to see my old home in Ohio. He refused, claiming it was too risky for me to be seen out in public. Especially in my hometown. What if someone recognized me?

Driving into my old neighborhood now, after a four-year absence, I understand the real reason he said no. It would have devastated me beyond repair.

It's early evening when I turn onto my street and any weariness I may have felt from the ten-hour drive instantly disappears the moment the house on the corner comes into view. My breath catches as I slow to peer in the windows.

Little has changed—there's the same sweep of flowers across the front porch, the same mailbox listing slightly by the curb. Lights blaze out of the downstairs window, highlighting the perfect scene of domesticity inside.

A family. Just like mine had been. The mother sweeping into the kitchen to grab something as the father and son take their places at the dining room table.

I wonder if they know what happened to the family who lived there before. Who measured the years in height marks on the wall in the hall closet. Who buried three goldfish, two hamsters, and a parakeet in the back garden.

Who are themselves buried in a cemetery at the edge of town.

I wonder if they realize how fragile it all truly is?

Somewhere nearby a car door slams, pulling me out of my reverie. I glance up to see a neighbor standing in his driveway, head tilted as he looks at me. He raises his hand, waving, the way you would to anyone else passing down the street. Automatically I lift my fingers from the wheel in greeting as I press on the gas and wend my way out of the neighborhood.

*Josh Reilly*, I think to myself. That's who waved at me. He's two years older than me and was part of the popular crew at school. I'd spent countless hours riding my bike in front of his house, hoping—and failing—to "accidentally" run into him. And here I am back in town less than fifteen minutes and there he is.

It actually makes me laugh. All these things that had seemed like such monstrous concerns at the time—like trying to capture Josh Reilly's attention—and now they're worth nothing.

I make my way out past the edge of town and park my car where no one will pay much attention to it. Holding my breath, I call the hospital to check on Shepherd but nothing has changed. They're still monitoring his condition, waiting for the swelling around his brain to go down. There's nothing I can do but wait. They'll call me if anything changes. I clench my teeth, hating how useless I feel.

There are still several hours yet before nightfall and I'm exhausted; I might as well try to grab some sleep while I can. But as I crawl into the backseat to take a nap, I can't stop thinking about what my life would have been like if we'd never stepped foot on that cruise ship.

I don't know if there's a proper time to dig a grave, but I figure that after midnight is a pretty good bet. So when the dashboard clock ticks over into the new day, I slip from the car and grab my tools from the trunk. It's cooler in Ohio than I've grown used to recently and my arms prickle into goose bumps as a dark breeze whistles past me. Soon enough, I know, I'll be sweating so I don't bother pulling on a jacket.

Overhead, clouds skitter across the sky providing me with a bit more cover. Not that it seems necessary, I think, scanning my surroundings. The cemetery's not a large one, but thankfully it's remote—tucked away past the outskirts of town.

I don't need a flashlight to find my way. I already know exactly where to find my family's plot nestled beneath the boughs of a drooping willow. Though Cecil refused to ever bring me here, that doesn't mean I haven't often thought about it. Planned it. Used pictures I found online to help me imagine what it would be like.

When I finally reach the gravesite, though, I find that I can only stare at the line of headstones. One for my mother. One for my father. One for me.

I'm stuck, frozen, the tip of my shovel resting gently against the ground. There's something about seeing my own name and the dates beneath it that causes my lungs to squeeze.

It's as though I don't exist. Perhaps I never have. I've somehow become neither Frances nor Libby, but some sort of in-between. Something cold and hard, impenetrable to pain.

And yet pain has found me just the same. It seems as though it's impossible to live a life without it.

I fall to my knees, curling over myself to press my cheek against the dew-stained grass. The layers of dirt between me and my parents are nothing compared to everything else that separates us.

The number of times my heart has beat when theirs has not. The number of breaths I've taken, steps I've traveled, words I've spoken. While they've been here. Motionless. Voiceless. Bloodless.

Dead.

*Because of Alastair Wells and Thom Ridger.*

But just as on the yacht when I lay on the bed where they'd placed Libby's body, I don't belong here. I am not dead the way Libby and Frances are.

Though somehow I'm not alive either.

I am nothing except this: a girl reborn of the deep ocean silence, meant for nothing but vengeance.

Which is what pushes me to my feet. I grab the shovel and thrust the bladed end into the ground. Letting anger bolster my courage and spur me forward.

Thankfully, it's a myth that a grave must be dug six feet deep. In actuality, most cemeteries only require twenty-four inches of dirt between the top of the coffin and the surface. Just enough to make sure the grass can grow back.

Which is a good thing because, even fueled by rage, my muscles begin to protest before long. By the end of the first hour, they're burning and at the end of the second they're screaming.

That's when the tip of the shovel connects with something solid. And I gasp. With relief and perhaps also a bit of dread.

Here's the thing about revenge: How many times does someone say, "I'll kill him," when they feel wronged? Their first instinct to lash back violently? But the truth of the matter is, death is too swift and sweet.

Living is more difficult. Living with pain, with guilt, with loss.

I'd rather my enemies live a long and healthy life. What better way for them to fully reap the rewards of their misdeeds?

## FIFTY-ONE

After the long drive back to the O'Martin estate, the first thing I do is call the hospital again to check on Shepherd. He's still unconscious—only time will tell if there's been permanent damage. The rage of it crashes over me like a tidal wave, robbing me of the last of my energy. I collapse into bed and sleep through the afternoon and evening. Waking only long enough to check in once more before passing out again.

When I finally do wake the next afternoon it's to my cell phone ringing. I fumble to answer, sleep making my voice raspy as I say hello. The caller explains she's one of Shepherd's doctors and I jolt in bed, my heart constricting painfully. But the news is good. Though Shepherd's still unconscious, the swelling around his brain has gone down enough for them to run several scans and the results have been encouraging. She's optimistic that, barring any complications, he'll make a full recovery.

I practically sob with relief thanking her over and over again before asking when I can visit. "Anytime," she tells me, and I let her know I'll be in tomorrow.

Even though I know it's a lie.

After hanging up I let out a long sigh, collapsing back onto the pillows. It isn't long before the implications of the news set in. Now that I know Shepherd will be okay, I can start the endgame.

I scroll through my call history, looking for the Senator's number from when he helped me locate my "lost" phone in his car. I spent much of the long drive back from Ohio planning through every detail, including what to text the Senator. I quickly type out the message:

*Senator Wells, this is Libby O'Martin. Certain information has come to light that I'd like to discuss. It's probably best done in person. Would this evening work? Maybe around 8?*

A bubble appears under my text, indicating he's typing a response. I wait for several minutes. When his reply finally comes through it's a curt *I look forward to it.*

Smiling, I roll onto my side and stare out at the ocean, contemplating how I want to spend my last day. There are still a lot of preparations to be done. I've had to scrap my original plan—come up with something new and speed up the timeline. But I'm content with what comes next.

I've made peace with my impending death.

A few hours later, my hand trembles as I tuck a stray strand of hair behind my ears. In front of me, a fireproof lockbox sits open on my dressing table. Inside I've stashed a variety of important documents: Libby's birth certificate, a baby book containing a lock of her hair from when she was an infant.

Next to it are two stacks of journals: Libby's from before the *Persephone*, mine from after. I flip through Libby's first, running my fingers across a random page. It's been strange to know her so well, parts of her that she shared with no one else. For a while I thought that by living her life I'd somehow kept her alive, but I've come to learn I've done just the opposite.

I've robbed her of her right to be remembered for who she'd been. Though I plan to remedy that soon—give her the chance to be mourned as she deserved.

The second stack of journals is written in my own hand, at first carefully crafted to mimic Libby's until it became my own by habit. Just like so much of her. These pages are too difficult to flip through. Too painful.

They're more the truth about who I've become than anything else.

I shove each stack into a separate waterproof bag and then pull my notebooks out from under the bed. The ones that so carefully lay out my research, that show every step of my original plan before it went off the rails. I'd spent several hours filling in the missing details—everything about Ecuador and DMTR. The Senator's corruption and Grey's complicity in covering it up. Enough to bring them all down. I shove it all into the second waterproof bag along with my journals, and a backup of the video from Grey's phone, making sure to seal it up tightly.

And then, with everything else taken care of, I look up, into the mirror. For the last time I slip free the picture of Frances and Libby taken on the cruise ship. I tuck it under the edge of the mirror so that once again I'm the ghostly reflection, hovering above the two smiling faces frozen in time.

What would those two girls think if they could see me now? Sitting in a house doused in gasoline, a box of matches in my pocket. Would they think me weak that after four years I'm ready to finally end this? To be done with both of them?

It's been hard to carry around the ghosts of *two* girls. Their expectations and dreams. Truthfully, I've failed both of them.

Behind all three of us, the ocean is reflected in the mirror, and for one longing moment, I wish I were back in that raft alone at sea.

Where life was a simple: one more breath. One more beat of my heart.

I sigh and stand. Leaving the photo tucked in the mirror. Leaving the reflection of the ocean. Leaving the fireproof box. Leaving the two waterproof bags. One of Libby's life, the other of Frances's.

For the past four years, my life has always been leading to this moment. I was spared from the ocean, but my body has only been on loan. I'm nothing more than a specter come back to haunt those who've wronged me.

It's too late for my own redemption. Maybe at some point I could have veered away—perhaps if I'd left Libby's ring sitting on the table and refused Cecil's offer. But now I've gone too far down this path of revenge.

I can't go back to who I was before—she doesn't exist. I'd known that going into this.

My death has already been written and there's no way to take it back. My only goal is to take the Senator down with me. I glance at my watch—I have an hour and a half before I'm supposed to meet him.

Just over an hour before I finally get to confront him. To ask him face-to-face what happened before finally making him pay.

I make my way downstairs to double-check that I have everything in place. But when I turn the corner into the kitchen, I realize that there's one contingency I never planned for. Someone's here.

"Hello, Libby," Thom says. He's standing casually next to the kitchen island. A large black gun rests on the counter by his hand.

Adrenaline pours into my system, causing my pulse to sky-rocket.

I take a step back and his fingers twitch toward the trigger. "You won't get far," he warns. "I'm an excellent shot." His lips shift into a slow grin. "But I guess you already know that."

Of course it's Thom. The Senator sent him to do his dirty work, which means the situation has just become infinitely more dangerous. This is not at all in the plan. My eyes dart around the room searching for a way to handle this new variable.

"You were expecting the Senator," Thom says matter-of-factly.

"I—" I cross my arms over my chest, buying time as I try to figure out my next move. "Why are you here?"

He laughs. "No, the question is why are *you* here. I'm guessing it has something to do with this?" He reaches over the papers scattered across the island—copies of the proof I have of the Senator's involvement—and picks up the old bat-tered phone. It's Grey's, from the cruise. After a few clicks, the sound of the attack fills the room.

My knees go weak and I brace a hand against the doorway. "Stop."

He lets out another laugh. "Oh, I'll do more than that." He spikes the phone on the floor. It shatters, pieces skittering in every direction. Then he smiles, satisfied.

"I made a copy, you know," I inform him.

He shrugs. "None of it's enough to cause anyone to take a second look. If you think any of this is proof"—he swipes his arm across the counter, sending the papers flying—"then think again."

Pages flutter to the floor, hitting gasoline-soaked puddles. I clench my jaw. "You'll pay, you know. So will Senator Wells."

His smile has no humor, only power and contempt. "That's the thing. No, we won't."

# FIFTY-TWO

He seems to enjoy watching the fear wash through me, causing my heart to scuttle so quickly that my breathing becomes feathery light and fast. "What do you want?" I ask.

Without any sense of concern or rush, he reaches for the box of matches nearby and strikes one, holding it out in front of him as the bitter puff of smoke snakes up to the ceiling. He sniffs at the air, smiling at my discomfort. "Smells a bit like gas around here, doesn't it?"

I lift my chin, trying to give a show of bravery, but the fact that it trembles doesn't help my cause. I say nothing.

He discards the burned match and lights another one. "I'm just trying to work out why you'd be planning to torch your own house. Though I do have to admit, you've definitely made my job tonight easier. No bullet, no way to trace the gun."

I swallow and press my lips together, trying to rein in my growing distress. I'd planned on dying tonight, but not like this. "I saw you on the *Persephone*, you know."

He laughs, letting the lit match slip through his fingers. I cringe, but the flame flutters out before it hits the floor between two gleaming rivulets of gas. *He won't torch the place while he's inside*, I remind myself. No one would be that stupid.

I hope.

"I assumed as much," he says, as though he hasn't a care in the world. "You have Greyson's mental breakdown to thank for your continued existence. I'd planned on taking you out a few weeks after the cruise, once the media died down, but Wells worried it might be too much for the poor boy's psyche. Plus, you seemed happy to play along with keeping things quiet."

He strikes another match. "Until now, that is. Which is a shame because it turns out I've got to break the poor kid's heart after all."

"He's as bad as the rest of you," I scoff. My eyes dart around the room, searching for a weapon. Or an exit. Anything. "The truth will come out, you know. Even if you kill me."

The corner of his mouth twitches. "*If* I kill you?" he asks, lifting an eyebrow. "I think you mean *when*."

I'm shaking my head, mouth dry. It's like being stuck adrift all over again, unable to swallow. "They'll tie it back to the Senator."

That had been my plan after all. If I couldn't pin the cruise attack on him, at least I could make him pay for killing Libby.

The match burns out against his fingers. He pulls three more free, striking them all at once. My heart gallops at the sting and *pop* of the flame coming to life. "You mean the Senator I just escorted with his family up to dinner at a very crowded restaurant, giving them a nice, tight alibi?"

I bolt. Before I can think twice about it. While he's still sitting all smug and sure of himself, tied up in his own boasting. My bare feet slap against the marble hallway as I careen out of the kitchen, little splashes of gas trailing in my wake, making the turns difficult to navigate.

With a roar, Thom thunders after me.

I race straight to the front door, cursing Morales for telling me to always keep it locked. I've just thrown the bolt, just started turning the knob when Thom crashes into me, slamming me hard against the door. Everything inside me jolts, my bones protesting the sudden pressure. Thom may be skinny, but he's made of muscle, all of it focused on taking me down.

But I know that if I give him room to maneuver, I'm dead. And so I throw my arms around him, keeping him close. He's not expecting it and he staggers a step, giving me just the opening I need.

I lift my knee, kicking hard between his legs. He's able to turn, deflecting most of the blow at the last minute. But not all of it. There's a whoosh of air leaving his lungs. A grunt. A moment where he's distracted enough that I'm able to pull away.

I'm halfway up the stairs when my gas-slick foot slips out from underneath me. My shins slam against the marble steps, sending lightning bolts of pain screaming up my body. I claw at the banister, scrambling, panicked, climbing like a dog on all fours. But Thom's legs are longer than mine and he can take them three at a time. I've barely made it to the top when he lunges. One hand wraps around my ankle, and with a forceful yank, he's pulled me down.

I let momentum carry me toward him, ceasing my struggles for the barest moment so that I can gain leverage. This throws him off balance. Just enough that I slam into him and he bobbles the gun, dropping it in order to grab the railing to keep from falling. It clatters to the floor of the foyer below, well out of reach.

Recovering quickly, he backhands me, sending me crashing onto my side. With a vicious yank of my waistband he flips me onto my stomach and digs his knee into the middle of my back. I'm facedown on the staircase, my throat pressed hard against the lip of one of the stairs, making drawing a breath impossible.

He doesn't need the gun to kill me. Gurgling sounds bubble in my throat as I struggle to wedge my hands under my chest, pressing hard against Thom's weight to ease the pressure on my windpipe. I've just enough strength to lift my head and gulp in a lungful of air. But that's all I can do. I can't move my hands to swipe at him or else I won't be able to breathe. He has me pinned, unable to do anything but kick at the empty air.

Thom fists his hand through my hair and slowly pulls my head back, digging his knee between my shoulder blades. Forcing an unnatural arch into my neck until my body threatens to break. My fingers scratch at the marble of the stair, struggling to keep as much of the pressure off my throat as possible. But even so, I'm choking. Helpless.

The rigid edge of his teeth presses against my ear. "Say good night, Libby."

My eyes whisper closed. *For nothing*, I think. All of it for nothing. What's the point of struggling anymore? After all these years, I'm exhausted. Ready to be done with it.

There's no one left to mourn me.

*Say good night, Libby.*

*Libby.*

My heart jolts. I'm thrown back to that moment on the life raft when Libby gave up. The way her eyes dulled, dried trails of red tears staining her cheeks. She was just done. There was nothing I could do to convince her to keep fighting.

And it was so shocking to me because that's not who Libby was. Libby was vibrant and full of life—she was everything I wasn't. Everything I wanted to be.

Except in this one thing.

Libby wasn't a fighter.

But Frances was.

And I still am.

## FIFTY-THREE

I explode, throwing elbows, arching to buck him off. But his grip is too tight, his knee digging harder into my back, keeping me pinned. He slams me against the stair once and then twice. I brace for a third, but something causes him to hesitate. His fingers twitch against my scalp. A second later, I understand.

*Smoke.* Through the blurry slits of my eyes I peer past the banister to where a curling finger of black snakes its way into the foyer.

Thom curses.

I remember him lighting the three matches, just before I ran. He must have dropped them when he came after me and the flame hit one of the puddles of gas.

*The house is on fire.* And with accelerant doused all over the place, it won't be long before the entire thing blazes uncontrollably. I struggle harder, thrashing. But Thom has something else in mind. He swipes at my hands, yanking them behind my back. Taking away my leverage.

My throat crashes against the lip of the stair and he braces his forearm across the back of my neck, increasing the pressure and choking me in earnest. My windpipe feels like it's being crushed and I can't breathe. I can't breathe. I can't breathe.

Starbursts explode in my vision. Lungs screaming in agony, my mind becomes a blur of light-doused panic. With the last of my energy I flail, doing everything I can to just please— *please*—draw another breath.

Thom doesn't relent. It's obvious what his plan is: choke me to unconsciousness and leave me to burn. Which means the only way to have a chance at survival is to let him think he's succeeded.

It takes everything I have to stop struggling. To somehow override the primal urge for air. I go limp, letting the fight seep from my limbs. He continues the pressure a few heartbeats more and then, finally, he relents.

My first lungful of air burns—from the pain of my bruised throat and from the sting of smoke. But even as I choke and sputter, I continue to feign helplessness. Let him think that I'm too oxygen-starved and weak.

I don't fight as he drags me up the final few stairs by my hair. The air's thicker up here, heavy with smoke billowing from below. Orange light already flickers along the hallways, chewing its way up the walls.

He's running out of time if he wants to get out safely.

I'm running out of time as well.

He's just pulled me around the corner when someone screams my name from downstairs. Thom pauses, listening.

"Frances!" the shout comes again. This time closer and more panicked.

*Grey.*

And at the sound of that name on those lips, a memory shifts into focus. The night of Shepherd's accident—the texts from Grey. He'd said, "Thank you, Libby."

But at that point Grey already knew the truth about me. He'd have never called me Libby. Not even to keep up the charade.

Which means that he wasn't the one to send those texts.

A jolt passes through Thom, his eyes going wide as he recognizes the voice. "Shit," he growls.

I pounce on his hesitation. "Grey!" I try to scream. But the sound comes out limp and scratched. It's nothing against the buffeting roar of the fire.

Thom hauls me to my feet, pulling my back to his chest as he wraps his forearm around my throat. Cutting my air. He drags me down the hallway and into the first room he comes across.

Mine.

I know the instant he sees the bed because he draws a horrified gasp and stumbles to a stop. His arm goes slack in shock and I force my elbow back, jamming it into his stomach. I try to pull free and pivot but my air-starved muscles refuse to cooperate. I make it only two steps before falling to my knees.

"What the *hell* is that?" His voice wavers as he points to the bed.

Behind him, the hallway pulses orange, heat causing sweat to drip down my cheeks. Any moment the flames will ignite the trail of gas into this room. And when it does, that's the end of everything.

That's the endgame of it all.

There's no escaping.

"*What is that!*" he screams louder, advancing toward me.

"I . . ." There's barely anything left to my voice, which is fine because what would I say anyway? That's it's me?

A large groaning noise comes from below as some integral internal structure gives way. The floor shudders and tilts.

He lunges. "What—"

But he doesn't have a chance to finish. There's a loud *POP*. A red gash tears along the side of his throat, blood spraying in a wide arc. Thom clutches at what used to be his neck, eyes wide and mouth gaping as he falls to his knees.

Grey stands behind him. Thom's gun clutched in his hands. He looks at me, face frozen in shock. Not processing what he's done and where he is. He starts to turn and I know that if he does, he'll see the bed.

I stumble, half standing, and lunge for him. When I grab his hand, a bright flare of orange roars up in the mouth of the doorway. It races toward us, spitting sparks and chewing everything in its path. Pulling Grey behind me, I dive for the door to the balcony and struggle to pry it open.

A sharp wind batters its way inside, tossing my hair as it rushes past. Behind me there's a sucking sound, as though the house were alive and breathing. I know what's coming next. The fresh air will fuel the fire, turning it monstrous.

I shove Grey across the balcony. "Jump!" I scream at him. He throws a leg over the balcony and I turn to go back inside.

"Wait, what are you doing?" He reaches for me, but I twist out of his grasp. All of my journals are still in my room—along with the proof I have against Senator Wells. I can't let it get destroyed.

Heat rolls over me in waves as I force my way back into the burning house. My eyes sear from the smoke as I search for the two bags. They're still sitting on the floor by my desk and I grab them.

Grey's hand closes around my arm. "Get out!" He hauls me to my feet, throwing me toward the door. I crash onto the balcony, hit the railing with my hip. I drop the two bags to the ground and turn for Grey.

He's right behind me. "Come on!" I reach out a hand for him.

There's a moment when everything is perfectly still. The house no longer sucking in the fresh air. The flames retreating. Grey's fingers brush against mine.

And then it's nothing but fire. I'm thrown, no up and no down, just me twisting in the air and then my shoulder crashing onto the patio. Above me the sky explodes into a brilliant orange of shattered glass and smoke that swallows the balcony whole. Flames rip through what used to be the doors to my room.

"Grey!" I scream. I have no idea whether he jumped or whether he was caught in the blast. "Grey!" I scream again, pushing to my hands and knees, panicked.

In the distance I hear sirens approaching. I can't be found here, but I can't leave—not until I find Grey.

I can't be responsible for his death.

"Grey!" I shout again, spinning to scour the patio for him.

That's when I see the body, sinking through the ash-smudged water of the pool, limbs limp. "Oh God," I croak, scrambling toward him. I dive in after him and he doesn't fight or even react as my arms circle around his chest.

"Hang on, Grey," I tell him, when I get him to the surface. Except he doesn't cough. He doesn't even move.

I haul him out onto the edge of the pool deck, my hands moving by rote memory as my mind screams: *Not Grey. Not him too.* I pound at his chest, and water dribbles from his mouth and finally—*finally*—he draws a shallow, shuddering breath.

I'm kneeling over him, my hands wiping across his forehead, pushing wet hair from his face, when his eyes flutter open.

"You're okay," I tell him, the words coming out in a relieved sob. "You're okay."

A smile twitches along his lips. "*You're alive*," he whispers.

I'm trembling, my relief is so overpowering. I almost laugh, more of a choking cry than anything else. "I'm not," I whisper, pressing my hand against his cheek, letting my fingers dance across his skin. "I died in the fire—I never made it out. I'm just a ghost, I promise. This isn't real."

He raises his hand to mine, but his grip is weak. "You feel real."

"*I'm not*." I try to smile but fail. "I never have been."

His eyes flutter closed and for a moment I'm worried I'm about to lose him again. But his breathing continues, slow and steady. "I saw the texts—I wasn't the one to send them. I'd never put you in danger like that," he murmurs. "I'm so sorry about Shepherd."

"Shh, I know it wasn't you," I tell him.

He struggles to focus on me. "Dad swore to me that you'd be safe—that you wouldn't get hurt. I shouldn't have believed—" His voice breaks. "Dad was just a pawn. Thom was the one behind it all. I tried to get here in time when I realized he'd gone after you.

"I'm sorry," he wheezes.

Sirens blaze from the front of the house as the fire trucks arrive. I only have moments left.

"I'm sorry too," I whisper.

But his grip tightens on my hand. "No, I mean for the *Persephone*. For Frances. For all of it."

I lower my face and press my forehead against his. "I know. And if Frances were still alive, she'd forgive you too."

He looks at me confused. "But you're Frances." He scores a thumb down my cheek.

I shake my head. "No, you were right before. I haven't been Frances for a long time."

"But—"

"I promise you'll understand soon," I whisper against his cheek.

I let my lips touch against his, lighter than a sigh. "Goodbye, Grey."

And then I'm gone. I grab the two waterproof bags and race down the boardwalk to the beach. To where there's a Zodiac anchored in the dark just beyond the breakers, waiting for me.

To a new life.

# FIFTY-FOUR

Shepherd's asleep, surrounded by an army of beeping machines, when I slip into his room at the hospital. I know it's a stupid risk for me to be here, but he deserves the truth. He's suffered enough because of me.

I set the stack of Libby's journals on a table beneath the window, a stray piece of paper tucked into the top one. All it says is

*For all old myths give us the dream to be.*
*We are outwearied with Persephone;*
*Rather than her, we'll sing Reality.*

I sit for a moment by his side, my fingers wrapped through his. Hating how bruised his face looks under the fluorescent lights. In a soft voice, I tell him everything Libby said about him at the end, when we were on the life raft together. About how much she loved him. How much he meant to her. Several times I have to stop, my voice cracking.

"She is yours again," I finally whisper, pressing a kiss against the back of his hand.

As quietly as I entered, I slip back into the hallway, keeping my head down and shoulders hunched. But my steps slow as I pass an empty hospital room, my attention caught by the television mounted on the wall.

It's turned to a twenty-four-hour news station and an image of my charred house flashes on the screen, the rubble still smoldering as firefighters pick their way carefully through it.

"Police have confirmed that two sets of remains were found in the wreckage," a young man reporting from the site says. "And while DNA tests will still be performed to confirm the identities, police believe one of the bodies belongs to Elizabeth O'Martin. According to an unnamed source with the arson investigators, they think she was in bed asleep when the fire broke out."

Glancing around, I move farther into the room. I press my fingers to my lips, trying to hide my giddy smile over such tragic news.

"And the second body?" the female anchor interrupts to ask.

"Well, that's the more interesting question. Again, these bodies were very badly burned so more tests will be needed before the police will officially confirm anything. But that same source tells me that the second body belongs to Thomas Ridger, a man who apparently worked as a special security consultant for Senator Alastair Wells."

"Speaking of Senator Wells," the female anchor continues. "We have someone on the ground over at his house as well. Let's check in."

The camera switches to a middle-aged man standing in a

swarm of reporters. Behind him, the Senator's house fills the screen, its front driveway cluttered with cop cars.

"It's been a busy morning at Senator Wells's house. Police have been speaking with the Senator for several hours, and just a few minutes ago, we started to see some activity." A buzz goes through the reporters as the front door to the house swings open. The camera shakes for a moment before zooming in as two cops step outside.

And then I see Senator Wells and it's the most amazing sight ever. Even handcuffed, he attempts to appear poised and put together, his back straight and face betraying nothing. But there's just enough off about his appearance to show he's shaken: His face is unshaved, casting his chin and jaw in shadow, and his hair is not as perfectly polished as usual.

I draw a sharp breath as the police escort him to a cop car. Reporters explode into a cacophony of shouted questions, but the Senator ignores them all.

"Wow," the reporter says, eventually stepping back into view. His expression is stunned. "I'm getting confirmation that the police have arrested Senator Wells in connection with the death of Elizabeth O'Martin."

"Is there any word on what the evidence against him is?" the female anchor asks.

The reporter glances down at his notepad. "So far, everything we're getting is off the record. But apparently his son may have been the one to implicate him."

At this my knees go weak and I sink into a chair. *Grey?* I press the heels of my palms to my temples, trying to understand.

I'm interrupted by a knock at the open door. I don't even think twice, I turn toward the noise.

"Nice haircut," Morales says. She's wearing the same old Carolina sweatshirt and jeans. A faint odor of smoke drifts around her like perfume. And though her voice may sound light, it carries an undercurrent of something stronger. "I almost didn't recognize you."

My hand lifts automatically to run my fingers through my new pixie-short hair. "I—" It comes out more as a squeak than anything else, which is fine because I have no idea what to say.

"Mind if I join you?" Morales asks, already stepping farther into the room. I glance toward the door. It's the middle of the night and this wing of the hospital is practically empty. Even so, I'm fairly certain there's no way I could outrun her. Especially given the state of my body after falling from the second-story balcony.

Morales notices my unease because she waves a hand and says, "Don't worry, this is all off the record. For now. I figure we have a few loose ends to tie up." She pulls a chair close to mine and sits, elbows braced on her knees and hands clasped.

For a moment, I can only stare, frozen like a rabbit caught in the sights of a predator. Finally I manage to find my voice. "Do you have word on how Grey's doing?"

She seems surprised at the question. "Cuts and scrapes, minor concussion—what you'd expect after what he's been through." She looks meaningfully at the scrapes visible across the backs of my knuckles. I tug the collar of my shirt higher, hoping to hide the bruises circling my throat from Thom strangling me earlier.

But Morales must notice them because she frowns. "Have you had anyone look at that?" she asks, motioning.

I shake my head. "I'm fine. How did you find me?"

She tightens her jaw and for a minute I think she'll argue, but she ends up letting it go. "Because I don't trust you," she answers. "Never have."

Her statement takes me aback and I frown, confused.

"There's a note in Shepherd's file that I'm to be notified of any visitors." She looks at me pointedly. "Imagine my surprise to get a call about a young female visitor who fit your description. You know, with you supposedly being dead and all." She glances toward the TV. It's now replaying a clip of the Senator's arrest.

We watch for a moment before she continues. "You were there earlier—at the O'Martin estate." It's a statement, not a question.

Cringing, I clench my fingers into fists. Not caring about the cuts that open along my knuckles. *So close*, I think. I glance again at the door but when I look back at Morales, she shakes her head.

I let out a long sigh, resigned. "Yes, I was there."

"The two bodies . . . ?" She leaves it as a question.

"The news is right—his name's Thom Ridger."

Her lips press together. "That's what Grey reported as well. We found a gun . . ." Again she trails off. She already knows most of this, but she wants to hear it from me.

"It was Thom's," I tell her, my voice bizarrely calm and even.

She nods and then frowns. "And the other body?"

I hesitate, swallowing before finally answering. "The other body belongs to Elizabeth O'Martin."

## FIFTY-FIVE

Morales bristles; she's not the kind of person who likes to be toyed with. "They're planning to do DNA tests, you know." The words are short and clipped, her tone testy.

I struggle to suppress a smile. "And the DNA will come back a perfect match to Elizabeth O'Martin."

For the first time since I've met her, Morales is flummoxed. Her eyes narrow as she leans back and crosses her arms. "How's that?"

I hesitate, not sure how much to share. But then I realize, what does it matter now? If I'm arrested, the truth will come out anyway. It has to. The DNA tests will prove that Libby's dead, and then all eyes will fall on me.

"I don't know how much you know about the *Persephone* disaster," I tell her. "But there were two of us who survived when the ship sank: Libby O'Martin and Frances Mace." I stare down at my hand, feeling the nakedness of where Libby's signet ring used to be. I had to leave it behind with the body. It never really belonged to me anyway—it was always hers.

"Only one of us lived long enough to be rescued."

Morales's eyes sweep over me and then she lets out a surprised breath. "You're Frances Mace."

It takes me a moment to figure out how to answer that. I meet her gaze head on. "I used to be."

"So the body that burned?"

"It's Libby's. She was buried in Frances Mace's grave." I hesitate, clear my throat. "I dug her up the other night. And then made sure the fire would burn hot enough that no one would be able to tell the body had been dead for years."

Morales blinks, trying to take this all in. "We arrested Senator Wells in connection with your—I mean Libby's—murder."

"I know," I say, nodding at where the TV still plays an endless loop of the charred wreckage and of the Senator being escorted out of his house in handcuffs. I still feel a jolt of satisfaction watching it.

Morales's expression is apologetic. "You know I can't let an innocent man go to prison for a crime he didn't commit."

I lean forward, hands clenched. "Trust me, Senator Wells might not be responsible for the fire last night, but he's still the reason Libby died. He killed her." My voice comes out tight and barely controlled.

We stare at each other, her waiting for me to say more, me wondering how much I can trust her. In the end, I tell her everything. The entire story: meeting up with Libby; me and Grey falling for each other on the *Persephone*; the attack; witnessing my parents' murder; the days adrift in the raft with Libby; the rescue that came after; and Cecil's proposal to switch identities.

And then I explain the why, laying out everything about DMTR, the Senator's corruption, the Ecuadorian oil. Morales takes it all in, her expression betraying nothing.

"Senator Wells just . . ." I struggle with the words, the familiar anger simmering. "He got away with it. There was never enough proof. No way to make him pay." I lift my chin. "The Senator deserves to pay for what he did. If he hadn't lied, we would have been rescued while Libby was still alive."

"Why not just let the FBI investigate—let him pay for his corruption then?"

"Because I don't trust the system," I argue. "I don't trust that he'd truly be punished the way he should."

She lifts her eyebrows. "For killing an entire ship of innocent people?"

This is where I bite my lip, glance at the TV for a moment. Bringing the truth about the *Persephone* to the light means bringing Grey's complicity. There may never be any official consequences for his lying, but society would judge him. Even if they understood the why of it.

While my intent has always been to out the truth, damn the consequences, now I'm not so sure. Because there are some consequences that aren't worth risking.

Grey is worth more to me than my need to let the world know the truth.

"Let the *Persephone* lie where she rests." Morales opens her mouth to argue but I don't let her. "Thom Ridger was responsible for the attack and he's dead now. The Senator will go to jail for Libby's murder as he should. It's over—all of it."

She draws a sharp breath, still uncertain. "Look," I continue.

"Think of all the families out there who mourned their loved ones four years ago. The truth would only dredge all of that up. Even worse, it would prey on them.

"It's easier to believe in the cruel hand of nature than the cruel hand of man. Trust me."

In the silence that follows, Morales taps her fingers against her knees, thinking. On the TV, the news cycles between clips of the Senator being escorted to the police car in handcuffs and the arson investigators sifting through the rubble of the burned house.

There's no way the Senator can escape this. Not with Grey implicating him. They'll find the texts that he was supposed to meet me last night. That his head of security was found in the wreckage with a gun only adds to the Senator's guilt.

He'll lose everything because of this: his job, his marriage, his son. Even his freedom once he's convicted of Libby's murder.

Finally Morales lets out a deep breath. "So what now?"

I lift a shoulder. "You take down the Senator—use it to advance your career. I walk away. So long as you let me, that is." I wait to see if she protests, but she doesn't. "I transferred most of my inheritance—or rather Libby's inheritance, I guess—to Shepherd and his brother. The rest I've set aside in a series of trusts that are pretty untraceable. It won't take much to develop a new identity—give her a history. I'll disappear—you'll never have to worry about me again."

With a wry smile, I add, "I've had practice sliding into someone else's life."

She nods, but there's still something concerning her and it makes me anxious. "So everything—from the moment you returned to Caldwell—was part of your plan. And we were all just pawns you pushed around to get what you wanted, regardless of the consequences."

A hot flush of shame creeps up my neck. "No."

But she's not done. "Doesn't that make you just like the Senator? Eye on the prize, damn the people who get in your way?"

"That's not the way it was," I protest.

"You broke Grey's heart, you put people's lives at risk, and Shepherd—" All she has to do is glance down the hallway to make that point.

"Shepherd wasn't supposed to be part of it," I say softly, chagrined. "And neither were you." I stare at the blood smeared along the back of my hand, one of the cuts on my knuckle opening up from having clenched my fists earlier. "Everyone's life will be better with me gone."

"Was it worth it?" she asks.

*Yes*, I want to tell her, but for some reason the word won't come. On the TV a red BREAKING NEWS! alert flashes and is replaced by the scene of a reporter standing outside the Caldwell County Hospital, cameras everywhere.

The hospital doors slide open and Grey steps out, his mom by his side. The media crushes toward them, everyone shouting questions at once. Mrs. Wells keeps her head down, repeating "No comment," again and again as she follows in Grey's wake, pushing toward the waiting car. Grey holds the door open for his mother, who slides gratefully into the backseat.

But he hesitates, and then glances up. He must have chosen the camera to look into at random—there's no way he could know I'm watching him.

And yet it feels like he's staring right at me. There are dark, sleepless bruises under his eyes and his hair's disheveled. A bandage covers his forehead and his cheek is scraped an ugly red. His shoulders sag under the weight of everything that's happened, and I know, I'm the one who did this to him.

Then he slips into the car, closes the door, and is gone. I let my head drop, closing my eyes tight against the tears. Morales still waits for the answer to her question. *Was it worth it?*

"*I don't know,*" I finally tell her, my voice barely above a whisper.

She says nothing, just taps her fingers against her knee. "You know," she finally says. "There was this kid once—lost his parents young but was taken in by a good family and seemed to be doing fine. Until his adoptive mother died and his adoptive father started spending all of his time out of the country, taking care of his adoptive sister who'd been in a pretty horrific accident."

I clench my teeth, knowing that I'm the girl who took the father away from that boy. That the boy in question is Shepherd. But I listen anyway because this is a woman who could throw me in jail right now if she wanted and it's probably best that I don't tick her off.

"See, the problem was that everyone he'd ever seen as family had just up and left," she continued. "Either dead or gone voluntarily. And that left him pretty angry and he didn't know what to do with that anger so he started getting in trouble.

Which got me involved and I started to pay attention.

"You know what I realized?"

She waits for me to answer, but I shake my head, gaze still focused on the ground.

"He just wanted someone to *see* him. Even if it was the cops."

I press my palms against my eyes, struggling to draw jagged breaths. Knowing this was all my fault. Cecil was taking care of me when he should have been home taking care of Shepherd.

She leans forward, the tips of her fingers just barely brushing my shoulder. "I told him the same thing I'll tell you: You can't be seen when you're constantly pushing people away. You've got to let people in. Even though it's a risk. Even though it's scary. That's what life is."

I'm so wrapped up in the memory of Shepherd telling me the same thing that I don't even realize she's gone until I look up to find the waiting room empty. I wipe a hand down my face, trying to figure out my next move.

Because that's the thing—everything in the last four years has been geared to a moment that's now passed. I never considered what would come after. And now that my revenge is wrought, now that retribution is complete . . .

I have no idea what's next.

Life still grinds forward. I still have to figure out who I am and what I want.

And though I reach for answers, I come up empty.

# EPILOGUE

In the end, though I've spent hours—days—agonizing over it, my letter to Grey is simple. I write it on plain paper, with my new address at the top, and tuck it under the ribbon tying my journals and notebooks together along with the only back-up of the video from his old phone.

> *You want to know who I am, here it is. This is me— every thought, every fear, every truth. I leave myself in your hands. You can turn me in, you can condemn me, you can ignore me.*
>
> *You can come find me.*
>
> *I'll be waiting, for whatever it is you decide.*
>
> *But know this: I've lied about most everything in my life, but never about my love for you. It is as strong now as it ever was. There is a reason your heart found mine. It is my sincerest hope you find me again.*
>
> *Yours always,*

I struggle in the end, not knowing how to sign it. And so I leave it blank. But that's the thing about silences and futures; someone always comes along to fill them in. If you let them.

# ACKNOWLEDGMENTS

I love that I get to spend my days in the world of books. Thank you to my passionate readers for making this possible—you are a dream come true!

The very first seeds of this book were planted around Ally Carter's breakfast table, and I owe her a huge thanks for saying, "Yes, write that!" and for cheering me on ever since. Thanks also to Jennifer Lynn Barnes, whose quick plot adjusting not only helped to sell the book, but also spawned a cult following of eight box plotters, and to Melissa de la Cruz who gave me great advice when I needed it. Sarah MacLean and Diana Peterfreund not only read, but listened many, many times as I talked through plot details. Several other folks read this book at various stages and helped me work through the snags: Beth Revis, Holly Black, Sarah Rees Brennan, Kami Garcia, and especially the Bat Cavers. Thanks also to the Debs who have been there from the beginning.

I'm so grateful to have had the chance to work with editor extraordinaire Julie Strauss-Gabel, whose keen insight teased out themes I didn't even realize were there. She's brilliant! The entire Dutton and Penguin Young Readers team is amazing, especially Melissa Faulner, Anna Jarzab, Lisa Kelly, Carmela Iaria, Venessa Carson, Rachel Cone-Gorham, Erin Berger, Emily Romero, and Doni Kay. It's a huge honor to have their creativity and enthusiasm behind this book and a delight to be working with Jessica Shoffel once again.

Merrilee Heifetz excels in her many roles as agent: fear-alayer, fire-putter-outer, advice-giver, advocate, and confidant (to name a few). I'm thankful to have her in my corner! Thanks also to Sarah Nagel, Cecilia de la Campa, and the Writers House crew for championing my books home and abroad.

As always, my family is a continued source of love and support (whose patience is boundless!). Thank you never feels like enough to show how much I love you all!

There were many hurdles in the way of getting here, but JP was there at every one, ready to catch me if and when I tripped. Thank you, my love!